The
# ESKIMO
# SLUGGER

## Brad Boney

Dreamspinner Press

Published by
DREAMSPINNER PRESS

5032 Capital Circle SW, Suite 2, PMB# 279, Tallahassee, FL 32305-7886 USA
http://www.dreamspinnerpress.com/

The Eskimo Slugger
© 2014 Brad Boney.

Cover Art
© 2014 Paul Richmond.
http://www.paulrichmondstudio.com
Cover content is for illustrative purposes only and any person depicted on the cover is a model.

ISBN: 978-1-63216-226-7
Digital ISBN: 978-1-63216-227-4
Library of Congress Control Number: 2014944478
First Edition September 2014

Printed in the United States of America
∞
This paper meets the requirements of
ANSI/NISO Z39.48-1992 (Permanence of Paper).

"If you want a happy ending, that depends,
of course, on where you stop your story."
— Orson Welles

# ONE

IN THE bottom of the seventh inning, Trent Days stepped into the batter's box and tapped home plate. He loved ball games in the Astrodome, despite the fact that some players complained about the artificial turf. It was a Saturday afternoon in early July, just after the All-Star break. Their opponents were the Atlanta Braves, who put Craig McMurtry on the mound and Bruce Benedict behind the plate. Trent's Astros were down 3-1, but he had Doran on first and Puhl on third, with two outs. That was one of Trent's favorite setups, because the ball could only be in one place at a time. The key was for Doran to lead with the steal so that McMurtry would have to throw to second, leaving Puhl free to come in for the run. Or Trent could hit a homer. That would work too.

Trent looked around at the lights and cameras. This was NBC's *Major League Baseball Game of the Week*, televised live across the nation, with Vin Scully and Joe Garagiola in the booth.

—*Joe, a hush has fallen over the Astrodome as Trent Days, wearing lucky number eight, takes his turn at bat.*

—*The kid is having an incredible rookie season so far.*

—*I'll second that. The press dubbed him the Eskimo Slugger back in May, because he was raised in Alaska and has a .550 slugging percentage.*

—*Unbelievable. Nineteen home runs, Vin, and we're only halfway through the '83 season. I got a feeling we may see number twenty right here.*

*—Well, the fans certainly love him, and I was talking to Nolan Ryan the other day, and he was singing his praises too. Said Days is a natural-born leader and a huge morale booster in the clubhouse.*

*—I think if you asked most of the kids here today, they'd tell you they came out to see Trent Days hit a home run.*

*—No question about it, Joe.*

Benedict, the catcher for the Braves, stepped forward and went through an elaborate series of hand signals, communicating his strategy to the other members of the nine. Then he lowered his mask, squatted down behind home plate, and said, "Time to strike this Eskimo out."

Trent ignored him and the first three pitches as well. He liked to work the count, because the more McMurtry had to throw, the more likely he was to make a mistake. When he had the count at 3-2, Trent tapped the plate again and stared the pitcher down. The final toss came in right above his knees, just the mistake Trent had been waiting for. He sliced it perfectly and sent it flying toward the fence. The ball disappeared into the stands and the crowd leaped to its feet.

*—There it is, baseball fans! Trent Days has hit home run number twenty, moving the Houston Astros into the lead and turning this into a real ball game.*

*—Did I call it, Vin, or what?*

*—Yes, you did, Joe. This kid looks determined to never disappoint his growing legion of hometown fans. What a spectacular hit that was.*

Trent jogged around the bases and met Doran and Puhl at home plate. The Houston dugout emptied and Benedict got shoved aside. He threw a punch at Jose Cruz, and a small scuffle broke out. It didn't last long, but the Braves were clearly pissed off that the Astros were now up 4-3.

By the time McMurtry managed to strike out the next batter, Trent had already put on his shin guards and padding. He grabbed his face mask and trotted out to the mound to chat with Kieran Harrison, a pitcher for the Astros—and his best friend.

*—Days and Harrison are now talking on the mound. The two are old high-school buddies and played at the University of Texas together.*

*—If I were going to build a franchise on a pitcher and catcher combo, I'd start right there, Vin.*

*—They're quite the dynamic duo. Harrison with his Texas-size ego and Days with the self-deprecating humor.*

*—They were really cutting it up in front of the cameras earlier today. They give highly entertaining press conferences.*

"Let's put them down right in a row, Kieran. One, two, three. Sound good?"

"I'm not feeling the slider today, Trent, so don't ask for it."

"I heard you the first fifty times you told me that. Hey, did you hear the one about the Eskimo who got dragged into the police station on suspicion of robbery?"

Kieran shook his head and laughed. "No, I haven't heard that one."

"They wanted to know what he was doing on the night between September and March."

Kieran groaned. "Okay, enough with the Eskimo jokes. I'm loose. Get behind the plate and let's play ball."

They didn't put the batters down one, two, three. Brett Butler, the Braves' young left fielder, hit a long ground ball down the third-base line and scrambled all the way to second. Bob Horner followed him and popped a fly into right field. The first-base ump inexplicably called Horner safe, and Butler advanced to third. Trent found himself smack in the middle of the same setup he loved as a hitter, but hated as a catcher. He walked forward as Glenn Hubbard stepped into the batter's box. Trent went through his own hand motions and then returned to his position behind the plate. Hubbard wasn't a great hitter, but he was having the best season of his career. Trent knew he couldn't take anything for granted.

Hubbard let two pitches go, but then smacked a line drive right over Dickie Thon's head. The Astros' shortstop had such excellent reflexes that he jumped up and caught the ball. Dickie tagged out Horner at second as Trent saw Butler barreling toward him. He blocked the plate as Thon threw the ball, and when Trent caught it, he felt Butler hit him at full speed. Trent fell backward and his head slammed against the dirt. Butler landed on top of him, and Trent felt a stab of pain in his ribcage. He grabbed his right side and screamed. As Butler jumped up and Trent curled into a ball, he heard the umpire call, "Out!"

—*Trent Days is down, ladies and gentlemen, and it looks bad.*

—*What an amazing catcher he is, Vin. Days never flinched as Butler came at him, and Butler's got at least thirty pounds on him.*

—*What a game this has been, but it looks like the Eskimo Slugger isn't moving. What a terrible twist of events it would be if this turns out to be serious.*

—*It looks pretty serious from up here, and.... Yep, there comes the stretcher.*

Trent had made the play. That was all that mattered, and it was the last thing he remembered as he closed his eyes and blacked out.

# TWO

ON MONDAY afternoon, Trent opened the door of the record store, removed his sunglasses, and stepped across the threshold. A bell rang above his head. It was the same cramped, almost claustrophobic space he remembered from his college days. Back then he had been more into hard rock like Aerosmith, Rush, and Kiss, but lately he'd embraced new wave and electronic music. He looked around at the empty shop and heard someone rustling in the back.

"I'll be right out," a male voice called.

"Take your time," Trent said. "I'm in no hurry."

Trent moved down the aisle and thumbed through a stack of albums: Culture Club, the B-52's, R.E.M., Stray Cats, Modern English. *I melt with you*, he said to himself. He noted the albums were still stocked haphazardly and not in alphabetical order. He looked up as a young man appeared behind the counter. Trent noticed his red hair first—which was really more a dark copper—and his beaming smile second. He was taller than Trent—probably around six foot—with broad shoulders and powerful arms. His skin was perfect and freckle-less, his ears stuck out just a bit, and his chin had a tiny cleft in the middle.

"Oh my God. You're—" The young man stopped himself, and then he must have recognized Trent's concerned look, because he switched gears and said, "Sorry about that. I didn't mean to sound like a teenage girl meeting C. Thomas Howell. We don't get many actual celebrities in here. Joan Jett dropped by last year when she was in town for a concert. One of the nicest people I've ever met. She was so down-to-earth I felt like I was talking to my sister. And I don't even have a sister. Anyway, welcome to Inner Sanctum Records. Have you been here before?"

"Yes," Trent said. "I went to school at UT."

"Of course. I read that. You still live in Austin, right?"

"Yeah. I bought a house in Travis Heights."

"Why didn't you just move to Houston?" Brendan asked.

"Because. This has been my home for eight years. I'm not ready to give that up yet."

"Very cool. Are you looking for anything in particular?" Trent blushed. He didn't understand why, but he could tell the young man noticed. "Music-wise, I mean."

"Yes. The latest New Order album. I don't remember the name."

"*Power, Corruption & Lies.*"

"That's the one."

"It's over here." He came around from behind the counter and walked past Trent to the end of the aisle. He pulled the album from a bin and held it out. "You know this doesn't have 'Blue Monday' on it, right? We've had some angry customers who just assumed it was on here. We do have the twelve-inch of 'Blue Monday,' though, if you're interested."

Trent reached out and took the record.

"Yeah, I'll take both."

The young man walked over to another bin and pulled out a second record. He turned and handed it to Trent, who said, "Thank you."

"You're welcome. I'm Brendan, by the way." He held out his hand.

Trent shook it. Brendan's grip was firm and sturdy. "It's nice to meet you."

"It's eight bucks total. You need a bag?"

"No. I'm good." Trent reached into his back pocket and pulled out his wallet. He handed Brendan a ten-dollar bill. Brendan walked to the counter and reached into the open money drawer. He pulled out two ones and handed them to Trent.

"I'm sorry about your injury," Brendan said.

Trent took a deep breath. "That's the game."

"I know. Still. You had Rookie of the Year all sewn up, man. Maybe even MVP."

"You don't know that. A lot can happen in two and a half months. Besides, I'm not out for the season."

"They put you on the twenty-one-day disabled list, right?"

"Yeah."

"Sorry. I'm sure the last thing you need is some dopey law student playing twenty questions with you."

Trent laughed. "I think hitting a ball with a piece of wood is a lot dopier than studying the law. How far along are you?"

"I'll be starting my second year in September."

"Why do you want to be a lawyer?"

"Why not?"

Trent grimaced.

"What's that look?" Brendan asked.

"I don't know what you're talking about."

"You don't like lawyers?"

Trent shook his head. "Not particularly."

"You've probably only dealt with contract lawyers. That kind of stuff doesn't interest me."

"What? You want to be the next Perry Mason?"

"Fuck that. I want to be the next F. Lee Bailey."

Trent laughed again and buckled over in pain.

"Sorry," Brendan said. "Does it still hurt?"

"A little."

"He got you good."

"You saw the game?"

"No, but I saw the highlights on the ten o'clock news. Home-plate collisions, man. I don't know. They should outlaw those. Sometimes I think catchers aren't too bright."

"Why do you think they call all that padding the *tools of ignorance*? You play any sports?"

"Do you mean, do I play any sports currently?" Trent nodded, and Brendan shook his head. "No. I played football in high school."

"You're built like a quarterback."

"Good guess."

"Were you any good?"

Brendan grinned. "No way. I'm not going down that road."

"What road?"

"Stacking my athletic ability up against yours."

"How old are you?" Trent asked.

"I'll be twenty-four in a few months."

"Really? We're the same age. I'll be twenty-four in a few months too."

"Thanks for rubbing it in."

"I wasn't trying to—"

"You're almost twenty-four years old and one of the most famous baseball players in America. I'm almost twenty-four years old and I work in a record store. I'm just saying."

"I'm not one of the most—"

"Come on. Three months in the majors and you're already on the cover of *Sports Illustrated*. And a rookie All-Star. Look, I get the whole humility act, but you may be one of the most talented players to ever grace the diamond. They were calling 1983 the year of the Eskimo Slugger before…."

Trent cringed when he heard the nickname. "You know my batting average too?"

Brendan hesitated at first, but then he said, with a fair amount of certainty, "Um, .358?"

"That's scary."

"Relax. I'm not a stalker. You walked into my record store, remember?"

Trent didn't answer at first. He took a good look at Brendan. "I remember."

"It's not like I'm the only red-blooded American male walking around with a bunch of useless baseball statistics in his head. Anyway, I didn't mean to keep you. Enjoy your records. And heal up fast. The Astros are falling apart without you."

"Thanks. I'll do my best." Trent started for the door, but then stopped and turned back to Brendan. "I didn't mean to bad-mouth lawyers."

"That's okay. People have been bad-mouthing lawyers since Shakespeare. *Henry VI, Part 2.* 'First thing we do, let's kill all the lawyers.' It was nice to meet you, Mr. Days."

Trent smiled at the formality. "You too, Mr....?"

"Baxter."

"Take care, Brendan Baxter." He put on his sunglasses, opened the door, and left the shop.


WHEN HE arrived at his house in South Austin, Trent put "Blue Monday" on the turntable and lay down on the sofa. He closed his eyes and listened to the song. There was something about the steady beat that relaxed him. He squirmed left and then right. He tried to find a comfortable spot where his ribs didn't hurt, but he failed.

He sat up and grabbed a bottle of painkillers off the coffee table and went into the kitchen. He retrieved a glass from the cupboard over the sink, filled it with water, and then swallowed two of the little white pills. He looked out the window into the backyard. The grass was turning brown, but at least the kid down the block was keeping it mowed. He returned to the living room and the sofa. As Trent was about to close his eyes, the record skipped.

"Shit."

He got up and reached into his pocket. He pulled a penny out and walked to the turntable. Trent gently laid the penny on the needle. He lifted it up and placed it a few measures before the skip. Sometimes it worked, and sometimes it didn't.

This time it didn't.

Trent removed the penny and then the needle. He pulled the record off the turntable and pushed it back into the sleeve. He grabbed his sunglasses and the keys to his truck, then headed out of the house.

WHEN TRENT reentered Inner Sanctum Records, Brendan was sitting behind the counter, reading a copy of *In Search of Excellence*. He looked up and grinned. "Back already, Mr. Days?"

"Yes, Mr. Baxter."

"Couldn't resist my charming repartee?"

"Not exactly." Trent handed the record to Brendan. "The twelve-inch of 'Blue Monday' has a skip."

"Crap." Brendan laid down his book and took the faulty record. "Sorry, I hate when that happens. Let me pull you another copy."

As Brendan came out from behind the counter, Trent shook his head and blinked. The floor felt like it was shifting underneath him.

"You okay?" Brendan asked.

"Yeah. I forgot that I took some painkillers before I left the house. They make me a little dizzy sometimes."

"And you thought it was a good idea to get into a car and drive?"

"A truck, actually, but yeah. I wasn't really thinking. I'm a catcher, remember? Not too bright."

"Well, no way am I letting you get back behind the wheel while you're feeling dizzy. I won't have any Roberto Clemente-style tragedy hanging over my head for the rest of my life."

"Do you mind if I sit down for a minute?"

"Not at all, man." Brendan grabbed a chair from behind the counter. Trent sat and rubbed his eyes. "I'm off work in"—Brendan turned his head and looked at the clock—"five minutes. You want to go next door and get some lasagna?"

"Lasagna?"

"Yeah. Les Amis has great lasagna. Putting some food in your stomach will make you feel better. Unless you have somewhere else you need to be."

"No. I was going half crazy alone in the house. But is lasagna all they serve?"

"You don't like Italian food?"

"Not really," Trent said.

"What's wrong with you?"

"It's all the cheese. I don't like cheese. It slows me down."

"Fine. I'm not going to force a plate of lasagna down your throat. They have other stuff."

Trent felt his head clear a bit. "Sorry about this. I'm sure you have better things to do than babysit me."

Brendan chuckled. "Not really. I eat there most days after work, anyway. And I'm pretty sure the clientele will have no idea who you are, if that Longhorns cap and those sunglasses are your attempt at traveling incognito. Les Amis is part of the intelligentsia triangle."

"What's that?"

"Les Amis, the Cactus Cafe in the Union, and Quack's. Three academic hotspots. I made the triangle name up."

"What's Quack's?"

"Captain Quackenbush's Intergalactic Dessert Company and Espresso Café. It's the first coffeehouse in Austin. Just opened a few months ago on the Drag. They only serve espresso-based drinks. Kind of pretentious, if you ask me, but nobody did. I mean, we're suddenly looking down our noses at coffee? If you want a hangout to discuss Kierkegaard or debate Freud versus Erikson, you go to one of those three places. On the other hand, I doubt anyone knows the difference between a slider and a curve ball."

"Sounds like I'll fit right in."

"Sarcasm. I like that."

FIFTEEN MINUTES later a heavyset young woman with pink hair and a nose ring showed up to take over Brendan's duties behind the counter. "Thanks for being late, Fiona," Brendan said. "Again."

"What's the big deal?" she asked, plopping down her huge bag. "You got a hot date or something?"

"Please. I don't expect you to know who this is," Brendan replied as he nodded toward Trent, who stood up and said, "Hello."

"Are you a movie star?" she asked him. "You look like you could be a movie star."

Brendan answered for him. "This is Trent Days, the baseball player."

The young woman's blank expression remained unchanged.

"The Eskimo Slugger?" Brendan continued.

"Sorry, Trent Days, the baseball player, aka the Eskimo Slugger. I've never heard of you."

Trent forced a smile. "There's no reason you would have."

"Why do they call you the Eskimo Slugger?" she asked. "Isn't that the name of a cocktail?"

"I'm from Alaska. My mother is a native Inupiat."

"Really? My sister dated a guy from Alaska once. You don't look anything like him."

"My father is from Texas."

Fiona made a framing gesture around his face. "That explains the black hair and blue eyes. Your bone structure is very unique, though. Sorry, I'm a photographer, so I notice these things. You could be a model if the baseball thing doesn't work out. You from Anchorage or Fairbanks?"

"Neither. I'm from Barrow."

"Where's that?"

"The north coast."

"Funny that your mom is from one of the coldest places in the US and your dad is from one of the hottest. I bet you run hot and cold. Ha! Get it? Texas and Alaska? Hot and cold…?"

"Hysterical," Brendan said.

"Why were you sitting in a record store?"

Brendan raised his hand. "Enough with the inquisition. He's not feeling well, okay? I'm taking him next door to get something to eat."

"Fine. Don't let me stand in your way, Baxter. I'd rather not look at your ugly mug anyway."

"Charming, as usual. Can you walk?" he asked Trent.

"Yes, I can walk. I'm not a cripple. But what about my new copy of 'Blue Monday'?"

"Right," Brendan said. "I forgot all about that." He crossed to one of the bins, grabbed the record, and handed it to Trent. "Here you go. Now, let's get something to eat. I'm starving."

Trent stepped aside and gave his chair to Fiona, who narrowed her eyes and asked, "Did he warn you about Quincy?"

# THREE

"IGNORE HER," Brendan said as he opened the door. Together, they stepped into the blinding sunshine of a Texas afternoon. After spending his entire childhood in freezing temperatures, Trent basked in the heat. Next door, he and Brendan passed through the gate of a white picket fence and continued under a sweeping red awning to the door of the cafe. When they walked in, a fortysomething man sitting in one of the far booths stood up and crossed the room to greet Brendan. He wore shorts and a loud Hawaiian shirt, but no shoes.

"Jesus, Brendan, where have you been? We haven't seen you in three days. I was starting to get worried."

"Sorry, I've been fixing up my new place."

"Who's this?"

Brendan turned and introduced them. "Trent, this is Quincy. He owns the cafe."

Trent reached out his hand. "Nice to meet you."

Quincy hesitated at first, but then shook it. "Where do I know you from?"

"Shhh," Brendan said. "We're trying to fly under the radar. You've probably seen him on TV. He plays for the Houston Astros."

Quincy's face scrunched up. "What's that? Football? Soccer? Badminton?"

Brendan laughed. "No, baseball."

"Baseball?" Quincy exclaimed. "When have I ever cared about baseball?" He stopped a waitress as she passed them with three plates of food. "Monica, in all the years you've known me, have you ever once heard me talk about baseball?"

"Do you mind?" the waitress said. "I'm trying to serve customers here."

"Oh, please. No one comes here for the service. Have you ever heard me talk about baseball?"

"No, never. Now leave me alone."

The waitress continued on her way, and Quincy said, "My staff has no respect for me."

Brendan nudged him. "And you wouldn't have it any other way."

"Of course not. Respect is the love child of convention and boredom." He looked at Trent again. "No, you definitely look familiar, but it has nothing to do with baseball. There's something in your aura. Don't worry, I'll figure it out eventually."

*Aura?* Trent began to see what Fiona was talking about and wondered if he should make his escape, but Quincy ushered them toward his booth before Trent could act on the impulse.

"Monica," Quincy yelled across the room. "Two lasagnas. Pronto."

"No," Brendan said. "Trent's not having lasagna."

"Why not?"

"He doesn't like cheese."

"What do you mean, he doesn't like cheese? Who doesn't like cheese?"

"I don't," Trent said. "Do you have any fish?"

"We have a blackened catfish, but sometimes Tony burns it if he gets too stoned. I mean, there's blackened and then there's *blackened.*"

Brendan shook his head and chuckled. "Would you ask him to be careful, please?"

"Monica," Quincy called. "Make that one lasagna and one catfish. And keep an eye on Tony to make sure he doesn't burn it."

"The lasagna or the fish?" Monica called back.

"The fish, smartass."

Quincy sat down on one side of the booth, while Brendan and Trent settled into the other. Trent put the copy of "Blue Monday" on the table and leaned it against the window. "Don't let me forget this," he said to Brendan.

"I won't."

"So," Quincy said, "what is a Houston Astro doing in my humble cafe?"

"I don't know," Trent replied.

Brendan stepped in. "He was buying some records in the shop and one of them had a skip. So he brought it back, but then he almost fainted from some painkillers. Personally, I think he needs some food."

"I didn't almost faint."

"Close enough."

"I meant, why aren't you playing?" Quincy asked. "Even I know summer is baseball season."

"I'm on the DL."

Quincy's smile went crooked. "What's the DL?"

"The disabled list," Brendan said.

"You're disabled?"

"No," Trent said. "Someone ran me over at home plate. I got a concussion and a couple of bruised ribs. Nothing too serious, but they tell me I need to rest. I'll be playing again by the end of the month."

"What position?"

"Catcher."

"Like Johnny Bench? Now, *that's* a baseball player. If Johnny Bench walked into my cafe, I would know who that is." Quincy turned his head and yelled across the room. "Monica, do you know who Johnny Bench is?"

The waitress looked up as she stood over a cash register in the corner. "Isn't he the lead singer of the Sex Pistols?"

"That's Johnny Rotten," Trent said.

Brendan leaned in and whispered, "I think she's joking."

Monica grinned. "He's a baseball player."

"See what I mean?" Quincy said, turning back to Trent. "Household name. Have you ever met Johnny Bench?"

"Yes, we've played the Reds a couple of times already. But he's not a catcher anymore. He's retiring this year."

"Why isn't he a catcher anymore?"

"His knees gave out. He's practically an old man at this point, and you can only take the squatting up and down for so long. It happens to everyone."

"I see," Quincy said. "So being a catcher has an expiration date."

"Everything has an expiration date," Trent said. He couldn't help but notice that Quincy kept looking at him and Brendan, back and forth, like he was trying to figure something out. Brendan must have noticed too, because finally he said, "What's wrong with you?"

"What do you mean?" Quincy said.

"You keep staring at us like you're looking for something. It's creepy."

"Am I being that obvious? I apologize, but that shade of blue is extremely rare. And the color of the sparks—"

"What sparks?" Brendan asked. Then he turned his head and said to Trent, "This is the part I should have warned you about. Quincy thinks he sees colors around people, and that they're some sort of window into the soul."

"You make me sound like a ridiculous hippie from the '60s."

"You are a ridiculous hippie from the '60s."

Trent put his elbows on the table. He figured if he had to sit and eat catfish burned by someone who smoked too much weed, he might as well make the most of it. Besides, his mother believed colors had meanings too. So he asked, "What shade of blue?"

Quincy looked surprised, like he didn't expect a knucklehead jock to be curious about such things. "Have you ever been to San Diego?"

"Yes, I have," Trent said. "The Padres are in the same division as us."

"The National League West," Brendan added.

"We play them a lot."

"The color of the ocean in San Diego. Do you know what I'm talking about?"

"Yeah. I always thought it looked like the Texas sky, only in the form of water."

Quincy smiled and looked even more surprised. "Exactly. That's the color of your aura. Very powerful. When you two sit next to each other, well, you're both blues. Most people are either reds, greens, or blues. Reds are the movers and shakers of the world, the ones who get things done. Greens are creative, like artists and musicians. Blues are negotiators. They can adapt to new situations and help other people adapt as well."

"Brendan is a blue?" Trent asked. "But he wants to be the next F. Lee Bailey. That sounds like a red to me."

"Just because someone's a blue doesn't mean they lack drive or ambition. Henry Kissinger is a classic blue, and he's very ambitious. When you sit next to each other like that, the edge where your colors mix has sparks of gold in it."

"Like the sand in San Diego." Trent turned to Brendan. "If you go down to the beach in Coronado, the sand has tiny flecks of gold in it."

Brendan looked at Quincy. "What do the sparks mean?"

"No earthly idea. Never seen the gold ones before. You two.... Never mind."

"What?" Brendan said.

Monica appeared at their booth with a plate of lasagna and garlic bread, and another of catfish and grilled vegetables. She placed the second plate in front of Trent and said, "I made sure he didn't overdo the blackened part. Can I get you something to drink?"

"Just a glass of water," Trent said. "Thank you."

"Brendan, what about you?"

"I'll have a Coke."

Monica walked away, and Trent took a bite of the catfish. "It's really good."

Brendan stuffed a piece of bread into his mouth and mumbled, "What were you going to say, Quincy?"

"Nothing."

Trent speared some vegetables with his fork. "Come on, tell us."

"Not yet. Like I said, I've never seen that color of sparks before, so when I figure it out, I'll let you know. And trust me, I will figure it out. Are you a religious man, Trent?"

"Not really. In Alaska—"

"Is that where you're from?"

"Yeah. Up there, everyone is mostly Christian now, but kind of a half-assed Christian. My mother raised me and my brothers in the Inupiat traditions, and we have a large extended family on her side. My grandfather always said, 'Eskimos don't believe in anything, but we fear everything.' Respect nature or she'll snap your head off. That's the only religion an Eskimo needs."

"What about the soul?" Quincy said.

"The Inupiat are a very spiritual people. We believe everything has a soul. Living creatures, rocks, snow, the wind, everything. No matter what you eat, you're eating a soul. When a person dies, the soul is freed from the body and continues to live on in the spirit world."

Quincy nodded. "Do you have a concept similar to the collective unconscious?

"Yeah, kind of. Each soul is individual, but they're connected. There's no God in the Christian sense. It's hard to explain."

"God is the grand total of the individual souls?"

Trent nodded. "That's a good way to put it. God is all of it. Everything you see. We are the Great Spirit."

"What about hell?" Brendan said.

"We don't have one of those. No heaven either, just the spirit world. There's no punishment for the crappy things you've done in this life. I think we believe that having to live with them for all eternity is punishment enough."

"Do you have shamans?" Quincy asked. "Priests who can communicate with the spirit world?"

"Yeah, but all that is mostly ceremonial these days. The songs and the dances and the masks. We do it for the tourists."

"Do Eskimos believe in reincarnation?" Quincy asked.

"No, not really. Some tribes, like the Caribou, believe in a dual soul. And there's also a ceremony where a child is bound to the soul of a recently dead relative—by giving the child the relative's name. Supposedly the birth-soul is too weak in the beginning, so the name-soul serves as a guardian until the child becomes a teenager."

"Interesting," Quincy said. "I believe in reincarnation. I think souls work in pairs and groups. Across centuries we come back, over and over again, and find each other."

"So you think Brendan and I are soul mates or something?"

"No, I didn't say that. In fact, I suspect your soul paths have never crossed before today."

"Really?" Brendan said as he took a bite of lasagna. "How can you possibly know that?"

"It's a gift I share with Shirley MacLaine."

Brendan chewed and swallowed. "It's bullshit is what it is, plain and simple. You know I'm an atheist."

"You are?" Trent said.

"God is a story," Brendan continued, "and not even a very good one. Genesis is strewn with contradictions and inconsistencies. All origin stories are. And *soul paths*? The idea that our energy and memory remain some kind of discrete unit after we die is just absurd. And then, to add insult to injury, we make up this story that our souls can jump from one body to another. There's not a shred of empirical evidence to suggest such a thing is possible. Only your vivid imaginations."

"However the world works," Quincy said, "it works that way whether you believe it or not."

Monica returned with a glass of water and a Coke.

"Can you tell Tony the fish is excellent?" Trent said.

"I will tell him, thank you. What's your name?"

"Trent."

"Brendan, how's the lasagna?"

"Delicious, as always."

After she walked away, Trent turned to Brendan and asked, "Don't you even believe in some kind of central intelligence to the universe? You think it's just random or something?"

Brendan finished chewing a large mouthful of lasagna and swallowed. "This is a big conversation. Are you sure you want to have it now? Can't we talk about home runs and stealing bases instead?"

"It just seems ridiculous not to believe in anything bigger than yourself."

Quincy nodded. "I agree. There are still questions science can't answer. It can explain everything about the beginning of the universe except *why*. Why did everything go from a singularity to—bam!—inflation? What, or who, put the universe into motion? If it's expanding, what's it expanding into? Before the big bang, when the universe was the size of a pinhead, what surrounded it? And don't even get me started on time. I can tell you right now, there isn't a scientist alive who understands time. Only the poets."

Trent took a drink of water. "Are these the kinds of conversations you always have in this place?"

"Yes," Brendan said. "Les Amis is a cathedral of the mind."

"I don't think I'd fit in here very well."

"Nonsense," Quincy said. "Blues have a natural curiosity about the world, and that's all it takes to fit in here."

Brendan pointed behind them. "Did you see the wheel?"

Trent swiveled in his seat and saw a spinning wheel mounted on the far wall. It was divided into twelve sections, each labeled with a different topic.

"It's a Les Amis tradition," Quincy said. "I'm Pat Sajak and Monica is Vanna White. People come in here with their friends and spin the wheel. Then Monica gives them a discussion question from whatever topic it landed on."

Out of the corner of his eye, Trent saw someone approaching.

"Nu-uh!"

Trent turned his head and a young man in his twenties walked right up to their booth. He was a little runt of a guy with long brown hair pulled into a ponytail and an unkempt goatee. His jeans and yellowed T-shirt were covered by a greasy white apron. From his slightly bloodshot eyes, Trent figured this was Tony.

"Well, I ain't never. Monica told me someone named Trent was talking sweet about the catfish, but she failed to mention it was Trent Days, the Eskimo Slugger! Wait right here, Mr. Days. Don't move a muscle." Tony ran back into the kitchen and returned a moment later with a thick black marker. "Please, will you sign my apron?"

Brendan stood up to let Trent out of the booth. Everyone around them, including Monica, stopped to watch. Trent took the marker from Tony, uncapped it, and scribbled his name onto the front of the apron. He handed the marker back to Tony and said, "Thanks for the fish."

"My pleasure. Right now, I'm just about as happy as a gopher in soft dirt. When my boy comes, I'll be able to tell him all about the time I met the Eskimo Slugger. I hope to hell you got lots more seasons of baseball left in you."

"Thank you. You're Tony?"

"Yes, I am. Tony. Tony Atwood."

Trent reached out and shook his hand. "Nice to meet you, Tony Atwood."

"Best day of this redneck's life, Mr. Days. One hundred and ten percent serious. Trent Days walks into fucking Les Amis. Okay, I'm fixin' to head back to the kitchen now and leave y'all in peace. I didn't mean to disturb nothing. Enjoy your dinner. Thanks for the autograph. I ain't never washing this apron again." Tony turned around and hugged Monica before he retreated to the kitchen.

"I hope he didn't mean that," Quincy said. "About not washing the apron."

Trent slid back into the booth. "He's a colorful character."

Brendan followed and returned to his plate of lasagna.

"I can see we have a bona fide celebrity in our midst," Quincy said, "if not yet a household name. The meals are on the house, gentlemen. Now, I must head into the office and take care of some bills. I predict you will find getting to know each other quite the game changer."

"What does that mean?" Brendan asked.

Quincy stood up and said, "Nothing, except please note the sports reference. Au revoir."

Brendan leaned over. "That's French for 'good-bye.'"

"You think I don't know what 'au revoir' means?"

"Do you speak French?"

"No, but people use 'au revoir' all the time. You don't have to speak French to know what 'au revoir' means."

"Brendan," Quincy said, standing next to the table, "you're acting like a moron. Stop trying to impress everyone." He turned and walked away. Brendan got up from the booth. He pushed his plate and Coke to the other side and moved into Quincy's now vacant seat, so that he and Trent were facing each other.

"I wasn't trying to impress you," Brendan said.

"You think a baseball player couldn't possibly know what a common French greeting means. I did go to college, you know."

"I'm sorry. I was being an asshole."

"That's okay. I like assholes. I mean—I don't mean I like actual—" Brendan flashed his smile. Trent shook his head and said, "Do you know you have this really evil grin?"

"Yes. I use it to talk people into all sorts of things."

"Like what?"

Brendan laughed. "No comment."

"There's something about you I just haven't figured out yet."

"I'm telling you, Mr. Days, I'm like an onion—one layer of mystery after another. Do you know what Les Amis means?"

"No. What?"

"Friends."

Trent raised his glass of water. "Here's to friends, then."

Brendan smiled and raised his Coke. "To friends."

Trent ate the last bite of fish on his plate. "Thanks for the meal. You were right, I definitely feel better."

"See? I should have been a doctor instead of a lawyer."

"What are you up to now?"

"I'm going to catch the bus home. I just moved into this garage apartment. The landlord is a little off the reservation, but the place is pretty cool."

"Oh, yeah? Where is it?"

"North Campus, just off Red River."

"Let me give you a ride. I'm more than capable of driving now. I promise. It's the least I can do to repay you for bringing me here."

"Okay. That would be great."

"What's wrong with your landlord?" Trent asked.

"Nothing. He's just a little outgoing for my taste. On the day I moved in, I found a joint taped to my door. A friend of mine told me about some book set in San Francisco, with a crazy landlady who tapes joints to her tenants' doors. I don't remember the name of the book, but he must have read it and thought it was cool or something."

"Did you smoke it?"

"Of course. It was really good weed, I'll give him that."

Trent smiled. "Doesn't sound all that bad to me."


TRENT LEFT a ten-dollar tip on the table and grabbed his copy of "Blue Monday." He and Brendan walked to Trent's truck, which he had parked a few blocks from the record store in West Campus.

"Can I drive?" Brendan asked.

"What?"

"Come on, please. I don't have a car and I miss it. Besides, this way I don't have to give you directions."

"I told you, I feel fine."

"And I believe you. This has nothing to do with your fainting spell. I just can't afford a car while I'm in law school."

"You know how to drive a stick?"

"Of course."

Trent retrieved the keys from his pocket. "Is this what you mean by talking people into things?"

"This would be an excellent example, yes."

Trent tossed the keys to Brendan. "No speeding, Hotshot."

"A little speeding."

"No."

"Ten miles over the limit. Fifteen, tops."

"I'm a very safe driver. No speeding."

Brendan unlocked the passenger door and opened it. "You're no fun."

"I'm all sorts of fun. My middle name is 'fun.'"

"Your middle name is Benjamin. That was in the *Sports Illustrated* article."

Trent climbed in and set the copy of "Blue Monday" on the seat next to him. He waited as Brendan walked around and got behind the wheel. Trent drove a 1978 red Ford F-150 Ranger XLT 4x4 with red interior, a bench seat, and wood-panel accents. His father had bought it for him when he got a full baseball scholarship to UT. He loved this truck and was a little nervous about someone else driving it.

"Wow," Brendan said as he settled in. "It's a beauty."

"This truck is how you know I'm half-Texan."

"I'm not any Texan. I just live here."

"Where are you from?"

"Ohio. My family moved to Houston after I graduated from high school."

"Where did you go to college?"

"Rice."

"You must be smart."

"Smart enough to get into UT Law, but not smart enough for Harvard or Columbia. That was my dream."

"Where did F. Lee Bailey go to law school?" Trent asked.

"Boston University."

"See? He didn't need Harvard."

"I know. It just sounded like fun."

Brendan started the engine and pulled out into traffic.

"Careful," Trent said.

"Yes, Dad."

"Did your father teach you how to drive?"

"Yep. I almost gave him a heart attack. He took me out to some country road and said, 'Okay, there's the gas.' I didn't know it was sensitive, so I laid my foot down and drove right into a soybean field. I thought it was kind of funny, but he had a different take on the situation."

"You have a twisted sense of humor."

Trent sat back and allowed himself to relax and enjoy the ride. Brendan used Thirty-Second Street to cut across town, and then turned left onto Red River. He headed north a few blocks and turned right onto a street with not one, but two NO OUTLET signs. He drove to the end of the block and pulled into a driveway on the left. As they approached the garage, Trent saw a man reading in a lounge chair.

"That's him," Brendan said.

"Your landlord?"

"Yep. Brace yourself. He's definitely going to recognize you."

"Uh-oh."

"Do you want me to get you out of this?"

"No, I'm fine. Maybe I can score you some points, if you want."

"Couldn't hurt. Get him to knock fifty bucks off my rent."

Trent got out of the truck. The man looked up from his book, then he covered his mouth with his hand, and a shocked expression bulged from his eyes. He removed his hand, pointed, and said, "You're Trent Days."

"Yes, sir, I am."

The man fumbled with his book as he jumped up from the chair. He walked over to Trent and shook his hand.

"Bill Walsh. Am I dreaming?"

"No, sir, you're not dreaming."

"Oh, please, call me Bill."

"Okay, Bill."

Brendan came around the truck and said, "Guess who walked into the record store today?"

"You mean you two aren't friends?"

Brendan shook his head. "No."

Trent looked at him. "Yes, we are."

Brendan paused for a moment. "Okay, but we just met this afternoon."

"Why aren't you with the team?" Bill asked. "You're still allowed to suit up and sit in the dugout, even when you're on the DL."

"I'm being punished. Lillis decided a break would do me good. He said I needed to think about my aggressive behavior."

"Horseshit," Bill said. "Your behavior is fine. What were you supposed to do, just step aside and let Butler score a run?"

"That's what I told him. But if I can't stay healthy, I can't play. So he's got a point."

"Are you coming to the party tonight?"

"What party?" Trent asked.

"It's my birthday," Bill said.

Brendan slapped his palm against his forehead. "I forgot all about that. Trent was just giving me a ride home. I don't think he wants to—"

"How many people will be there?" Trent said.

"It's nothing big. Me and my wife, Grace. Jon and Edith Wright from across the street. One of the other professors I work with at UT, and his wife. You two would make eight."

Trent smiled. "You teach at UT?"

"Yes, I do. English literature. Doesn't your dad teach English in Barrow?"

"Yeah, he does. You read the *Sports Illustrated* article too?"

"Every word. Did you really hit a home run your first time at bat?"

"That's a true story, but it wasn't quite as dramatic as the way the writer described it. I don't recall my father saying those things."

"Your swing reminds me of Ted Williams."

"Thanks, but you just compared me to the greatest hitter of all time."

"Greater than Ruth?"

"Yes. And Cobb. And DiMaggio."

"Hot dog," Bill said. "Talking baseball with the Eskimo Slugger. So, what about the party?"

Trent nodded. "I would love to come. Thanks for inviting me."

"I need to go in and call my wife. Eight o'clock. Is that okay?"

"Yes. That's easy to remember."

Bill Walsh turned to Brendan and said, "Best birthday present ever." He patted both of them on the arm and walked into the house.

Brendan waited until Bill was out of earshot before he said, "I'm so sorry. Of course, you don't have to come to his stupid party. I was looking for an excuse to get out of it myself. I mean, I just moved in last week. I don't even know the guy."

"I like him. Don't you want me there?"

"I didn't say that. You're Trent Days. You can pretty much do whatever you want."

"Well, I'd like to come to the party, then."

"Okay. I suppose that's settl—"

"On one condition."

"What's that?"

"You drop this 'you're Trent Days' stuff. It's the worst thing about my life, Brendan. Really. If we're going to hang out for even one night, you can't treat me like I walk on water. I'm not the Eskimo Slugger. I'm just a kid from Barrow, Alaska. Deal?"

Brendan thrust out his hand. "Deal."

Trent shook it. Still firm and sturdy. "I'll be back at eight. Everyone I know is either playing baseball or in Alaska, so I could use the company."

Brendan grinned. "Okay, then. But do you mind if I tell you something?"

"Not at all. What is it?"

"This is turning out to be one of the best days of my life."

# FOUR

TRENT WENT home and lay down for a short nap, which cleared the remaining cloudiness from his head. Afterward, he took a shower and put on a clean pair of jeans and a blue button-down shirt. He turned on the radio to listen to the first few minutes of the game. His name came up immediately. One of the announcers wondered if the Astros would be able to hold on until he returned in August.

His stomach tied itself into a knot. This had been his life since April, when he experienced his first opening day in the major leagues. Since then his rise had been meteoric. Sure he loved the game, but it wasn't in his blood like Kieran and his other teammates. The mania surrounding his rookie season made him wonder if he was cut out to be a baseball star. Fans hounded him for autographs and pictures wherever he went. He enjoyed signing gloves or cards for the kids, but the grown men could be creepy, and the women even more so. He and Kieran kept a fish bowl on the shelf between their lockers, where they tossed all the women's phone numbers they'd collected since spring training.

When the *Sports Illustrated* article hit the previous month, things got even worse. Trent felt deeply uncomfortable with the added attention, not to mention the comparisons to greats like Mickey Mantle and Willie Mays. He agreed with some of the beat writers who said it was too soon for such comparisons—he simply hadn't played enough games yet. But the sport loved a rookie sensation, and in July of 1983, Trent was the most talked-about player in major league baseball. No question about it.

Coming back to Austin was a break from all that. Maybe at this party he could be a normal person again, even if it only lasted for one night. He got up and checked his appearance in the hallway mirror. He stared at his reflection and said, "Who are you kidding?" Trent knew there was only one reason he was going to this party, and it had nothing to do with feeling like a normal person again.

At seven forty-five he turned off the radio, hopped in his truck, and headed north to the Walsh residence. He didn't know if he should check in with Brendan first, but he decided it was best to knock on the front door. A beautiful, dark-haired, and very pregnant woman answered.

"Excuse me, ma'am, but I'm here for the party."

"Are you the ballplayer?"

"Yes, ma'am, I am."

The woman pushed open the screen door and invited him inside. She offered her hand and said, "I'm Grace Walsh. My husband told me all about you."

"Trent Days." He shook her hand as he stepped inside. "This is a beautiful house you have."

"Why, thank you. We just bought it last year. There's still so much work to be done. The wallpaper looks like it's from the '60s, but I haven't gotten around to replacing it yet. I keep saying, 'After the baby comes.'"

"When are you due?"

"Next week. Bill!" she called. "The baseball player is here. My husband's in the kitchen."

Brendan appeared from another room inside the house. "You made it. I wasn't sure if you would show or not."

"I told you I needed the company. Besides, I'm a man of my word."

"I like you already," Grace said. "Can I get you a beer?"

"Yes, ma'am, that would be very kind of you."

She headed for what Trent assumed was the kitchen, leaving him alone in the foyer with Brendan.

"Nice shirt."

"You like it?" Trent said.

"I didn't know you were going to dress up."

"What are you talking about?"

"Your shirt has a collar. That's dressing up to me." Brendan was wearing a pair of shorts and a red T-shirt that said, *Liberty Lunch*.

"Do you want me to go home and change?"

"No, you look nice. Sorry I'm such a slob."

"Is everyone else here?"

"Yeah, they're in the living room. Want me to introduce you?"

"Sure. Let's get it over with."

Brendan led him into the giant living room, where two couples sat on an L-shaped sofa. One of the men jumped up immediately and thrust his hand toward Trent.

"Jon Wright," the man said. "Big fan."

Trent shook his hand. "Thanks, Jon. It's nice to meet you."

The other three people stood up and Trent introduced himself. Jon's wife, Edith, was a plump woman with brown hair the color of dishwater. Charlie and Cindy Henderson were a handsome young couple, but Cindy looked like she was enduring, rather than enjoying, this social outing. It was clear neither of them had a clue who Trent was.

The six guests sat down, and Charlie said, "Bill tells us you're a baseball player, Trent."

"That's correct."

"I'm sorry to say I don't follow sports. I've always been more academically inclined."

"That's okay. I'm actually not a big sports fan myself."

"Really?" Brendan asked.

"Nope."

Jon Wright cleared his throat. "Well, I'm a sports fan, and let me just say, you're sitting next to the finest catcher since Yogi Berra."

"Don't believe the hype," Trent said.

"Horseshit." The voice belonged to Bill Walsh, who had entered the room with his wife. "You're being modest. Charlie, we're taking a road trip to Houston next month to see the Astros play. I need to teach you about baseball. Get your head out of those books. You can come too, Jon."

"Well," Charlie said, "I don't know if—"

"Trent," Bill said as he handed him a bottle of beer, "Brendan told me you like fish. So I grilled some red snapper for dinner."

"That sounds delicious. I was raised on fish and still eat it pretty much every day."

"We had to squeeze two extra chairs around the table," Grace said. "It's going to be a tad cozy. I hope that's okay."

Edith Wright waved her hand. "Don't you fret, Grace. We'll fit just fine."

The guests filed from the living room to the dining room, where a table for six had been modified to seat eight. Brendan pulled out a chair, and Trent slid into the seat next to him. He noticed the plates were mismatched. In the center, large platters of fish and vegetables, salad, and bread were laid out for a family-style feast. Everyone filled up their plates, and before anyone could start eating, Bill began a prayer that Trent had heard many times before meals.

"Bless us, oh Lord, and these thy gifts, which we are about to receive from thy bounty, through Christ our Lord."

Everyone followed with an "Amen" and then started to eat.

Grace began the conversation: "Bill tells me you're from Alaska, Trent."

"That's correct."

"Is it common for baseball players to come from Alaska?" Charlie asked.

"No, it's not common at all. I didn't start playing until I was fourteen."

"Tell the story," Bill said.

"Well, my father is from Texas, so we usually visited his family at Christmas."

"How did your father end up in Alaska?" Edith asked.

"He went to college in Anchorage. He says he was always drawn to Alaska, for some reason. After he graduated, he took a job teaching at the school in Barrow. He met my mother shortly after that."

"Is she a native Eskimo?" Cindy Henderson asked.

"Yes, she's a full-blooded Inupiat."

"Oh, I apologize. Is Eskimo an offensive term?"

"I don't really mind either way. I'm not easily offended."

"So, you were fourteen...," Bill prompted.

"Yes. When I was fourteen, we finally visited my dad's family during the summer. My father has six half brothers and sisters, so I have lots of cousins in Texas. They were starting up a baseball game, and that's when I picked up a bat for the first time. We played in the open field next to my grandmother's house, and they designated where the corn began as the home run fence. So I stepped up to the plate. Strike one. Strike two. Then right into the corn. That got everyone's attention."

Cindy Henderson looked confused. "But how did you keep playing baseball when you went back to Alaska?"

"I didn't. I moved down here to Austin a year later."

"You left your family?" Edith said.

"Yes, ma'am."

"That's part of the legend," Bill said. "He lived with his father's best friend from high school, Brent Harrison."

"Bill," Grace said, "let the boy tell his own story."

"Oh, of course. Sorry about that."

Trent laughed. "It's okay. Jump in anytime, Bill. I keep forgetting that my biography is public knowledge. Anyway, Mr. Harrison had a son too. He was the same age as me."

"Kieran Harrison and Trent Days," Jon Wright said. "They're like the Hall & Oates of the baseball diamond."

"Hmm," Trent murmured. "Which one am I?"

"Kieran is a pitcher," Brendan explained.

"And like Jon said, I'm a catcher. We played together all through high school and college."

"And now they play for the Astros," Jon added.

"Both of you?" Cindy asked.

"Yes," Trent said. "Baseball is a business first, and we sell more tickets together than we do separately. The suits in Houston recognized that right off and worked a backroom trade so they could draft us together. It was a big deal in the press. Of course, Kieran and I had no complaints. We love playing together, but it's been tough on him, being in the rotation with someone like Nolan Ryan. He's used to getting all the attention."

"Does your family still live in Alaska?" Grace asked.

"Yes, ma'am, they do. I have three younger brothers."

"Really?" Grace said. "What are their names?"

"Dopey, Sleepy, and Grumpy."

Everyone laughed.

"Sorry about that. Their names are Stephen, Jeffrey, and Mickey."

"How often do you see them?" Cindy asked.

"Not as often as I'd like. I miss them something awful."

Charlie nodded. "That was quite a sacrifice for a fourteen-year-old boy."

"Well, actually I was fifteen when I moved here. After I picked up that first bat, though, my whole life became about baseball, and it's been that way ever since."

"It's nice that Kieran is a pitcher," Brendan said. "That way you two are never in competition with each other. I imagine it makes the friendship easier."

"That friendship has never been easy. We fight like brothers."

"That's good," Bill said. "Brothers should fight."

Grace slapped him on the arm. "What's wrong with you?"

"I hate when he shakes me off," Trent said.

"Shakes you off?" Charlie asked.

"In baseball," Bill said, "the catcher calls the game. He decides what kind of pitch the pitcher will throw. You know, a fastball or a slider, that kind of thing."

"What's the difference?" Edith asked.

"Well," Trent said, "a fastball is just that. Its power is in its speed. A slider is a breaking ball, which means it breaks down and out, or slides, at the last minute."

"How is that different from a curveball?" Charlie asked.

"A slider has a shorter break."

Cindy looked puzzled. "Why does the ball do that?"

"It's a combination of the way it's thrown and the seams. If the ball was completely smooth, most pitches wouldn't be possible. That's the thing about baseball: so much of it is an accident. Like the distance between bases. Ninety feet is perfect. A few feet one way or another and the game wouldn't work."

Charlie wiped his mouth with a napkin. "Let's go back to calling the pitches. How do you communicate those calls?"

Bill smiled and slapped him on the back. "There you go, Charlie. We'll make a baseball fan out of you yet."

"A catcher uses hand signals between his legs," Trent explained, "so only the pitcher can see. Unless there's a man on second base. Then he has to be careful."

"If the pitcher doesn't like the call," Bill said, "he shakes his head."

"And that's the part I don't like. I spend a lot of time studying batters. I know what I'm doing when I call for a fastball on a 3-2 count. But Kieran says he has to *feel* it. Drives me nuts. But then I don't claim to understand pitchers. I do respect them, but that's different. It's nothing short of magic what they do. That's pitching in a word: *magic.*"

"These hand signals," Charlie said, "are they a kind of sign language?"

Trent nodded. "You could say that."

Bill set his fork down and pushed his chair back a few inches. "Each team develops an elaborate system of signals. That was one of the first things my father taught me when he took me to the ballpark."

"How old were you?" Trent asked.

"Eight. On the surface, baseball seems like a quiet game, but if you look carefully, there's a fascinating conversation happening underneath. The coaches are communicating with the catcher, the catcher is communicating with the other players, and the players are communicating with each other. All silently."

"What do you say to Kieran when you walk out to the mound?" Jon asked.

"I tell Eskimo jokes. I don't claim to be a comedian, but that's what makes my jokes so funny. They're pretty bad."

"Tell us one," Brendan said.

"Did you hear about the Eskimo girl who spent the night with her boyfriend?"

Brendan shook his head.

"She woke up the next morning and was six months pregnant."

Everyone laughed except Cindy. "I don't get it."

"In parts of Alaska," her husband explained, "the sun doesn't rise in the winter. One night lasts almost half the year."

Trent continued. "Kieran gets stuck in his head too much. If I can get him to laugh, it helps loosen him up a bit."

Edith giggled. "I always get so bored whenever I sit down and try to watch a game with Jon."

Grace nodded in agreement. "I come from a football family. Baseball's too slow for me."

"That's because it's a game of subtext," Bill said.

Charlie laughed. "Spoken like a true literary scholar. Always looking for the subtext."

"I'm serious," Bill continued. "In many ways, you're both right. The text is quite slow and boring. The game tends to drag from pitch to pitch, punctuated by bursts of excitement. But embedded in the fabric of the game is the promise of immortality."

"Oh, Bill," Grace said, "you are so full of shit sometimes."

Trent smiled at their playful interaction and said, "Actually, he's right."

"See? I'm right." Bill Walsh leaned over and kissed his wife. "Because baseball has no clock. It's the only major sport without one. An inning lasts until the third out, no matter how long it takes. That's the beauty of baseball. If you can keep hitting, you can keep playing. An hour, a day, a year…."

"Or forever," Brendan said.

"Yes," Bill said. "And if you can play forever, you can live forever. Besides, how can you not love a sport where the central metaphor is coming home?"

And that's when Trent felt it.

Under the table, Brendan's knee had come to rest against his own. His mouth got dry and he took a drink of water, but he didn't move his leg. Should he say something? There were a lot of people at the table, and the arrangement was pretty cramped. Maybe it was an accident. Then, before Trent could react, Brendan sat up and moved his knee away. He put his arm on the back of Trent's chair and whispered into his ear, "Sorry about that. Small table."

Brendan's breath was hot on Trent's skin. That was no accident. His mind raced back to Quincy's words from earlier in the day: "I predict you will find getting to know each other quite the game changer." *This is a mistake*, Trent thought, but it was one he desperately wanted to make.

"Bill," Charlie said, "your take on baseball is quite poetic."

Edith giggled again. "I don't see anything like that when I watch it on TV. I swear, Bill, you're too much for me sometimes."

After the meal, Grace brought out a birthday cake with thirty candles on it, and Bill blew them out with much fanfare. Trent passed on a piece of cake, with the explanation that he rarely ate sweets. The conversation turned away from baseball and toward current events, which suited Trent just fine. By the end of the evening, he felt almost normal. It didn't hurt that Brendan kept him entertained by cracking jokes and whispering side comments into his ear.

Shortly after midnight they said good night, wished Bill Walsh one more "happy birthday," and walked out to Trent's truck. He was nervous standing in the dark street with Brendan, under the warm glow of a streetlamp, and he hoped it didn't show.

"You working tomorrow?"

"No," Brendan said. "I'm off, actually. Why?"

"Do you want to go fishing?"

"Fishing? What is it with you and fish?"

"Ancient Eskimo proverb: No fish, no life."

"You really know how to play up the Eskimo thing, don't you? Even though I know you hate that nickname."

"How can you tell?"

"I see the way you flinch every time someone says it."

"Your friend Fiona was right. It's the name of a cocktail."

"What's in it?"

"Baileys, vodka, and peppermint schnapps. I've never had one, but it sounds disgusting." Trent unlocked the door of his truck. "You in or out? Fishing tomorrow, I mean. I'm not going to twist your arm."

"Do I need anything?" Brendan asked. "Hooks? Worms? Wading boots?"

"No. We'll just be bank fishing. Nothing complicated. I got plenty of gear and tackle. You can bring the coffee, though. Or make us some breakfast tacos."

"I don't know how to make breakfast tacos."

"We'll pick up something on the way out of town, then."

"How early we talking?"

"Eight o'clock. I'm not a crack-of-dawn fisher, but any later and the heat will get us." Trent got into his truck and rolled down the window. He looked at Brendan, who was smiling his big, infectious grin. "Thanks for helping me out today. I promise not to pop pills and drive anymore."

"I would appreciate that," Brendan said. "Thanks for coming tonight. It meant a lot to Bill. And to me."

"You're welcome. He and his wife are a great couple. I think you're going to like living here."

"I think you might be right. Good night, Mr. Days."

"Good night, Mr. Baxter." As Trent drove away, he yelled out the window, "Don't forget to set your alarm."

WHEN TRENT got home, he noticed the replacement copy of "Blue Monday" was still on the seat next to him. He picked it up and went inside. He put the record on the turntable and laid the needle down. He sat on the sofa and listened to the soothing beat.

Trent closed his eyes and saw Brendan's face smiling back at him. It had been a great day. No question about it. Houston was 160 miles away, and out of sight meant out of mind. Maybe it was time to take a chance. Maybe he could finally let his guard down. He felt something for the redhead with the playful grin, and he had plenty of reasons to believe those feelings weren't one-sided. It all came down to one question: Could he trust Brendan with his secret?

Trent was so tired, he almost fell asleep sitting on the couch. But then the record skipped. He opened his eyes and started to laugh. He continued laughing as he got up and switched off the turntable. He undressed and brushed his teeth—and laughed so hard that toothpaste sprayed all over the mirror. He set his alarm for six thirty, crawled into bed—and laughed some more. He loved baseball, but this was a different thing entirely.

This was a kind of joy Trent had never experienced before.

# FIVE

THE NEXT morning Trent awoke to the high-pitched buzzing of his alarm clock. He sat up and peered through the blinds. The sun had barely risen on what promised to be a beautiful day. He jumped out of bed, and his bare feet hit the cold wood floor—the cold being a byproduct of the new air-conditioning unit he had recently installed in his bedroom. He gently pressed a finger against his ribs. Still sore, but better. He took a quick shower, dressed, and then headed for the garage, where he gathered up his fishing gear and packed it in the bed of his truck.

After the lunch with Quincy, and Bill Walsh's birthday party, Trent was looking forward to spending some time alone with Brendan. Still, he had no experience in these matters and no idea how to proceed. Baseball had saved him from an awkward adolescence full of dating girls he had no interest in. His single-minded focus was all the excuse he needed for his lack of a girlfriend, but he suspected that focus was about to be challenged.

When Trent arrived at the Walsh house shortly before eight o'clock, Bill came barreling out the back door and cut him off in the driveway. He had a folded map of Travis County and a black magic marker in his hand.

"Morning, Trent. Great to see you again. Brendan told me you're going fishing today."

"Yeah. I thought we'd try Lake Travis. I've been fishing out there since I was a teenager."

"It's beautiful, isn't it? Some great swimming holes too. My parents used to take me and my brother Tommy to Windy Point. We were there every Sunday in the summertime. Would you mind if I give you a tip?"

"What kind of tip?"

"I know the perfect spot. Still a secret to this day, known only to a select few. If you go to one of the county parks, you're bound to be recognized, and then you'll have people pestering you all day. I can show you my spot on the map, if you want."

Trent heard a sound behind him and turned to see Brendan coming down the steps from the garage apartment. His red hair was still wet and he was smiling the Brendan smile. He carried two cups of coffee and a bag from Texas French Bread.

"I decided to pick up breakfast before we head out," Brendan said, "so for me I got a chocolate croissant and some sour cream coffee cake—my favorite." He paused to hand one of the cups to Trent. "And for you, since you don't eat sweets, I got a slice of quiche. Not only is it savory, but it's made with soy milk and soy cheese, which means zero dairy products. It's a huge slice, too. You can be pretty sure I'm not—" Brendan stopped and stared at Bill, then back at Trent. "What's going on?"

"Bill was going to show me a fishing spot out on the lake."

"Oh, right," Brendan said. "The top-secret place. How do we get there?"

"Let me show you." Bill walked toward the patio table near the back door and spread out the map. Trent and Brendan followed him and watched as he drew a route in black marker. "When you get to this intersection," he said as he pointed to an X he'd made on the map, "go straight, and then look for three houses in a row on the left. They won't have any numbers on them. They're identical, but painted different colors. Red, green, and blue. Park across the road from the blue house, on the shoulder."

"We won't get towed?" Trent asked.

"No. I've taken care of that. Walk about ten feet past the blue house and you'll see a path of stone steps. But you won't see the path until you're right up on it, so pay attention. It's easy to miss. Take that down to the water, and then.... Well, I don't want to give it away." Bill folded up the map and handed it to Brendan, along with the marker. Then, to Trent's surprise, he reached into his pocket and pulled out a joint. He handed that to Brendan as well. "Trent," he said, "don't you dare tell Grace about this, you hear? It'll just get me into a bucket of trouble, and there's no point in that." He patted them both on the arm. "No point at all. Y'all have a wonderful day."

Trent put out his hand. "Thanks, Bill."

They said good-bye and Bill went into the house. Trent took a sip of his coffee, which Brendan had left black.

"I got cream and sugar, if you want it."

"No," Trent said. "This is perfect."

"Really? The only way I can drink coffee is if I doctor it up enough so that it doesn't taste like coffee anymore."

"What's the point, then?"

"*Caffeine.* It's eight o'clock in the morning, and I don't become fully functional until after ten."

"You'll be thanking me later when it heats up. You ready to hit the road?"

"Yes," Brendan said as they started to walk down the driveway, "but I have a confession to make."

Trent laughed. "I know."

"What?"

"You've never been fishing before."

"I'm from Ohio, not Michigan. I don't come from the land of a thousand lakes. And, not to mention, my father wasn't particularly outdoorsy."

"Don't worry, Mr. Baxter, it's not rocket science. What we'll be doing is pretty simple. You should be thankful I'm not taking you ice fishing."

Brendan got into the passenger side and set the map and breakfast bag on the seat between them. "Do you mind if I eat my chocolate croissant?"

"Not at all. Did you get up early and walk to the bakery?"

"Maybe. Why?"

"Just an observation. Hand me that slice of quiche, will you? I'm starving."

TRENT AND Brendan fell into a comfortable silence on the drive to Lake Travis. The winding road of FM 2222 had a hypnotizing effect as it snaked its way into the Hill Country. Eventually, they turned onto a side road, which led them to their first glimpse of the lake. It stretched out in front of them in a series of steep, cliff-lined coves filled with sapphire blue water and reflections from the early morning sun.

Brendan opened the map. As they approached a stop sign, he said, "Turn right here." He looked out Trent's window at the view. "It reminds me of Italy."

"You've been to Italy?"

"Yeah, I was there last summer. They have a lake country in the northern part, up around Milan. It's got the same combination of hills and water." Brendan looked back at the map. "The intersection with the X is coming up."

They came to another stop sign, and then Trent continued forward until they saw the three houses Bill told them about. As instructed, Trent pulled onto the dirt shoulder and parked across from the blue one. They gathered the gear from the back of the truck and found the stone steps exactly where Bill said they would be. The steps ended in a dirt path that wound its way a short distance to the lake.

"Jesus Christ," Brendan said as he reached the rocky bank of the water's edge. "This is fucking amazing."

The map had led them to a secluded cove, untouched and unseen by the boaters on the lake. They were completely alone for as far as they could see.

"This is frigging awesome," Trent said. "Remind me to thank your landlord. But we want to keep our voices down, so we don't scare away the fish."

"Oh," Brendan whispered. "Got it."

Trent set up a rod and reel for Brendan and showed him how to cast and retrieve. He caught on fast, and within ten minutes they were standing side by side, waiting for their first bite.

"Do you know what occurred to me last night?" Trent asked.

"What occurred to you last night?"

"You know my whole life story, and I know practically nothing about you."

"Hardly seems fair, does it?"

"Hardly."

Brendan practiced casting his line. "Not really sure what there is to tell. If I wrote my autobiography tomorrow, it would be a pretty thin volume."

"What about your family?"

"My mom and dad live in Houston. My dad works for an oil company and Mom…. Well, she doesn't seem very happy with the way her life turned out. My dad works and travels a lot. She doesn't make friends easily, so she's alone too much."

Trent reeled in his line and recast it over the water with a flick of his wrist. "Any brothers or sisters?"

"Nope, I'm an only child. I don't know if more kids would have made things better or worse. My guess is, worse."

"Why are they still together if she's so unhappy?"

Brendan shrugged. "Habit, I guess."

"What was Ohio like, growing up?"

"I thought it was fine. But now that I've traveled a bit, I can see how closed-minded everyone is."

"Everyone?"

"Okay, maybe not everyone, but the Midwest's oppressive power is in its blandness."

"I can relate to that," Trent said.

"Still, lots of great writers and artists come from that part of the country. It's as if they need their creativity to recover from growing up there. Everywhere I go, I meet cool people from Ohio."

"You're one of the cool people?"

"Hey, I'm fishing with Trent Days. I think that makes me pretty damn—Oh. Sorry, I agreed not to do that."

"Thank you."

"I'm listening, I promise. Even when it probably seems like I'm not." Brendan's line tugged, and he yanked upward, but it turned out to be a false alarm. "Shit. At least we know there are fish out there. Sneaky bastard."

"What do you think that was about yesterday, with Quincy?"

"You mean the bullshit about the auras and the gold sparks?"

"Yeah. Was he just blowing smoke up our asses?"

"No," Brendan said. "He believed every word of it. Quincy is a trip, but he's an authentic trip. That's why I hang out there so much. He respects everyone's point of view, but he's also convinced the world works in a certain way, and I like that."

"Even when you don't agree with him?"

"Especially when I don't agree with him. Even if he does see gold sparks, which I highly doubt, I don't think they mean we have a destiny to fulfill. You're not Luke Skywalker and I'm not Han Solo."

"Maybe you're Obi-Wan Kenobi."

Brendan swung his rod like a lightsaber and imitated the buzzing sound from the movies. "Jedi master, I am."

"I said Obi-Wan, not Yoda."

Brendan tried to engage Trent in a lightsaber duel with their fishing rods, but Trent knew better. "You're going to scare away all the fish," he said, "not to mention getting our lines tangled up together."

"Sorry, Dad."

"That's the second time you've called me that."

"Well, that's the second time you've acted like an overly responsible adult."

"You don't consider yourself a grown-up?"

Brendan burst out laughing. "No, not by a long shot. I still have two more years of being a student and working at a record store. I plan to enjoy it."

"Speaking of record stores, I've been meaning to ask you. Why aren't the records at Inner Sanctum sorted alphabetically? I never could find anything I was looking for in there."

"Which made you do what?"

"I don't know. Ask whoever was working, I guess."

Brendan grinned. "There's your answer."

"You sort them that way so your customers will talk to you?"

"Yes. We want to know what people are listening to. Music, even buying records, should be a social experience. And no, before you ask, I don't go bank fishing with every guy who buys a copy of 'Blue Monday.'"

"That's good to know. What are your plans after you graduate?"

"I'm moving to New York. I'm not even bothering to take the Texas Bar."

"Really? From Ohio, to Texas, to New York. That's an interesting path."

"Ohio and Texas weren't my choice. I'm done with small towns."

"Austin's not that small."

"It's too small for me." Brendan started to say something else, but then stopped himself and took a long pause. "Look, I'm not delusional. I know I'm never going to be the next F. Lee Bailey. I'm not even in the top 1 percent of my class at a second-tier law school. But if I stay in Austin, I'll end up working for the state. If I move to New York, at least I'm in an exciting city with the possibility of an adventure."

"Sounds like you've seen too many movies. You don't need to move to New York for an adventure. Besides, there's a lot to be said for a less complicated life."

"That's easy for you to say. Everything you do is an adventure."

Trent huffed. "You have no idea what a pain in the ass my life has become."

"At least you're great at something. That's all I want, really. To be insanely, ridiculously, better-than-everybody-else great at something. Like you."

"It's not as fun as it looks."

"Excuse me if I would like to try it out and decide for myself."

"Well, how about in our next life we switch places?" Trent said. "You can be a hotshot lawyer from New York City, and I'll be a simple country boy who makes furniture or fixes cars for a living."

"Can you make that happen, please?"

"I'll see what I can do. I am the Eskimo Slugger, after all. Maybe it will give me some pull with the Great Spirit."

Brendan stamped his foot against the rock. "I knew you were going to play that card at some point."

"No autographs while I'm fishing, please."

"Okay," Brendan said, "I should be allowed to ask at least once. One time. I know you want me to treat you like a kid from Barrow, but I'm dying to ask. It's only fair."

"You want to know what it's like."

"Yes! Come on, man. You're living the American boy's dream. *What does that feel like?*"

"Okay." Trent took a deep breath. "First of all, keep in mind, I didn't grow up with that dream. But, truth be told, it's like nothing I ever experienced before. When I hit my first home run in the Astrodome, a part of me thought it wasn't real—that no one's life turns out that way. Not really. But then I started to believe my own publicity. I honestly thought I'd never get hurt or end up on the DL. Never. I was the greatest five-tool player since Mickey Mantle. Finally it all began to look surreal, like it was happening to someone else, and I was just watching from the sidelines. Trent Days became a character I play. I'm surrounded by people all the time, but I've never been so lonely. I don't feel like I'm in one piece anymore. I have nothing to anchor me to the ground, so half the time I feel like I'm about to float away."

Brendan was silent for a moment. "Wow. You're right, it doesn't sound like fun. I wish there was something I could do."

Trent smiled. "You're doing it. I haven't been this relaxed and happy in a long time."

"Really?"

Trent nodded.

"Have you seen *Return of the Jedi* yet?" Brendan asked.

"No. I haven't seen a movie since spring training."

"We should go."

Brendan tried again to engage Trent in a fishing rod duel, only this time Trent played along, tangled lines be damned. They continued fishing until late morning, alternating between conversation and contented silence. Trent felt the temperature push toward the century mark and he could tell Brendan was getting a little bored, especially since they weren't catching anything.

"You know what would make this a lot more fun?" Brendan asked.

"What?"

Trent looked over as Brendan reached into his pocket and pulled out Bill's joint. Trent knew that if he went all Nancy Reagan, "Just Say No," on Brendan, he'd get called "Dad" again. He hadn't smoked pot since college, even though drugs were everywhere in the clubhouse, especially cocaine. Some of the guys even played as high as a kite, which frankly pissed him off. He'd always said no to the white stuff, but he didn't see anything wrong with a little herb now and then, off the field.

"Spark it up," he said.

"Seriously? You're not going to object?"

"Nope. Regardless of how I got here, I'm on vacation."

"I don't have a lighter."

"There's one in the tackle box."

Brendan handed his rod to Trent and then squatted down. He rummaged around until he found the lighter. He stood up and lit the joint, puffed a few times, and then inhaled. He handed it to Trent, who took a long drag and held in the smoke. He exhaled and handed it back to Brendan, who took another hit and said, "Much better."

He offered Trent another drag, but he waved it off. "One's enough for me. I'm a lightweight."

"We'll save the rest for later."

Brendan put some spit on his thumb and forefinger and then quickly extinguished the blunt. He returned it to his pocket and took his rod from Trent. They stood fishing in silence for several minutes. It didn't take long before Trent felt the first wave of a pleasant buzz. He started to giggle, and soon Brendan was laughing too. "What's so funny?"

"Nothing," Trent said. "I was just thinking that if you could somehow get the fish stoned, they'd get the munchies and take the bait."

"Are you going to get silly on me now?"

"I hope so."

Brendan reeled in his line and set his rod on the ground.

"What are you doing?" Trent asked.

"Let's go swimming."

"But we didn't bring any trunks."

"So? There's no one around. Come on. It's as hot as hell out here. You can keep your underwear on if you're a chickenshit."

"That's the problem."

"What?" Brendan said. "No underwear? I guess we'll both have to go naked then, so you don't feel awkward."

"I don't think we—"

But it was too late. Brendan had already peeled off his T-shirt and tossed his sneakers to the side, and before Trent could say another word, he dropped his shorts and briefs to reveal a thick cock. Trent immediately turned away.

Brendan had a good laugh. "Aw, are you shy?"

Trent would have been angry, except he liked it when Brendan teased him. He tried to keep a straight face, but inside he was beaming. He reeled in his line and set his rod down. He took off his shirt and shoes, undid the top button of his shorts, and paused. Brendan didn't wait for him, but instead walked a few steps to a large rock and dove into the water. Trent unzipped his fly and let his shorts drop to the ground. He took two quick steps before he jumped into the air, tucked in his legs, and landed on the surface with a splash, cannonball-style. A stab of pain shot through his torso, and he screamed as his head came out of the water. Brendan was immediately next to him. Trent reached out and wrapped his arm around Brendan's neck.

"I got you," Brendan said. Their bodies pressed together under the water as Brendan kept Trent afloat. "You forgot about those bruised ribs."

Trent nodded. He held on to Brendan until his breathing steadied and the pain subsided. "What was I thinking, getting stoned and jumping into a lake?"

"It's my fault."

"No, it's not." Trent gritted his teeth and shook off the last of the pain. He closed his eyes for a moment and relished the feeling of Brendan's arms around him. A calm settled over him and he said, "Okay, I'm good now."

Brendan untangled himself and his hands lingered on Trent's body as he pulled away. "I'm sorry."

"Stop apologizing. I'm fine." Trent smiled as his buzz returned. He sent a splash in Brendan's direction.

"Hey! You're using your weakened state to lure me in, only to turn around and attack."

"It's a good strategy. The water feels great, doesn't it?"

"Yes, it does."

"This was a good idea," Trent said.

"Better than fishing?"

"Well, fishing is more fun when you actually catch something."

They treaded water and Brendan moved in a little closer. "Can I ask you a question?"

Trent didn't back away. "Sure. But when people ask if they can ask a question before they actually ask it, that usually means they want to talk about something serious."

"Hmm. I don't know if you'll think this is serious or not."

"What's the question, then?"

"Are you sure you're okay?"

"I'm fine. Was that the question?"

"No."

A dragonfly landed on Trent's arm, and he swatted it away.

"Are we on a date?"

Trent looked down at the water. Anywhere but into Brendan's eyes. "I don't know. Can I trust you?"

Brendan's response was certain and definitive. "Yes. I think you already know you can."

"What do you think?"

"It feels like a date to me."

"Yeah, I agree. It does."

Brendan was silent, but the smile on his face spoke for him.

"That's it?" Trent asked.

"For now."

Trent ducked under the water and then came up a few seconds later. Brendan cut the surface with his hand and splashed Trent in the head. He retaliated, and soon water was flying everywhere. "If there were any fish in this cove before," Trent yelled, "they're gone now." They swam the few yards back to the water's edge and climbed out. Brendan's body glistened in the noon sun, and Trent did his best not to stare at his cock.

Brendan, on the other hand, boldly checked Trent out. "You're uncut."

"Yeah. Sorry."

Brendan lay down on a big slab of rock under one of the nearby oak trees. "Why are you apologizing?"

Trent lay down next to him. "Because everyone I know is circumcised. I feel like a freak in the showers."

"That's ridiculous. When we're visited by aliens, we'll never be able to explain why we chop off a part of our sons' dicks. Never."

Trent closed his eyes. The combination of water, pot, and not much sleep the night before made him drowsy, not to mention it was nice and cool in the shade. He could tell from the sound of Brendan's breathing that they were headed in the same direction. Trent opened his eyes and turned his head. Brendan looked peaceful and handsome, with water dripping from his red locks. Trent raised his head and took one more look at Brendan's dick. Then he closed his eyes again and nodded off to sleep.

WHEN TRENT woke up, Brendan was sitting beside him, his knees pulled to his chest, his gaze toward the water. Trent stretched and sat up. The buzz from the pot was gone, and his ribs felt a little less sore. "How long were we out?"

Brendan rubbed his arm against Trent's. "You were out for about an hour."

"Really? Why didn't you wake me up?"

"No need. I've been enjoying the view."

"Are you hungry?"

"I'm starving. Do you eat barbecue? Or is it fish only?"

"I love barbecue."

"Are you a brisket or a sausage man?" Brendan asked.

"I'm a brisket *and* a sausage man."

"I should have guessed that."

They got dressed and gathered up the rods and tackle. They hiked back to the road and climbed into the truck, but before he started the engine, Trent asked, "Are you okay? You're not freaking out, are you? About the date thing?"

"Me? What about you? You're the one who plays major league baseball."

"I know," Trent said. "It's a lot to process, but I'm trying not to overthink it. Or think about it at all, frankly."

"Have you ever been with a guy?"

"Never. Have you?"

"Kind of," Brendan replied. "In high school. One of the players on the JV squad gave me a blow job."

"Really? Did you like it?"

"Sure. I think guys are genetically programmed to like blow jobs. But I didn't like the way I behaved afterward. We didn't talk or hang out much after it happened."

"And no one since then?" Trent asked.

"No. I can't say I've struggled with it, but I haven't been in any hurry to embrace it either. Until now."

"Well, you can understand why I've never been with anyone. If it ever got out, my career would be over."

"So why me?"

"I think you know the answer to that."

Brendan blushed. "We can un-date this thing, if it's too much."

"Is that what you want?"

"No, but at some point, it could get really complicated. And ugly. Then I probably will freak out. I don't want to do anything to jeopardize your career, but at the same time, this is happening to me too. It's not all about you."

"I know that." Trent stared out the window. "You want to hear something weird?"

"What?" Brendan said.

Trent turned his head and looked at him. "I really don't want this day to end."

Brendan laid his hand on the open seat between them. "That's not weird. What do you say we forget about the rest of the world and just enjoy ourselves today? We can sort out the rest tomorrow."

Trent looked down and placed his hand in Brendan's. They intertwined their fingers, and Trent said, "Okay. But for the record, I don't want to un-date this thing either."

# SIX

THEY STOPPED at Trent's favorite barbecue place on the way back to town. It was little more than a shack and a few tables outside, but the food was some of the best he'd ever had. Trent had been coming here for years and knew the lady who owned it. Betty was a Texas-size woman with a heart of gold and the mouth of a sailor.

"Well, will you look at what the cat dragged in?" she said as they approached the ordering window. "How you been, Trent? It's been too fucking long."

"I know, Betty. How you been?"

"Oh, you know. Same bullshit, different day. What can I get you?"

He ordered brisket and sausage by the half pound, plus barbecue beans, potato salad, white bread, and all the fixings. With a cold bottle of Shiner Bock for each of them, they chose one of the picnic tables in the shade and sat down to eat. Brendan speared a piece of sausage with his plastic fork and dunked it in a cup of barbecue sauce. He popped it into his mouth and started to chew, then nodded his enthusiastic approval. "That's sinful."

"Good, huh?"

"Delicious. Have you been coming out here since college?"

"Since high school. Kieran loves this place. If you ask me, Lake Travis is the best part about living in Austin. You can fish it, you can swim it, you can sail it. But it's been years since I've been here in July."

"What did you do in the summer?"

"Kieran and I played ball up in Cape Cod. They have a summer collegiate league. Really hard to get into, but probably the most fun I've ever had playing baseball. Is this your first time out here?"

"No. I've been to Hippie Hollow once before."

"I bet you went naked."

"How did you guess?"

Trent took a piece of the bread and piled it with several slices of brisket and sausage. He trickled a small amount of the sauce over the meat, and then added some pickles and onions. He folded the bread to form a sandwich, took a bite, and chewed. "So you've only been in Austin for a year?"

Brendan swallowed and took a swig of beer. "A year in September. I lived at home when I went to Rice. Then I backpacked across Europe last summer, before I started law school."

"I've never been to Europe. Where all did you go?"

"London, Amsterdam, Paris. I was supposed to go to Germany too, but Italy got in the way. I spent two months in Florence and Rome."

"Did you pick up any Italian?"

"Sì. Voglio mettermi il tuo cazzo duro in bocca."

"What does that mean?"

Brendan grinned. "I'll tell you later. What year did you move to Austin?"

"1974."

"We didn't move to Houston until '78. Just in time for the oil boom."

"Did you go to Europe alone?"

"No. I went with my friend Jennifer."

"Girlfriend?"

"No. She knew about me. She kept trying to match me up with Italian boys."

"And you resisted?"

"I did. Italian boys are gorgeous, but they're also pigs. Besides, I wasn't ready a year ago."

Trent took another bite of his sandwich. "Lucky for me. Do you have any gay friends?"

"No. Jennifer is the only person I've told."

"Not your parents?"

"Hell, no. What would I say? I haven't even been with anyone yet."

Trent swallowed a mouthful of beans and washed it down with a drink from his bottle. "I think my parents would be okay with it."

"Really?"

"Yeah. My dad is very open-minded. It's the rest of my family… and the team. That's never going to happen."

"Do you have a big family on your mom's side too?"

"Yeah. She has four brothers, and they all have kids. I have cousins as far as the eye can see."

"And your father has how many half siblings?" Brendan asked.

"Six. His mother has been married four times and buried all four husbands."

"And no one's gotten suspicious?"

Trent laughed. "No. She had my dad with her first husband, then he died of a heart attack. She had two girls and a boy with her second husband."

"How did he die?"

"Lung cancer. Then three more boys with the third husband. Car accident. And childless with number four. Natural causes."

"So you were born and raised in Alaska, but you visited your dad's family every Christmas? What was that like?"

"Strange. Me and my brothers, we don't look like my Texas cousins. Everyone thought we were Mexican. That was pretty annoying."

"You don't look Mexican. What about in Alaska? Did they call you half-breed, like Cher?"

Trent laughed so hard he almost spit his food out. "No. No one ever called me half-breed. My mother's family loves my dad. Everyone loves my dad. He's the coolest white man they've ever met. If he ever went to confession, he'd have to make stuff up."

"Was Alaska even a state when you were born?"

"Just barely. My dad was part of the founding class at the University of Alaska Anchorage in 1954."

"Wow. A real pioneer."

"I suppose. My grandmother says he saw the Territory of Alaska on a map when he was a little boy, and from that point on, it was all he ever talked about."

"Is your grandmother still alive?"

"She is. In fact, I was planning to visit her sometime this week, since I have a few days off. She's a real character."

Brendan followed Trent's lead and made a brisket and sausage sandwich, minus the onions. "Did you know anything about baseball before that first game with your cousins?"

"Not a thing. We didn't even have a television in Barrow. No sports at all. I think I would be more of a sports fan if I had grown up watching them on TV like other kids."

"What did you do up there? Never mind, don't answer that. You probably went fishing a lot, right?"

Trent nodded. "It's not a very exciting life. My dad would read to us every night. Family is everything. You're always with your family. As kids, we had to keep an adult in our sight at all times, especially during winter."

"Did you have electricity?"

"No, we lived in an igloo," Trent said with a straight face. Brendan gaped at him until Trent cracked up. "I'm joking. The military brought a lot of modern conveniences with them in the '40s and '50s. We had houses and electricity and heat by the time I was growing up, so you could escape the cold. But it wasn't the cold that drove me crazy."

"What was it?"

"In the winter, you don't see the sun for sixty-five days."

"But in the summer, it doesn't set for sixty-five days, right?"

"Best thing about Alaska. I loved the summers as much as I hated the winters."

"So how did you learn about baseball?"

"Kieran and his dad taught me. When I moved down here and lived with them, I could finally watch games on TV. I studied players and asked a million questions. Mr. Harrison would tell me stories about the greats, and I read every book I could get my hands on. It came naturally to me for some reason, even though I didn't understand the passion other kids had for it. Obviously, my dad never took me to the ballpark when I was a little boy."

"I get it. My father took me to my first baseball game when I was ten years old. Tiger Stadium. At that age, the scale of the place was overwhelming, like a field of the gods. It brands something onto your brain. Who was your favorite player when you first moved here?"

"Catfish Hunter."

"A pitcher?"

"Yeah. Since Kieran was already a pitcher, it made sense that I would become a catcher, but catchers need to know everything about pitching. Mr. Harrison used to say, 'Show me a great catcher and I'll show you a pitching coach.' So I studied pitchers, and in 1974, Catfish Hunter was the best in the game. I loved watching him, the way he worked the corners."

"He was kind of a slob," Brendan said as he shoveled some potato salad into his mouth.

"I know, with that gut and all the spitting."

Brendan put his finger on his nose and nodded. "You could write a book about baseball and spitting. When did you fall in love with it?"

"Baseball?"

"Yeah. I assume you fell in love with it at some point, the way you play. I know a lot of writers compare you to Johnny Bench, because you're a catcher, but your style reminds me more of Pete Rose. You're aggressive, man, the way you stretch singles into doubles. And how many stolen bases do you have so far this season?"

"Forty-two."

"When did you find that fire in your belly?"

"The same night everyone else did. October 21, 1975."

"Ah, right. Game six of the World Series. That would do it."

"The greatest major league baseball game ever played. No question about it. I was sixteen years old and had never seen anything like it. That's when I figured a lot of things out."

"Like what?"

"Baseball is a long game by design. It's a nine-act play. A marathon every afternoon, sometimes two in one day. Even the season is long. Great baseball players know that. They all leave something in the tank and save the best for last."

"Who did you root for that night?"

"The Red Sox. They tell a great story."

"The curse of the Bambino."

"Getting so close, only to have it snatched away. Being a Red Sox fan means getting your heart broken, over and over and over again."

"It's like a fucking Greek tragedy."

"And frankly, I hated the Reds. Still do."

"Great. Here I am comparing you to two players from Cincinnati."

"It's okay. I just wish people would compare me to Carlton Fisk instead of Johnny Bench. I'll never forget the way he willed that ball fair at the end of game six. Magic. Let's face it, baseball is all about the pitcher. Just look at the diamond. Everything revolves around him, and great pitching beats great hitting any day of the week. But game six was when I realized a catcher could be the hero of a team."

"That's one of the beautiful things about baseball—anyone can be a hero if given half the chance. Remember the pinch hitter who slammed the tying homer? I remember he had jersey number 1. What was his name?"

"Bernie Carbo."

"That's the guy. One at bat, one shot at glory, and he knocks it out of the park. You know who I really remember from that game, though?"

"Who?"

Brandon took a drink of beer. "Fred Lynn."

"What a year he had. The greatest rookie season of all time."

"I'm not talking about his playing."

"What? Did you have a crush on him?"

"Big-time. I even had a few scenarios I'd run in my head when I jacked off."

"Like what?"

"I don't remember the details."

"Come on, try."

Brendan looked at Trent, as if to ask, *Is this turning you on?* Trent smiled, as if to say, *Yes.*

"Well," Brendan continued, "it would probably start with me getting a job at Fenway Park or something like that. Maybe as a ball boy. All my fantasies growing up had to be within the realm of possibility."

"Why? That's the point of a fantasy. It can be anything you want it to be."

"I know, but for some reason I couldn't get off on, say, doing it with James Dean. He's dead, so there's no way that could ever happen. And even though the chances of me getting a job as a Red Sox ball boy were highly improbable, it was still technically possible."

"What happened after you got the job?"

"Hmm." Brendan pondered the question. "I guess, at some point, after a practice, I would stick around to double-check and make sure all the jerseys got hung up in the lockers for the next day. I probably thought everyone else had left already, except when I walked into the locker room, there was Fred Lynn, in nothing but his jock strap. I would stammer and look away, but he would say, 'Come here, kid. You mind rubbing my shoulders? Rough practice today and I could use a little massage. You mind, kid?' And I would say, 'Of course not, Mr. Lynn.' So he would sit down on the bench in front of his locker, and I would walk over and start rubbing his shoulders."

"I thought you didn't remember any of the details."

"I have a vivid imagination."

"I can tell. What happened next?"

"You're a horny little Eskimo, aren't you?"

"I'm not that little."

"What are you? Five eight?"

"Five nine." Trent knew he was blushing, but he didn't care. "Come on, keep going."

"Well, it probably didn't get much further than that. Just the thought of rubbing Fred Lynn's shoulders would've gotten me really close. Maybe he stood up at one point and I saw the bulge in his jock strap. He would say something like, 'You wanna play with it, kid?' And before I could say anything, he would pull down his jock and show me. Huge, of course. Then I would reach out and touch it and— bam! That's when I'd shoot a load in my eye. Stings like nobody's business."

"You can shoot all the way up to your face?"

"I've hit the headboard before. I have a money shot that belongs on film."

Trent wiggled in his seat. "We need to stop talking about this."

"You getting excited over there, slugger?"

"Tell me about your football career."

"That wasn't a career."

"How big was your high school?"

"About a thousand students."

"So you must have been big man on campus, being the quarterback of the football team and all. That's how it was at my high school, at least. Baseball players were nobodies. Especially in Texas."

"I guess. I had some natural athletic ability, but we weren't that good, and the expectations were pretty moderate. I always felt like an imposter."

"What do you mean?"

"I knew I was different, even back then. I was terrified. If anyone had discovered the truth, I would have been toast. Kind of like how you feel now. No matter how popular I was, I knew it was based on a lie."

"And if they found out, they'd all turn against you."

"Precisely. And, I admit, I also secretly wanted to be in the spring musical."

Trent laughed. "You can sing?"

"Sure. I can carry a tune. But that would have been social suicide for a football player. All the guys in drama club were fags. Everyone knew that."

"Tell me more about your blow job."

Brendan turned red. "I don't want to talk about that."

"Why not? Come on."

"I thought you wanted to get off the topic of sex."

Trent ignored the obvious contradiction. "What was his name?"

"Who?"

"The guy who gave you the blow job."

"Stanton Porter."

"Was he hot?"

"Not as hot as you."

"Okay," Trent said. "Good answer. But—"

"Yes, he was hot."

"What happened?"

"I don't remember."

"Try."

"He was two years younger than me. Not even on the varsity squad yet, but we lived in the same neighborhood, and our parents knew each other. Our fathers worked for the same oil company. One day, I saw him walking home after practice, so I offered him a ride. There was something about him. I can't explain it."

"Did he have a crush on you?"

"Probably. I don't know. It was a long time ago. I haven't thought about him in years."

"So he sucked you off on the drive home?"

"God, no. I didn't just say, 'Hey, give me a blow job.' We started hanging out after that. Movies, pizza, that kind of thing. Then one night I got ahold of some beer. There was a drive-in outside of town, so we went there."

"What was playing?"

"*Jaws.*"

"No way."

"I'm serious. I didn't even think about how appropriate that was, considering what happened. The movie had been out for a couple of years, but we both loved it and wanted to see it again."

"So you drank some beer...."

"Yeah, we drank some beer and watched the movie. I don't think he'd been drunk before. We were joking around, making fun of the mechanical shark. It's a great drive-in movie. I don't remember what he said, but I responded with something like, 'Yeah, and you can suck my dick.' And he said, 'Whip it out.' So I did."

"What were you thinking?"

"I wasn't. I was a horny, drunk teenage boy, and for some reason, I knew I could trust him. Just like you know you can trust me. He was that kind of guy. When he saw that I was hard, he just went for it."

"Right there in the drive-in?"

Brendan looked puzzled. "Well, yeah. That's what drive-ins are for, man. I think we both went there knowing it was going to happen. I remember watching Richard Dreyfuss getting attacked by a shark while he went down on me. That was kind of strange."

"What happened afterward?"

"I freaked out. Totally panicked. Wanted to leave right after I came. Brushed him off at school the next week. It wasn't like we had any classes together—he was a sophomore and I was a senior. It was easy to avoid him, but still…. I was a jerk."

"Is he gay now?"

"No idea. We moved to Houston right after I graduated, and I never talked to him again." Brendan ate the last piece of brisket on the tray. "Nothing like that's ever happened to you?"

"No. Too risky."

"What about Kieran?"

"What about him? He's married to a girl we've known since we were sixteen."

"I know that. But you never had a crush on him?"

"Gross. He's like my fourth brother. Did you have a girlfriend in high school?"

"Yes, but she was surprisingly low maintenance. All I had to do was take her to the movies every Saturday night and hold hands in the hallway at school. That's about it. She never expressed any interest in sex with me."

"Maybe she liked girls."

"I wouldn't be surprised."

"Do you keep in touch with anyone from your high school?" Trent asked.

"No. I did at first, but we never went back, so there was really no point. All my grandparents are dead except one, and she lives in Florida."

"And you don't have any other family?"

"My mom has a sister who lives in Boston, but she never got married. My dad is an only child like me, so that's the extent of it. I don't have any cousins."

"I can't imagine a life like that."

"I was okay with it. I'm not really a social animal. I do best with one person at a time. And I don't like being responsible for other people, so I'm not sure I would have made a very good brother."

"I don't believe that."

"Suit yourself. I'm telling you the truth."

"If you say so. Who's your favorite baseball team?"

"The Houston Astros."

"I'm serious."

"So am I," Brendan insisted. "Okay, maybe not when I was growing up. I was a Pirates fan back then. But when we moved to Houston, I went to the Astrodome a lot. They were pretty good in '80 and '81. And I believe in hometown loyalty. But let's face it, the whole game changed when they got rid of the reserve clause. I get it—the system was criminally unfair. But still, Carlton Fisk in a White Sox uniform? That's just wrong on so many levels."

"I agree. Greed is going to ruin the game, just like everything else."

They had both finished eating. Brendan wiped his hands with a paper napkin and asked, "Are you nervous?"

"About what?"

"The Cold War. What do you think? You and me. Later tonight."

Trent had thought a lot in the last twenty-four hours about having sex with Brendan, but he had no idea Brendan expected it to happen that night. His pause dragged into a silence, and Brendan deflated.

"Jesus, I'm sorry. I just thought…. Never mind. You must think I jump into bed with guys the day I meet them."

"We met yesterday, so I know that's not true. I didn't think it would happen tonight, but now that I know it might, yes, I'm a lot nervous. It would be a big deal for me."

"It doesn't have to be tonight. I didn't mean to rush anything."

"I'm not a kid anymore, Brendan. It's been on my mind all day. I want to. You know that, don't you?"

"I thought I did. That's the impression I got, at least."

"Good. That's the right impression. It's just, I'm not used to moving from fantasy to reality."

"I'm in no hurry," Brendan said. "I take it all back."

"You don't want to now?"

"Yes, of course, I—Okay, you're teasing me."

"A little," Trent said.

"Have you ever been with a girl?"

"Yeah. One summer in Cape Cod, I got set up with a young woman of questionable reputation. That's what my father calls a hooker. The whole team did it."

"The same hooker?"

Trent laughed. "No. There was a different one for each of us. I didn't know how to get out of it, so I just closed my eyes and thought of Warren Beatty. Have you ever… you know. With a girl?"

"No. Does that make me a virgin?"

"I don't think so. You just told me about a blow job."

"Oral sex counts?"

"Doesn't it?" Trent said.

"I don't know the rules."

"It's got to count. Virginity can't only be about a dick in a snatch. Otherwise, gay guys would never lose their virginity."

"So how do two guys define virginity?"

Trent thought the question over before he answered. "Let's say two guys are together their whole lives. They suck each other's cocks every night, but never do it in the backdoor."

"Never make a rear delivery?"

"Never pack the fudge."

"Never dance the chocolate cha-cha?"

"Never ride the Hershey highway. Would you say they each died a virgin?"

Brendan took one last swig from his bottle of beer and swallowed. "Obviously not. Is there a gay virginity and a straight virginity?"

"No," Trent said. "You only get one."

"Okay, so technically, I'm not a virgin. But I've never actually had full-blown sex with anyone, so this is a big deal for me too. I never thought I'd wait this long. It just never happened."

"How about you? Are you nervous?"

"Hell, yes," Brendan said. "I'm terrified. And excited. It's hard to wrap my brain around it."

"Which part?"

"You being here, with me. I know you hate when I say this, but right now it's worth repeating. You're Trent Fucking Days. You could have anyone you want. Even some straight guys would suck your dick."

"Do you know what my mother said to me when I left Alaska? I was fifteen years old, moving three thousand miles away on my father's hunch that I might be a great baseball player. She kissed me on the forehead and said two words. *Pay attention.*"

"That's what Bill said to us, about the stone steps."

"I know. And that's what I've been doing for the past twenty-four hours. You dropped into my life, Brendan, and I don't know why any more than you do. But I haven't felt this way in…. Well, I've never felt this way. Is that something you want me to ignore?"

"I didn't mean to sound like I was complaining."

Trent wiped his face. "It's okay. Like you said, it's scary and exciting at the same time. But at some point, can you move from being a fan to being a friend?"

"Why can't I be both? Or more."

Trent took a pause and decided he was overreacting. "You're right. I'm the one who needs to get over it."

"Give me another day or two. Eventually, I'll treat you like a nobody."

"That would suit me just fine."

Out of the corner of his eye, Trent saw two men approaching their table.

"Well, I'll be shit," one of them said. "You're that Eskimo Slugger who plays for the Astros, aren't you?"

Trent looked up. "Yeah, that's me."

"What's your name, boy?"

"Trent Days."

"Trent Days," the second man repeated. The two men sat down at their picnic table, the first next to Trent and the second next to Brendan.

The first man picked a stray piece of sausage off their tray and popped it into his mouth. "Do you know, Trent Days, that I used to play baseball? Isn't that right, Earl?"

"That's right. You were a damn fine pitcher."

"Do you hear that, Trent Days? I was a damn fine pitcher. I bet you a hundred bucks I could strike you out."

Trent looked across the table at Brendan. "I'm sure you could."

"You're damn right I could. Where did an Eskimo learn how to play baseball, anyway?"

His friend chortled and said, "Hey, Lloyd, I bet they play with snowballs up there."

"Who's this?" the first man asked as he pointed to Brendan. "You two on a date? Don't they make a cute couple, Earl?"

"Fuck off," Brendan muttered.

The second man grabbed him by the shirt. "What did you say, boy?"

Brendan started to struggle, and before Trent could react, he heard a door slam and saw Betty striding across the lot with a shotgun in her hands. The two men scrambled off the picnic table as she approached. She cocked the gun and aimed it at their heads. "If you rednecks want to keep your ugly mugs connected to your misshapen bodies, I suggest you get into your piece-of-shit excuse for a truck and haul your sorry, no-good asses out of here. You hear me?" She took a step forward and the two men retreated. They jumped into their nearby truck and sped away.

"Jesus," Brendan said to her. "That was badass."

She barked a laugh and patted Brendan on the back. "Sorry about that, Trent. We still got plenty of trash in these parts, unfortunately. You boys okay?"

"We're fine," Trent said. "It happens a lot more than you'd think." He looked at Brendan. "You shouldn't have aggravated them."

"Bullshit," Brendan replied. "It's better to stand up for yourself and get the crap beat out of you than sit back and take it."

"Betty, this is my friend, Brendan Baxter."

Brendan shook her free hand. "Thanks for the backup."

"My pleasure. I like your attitude, kid, but that's about all the excitement my ticker can take for one day. I'll get these trays out of your way." She gathered them in her arms and headed off.

They walked to Trent's truck and climbed in. "Is your heart still racing?" Trent asked.

"Yes."

"Mine too."

"She's pretty cool."

"Betty? Yeah, she's the best."

"Remind me not to get on her bad side anytime soon."

Trent started the engine. "Where to now?"

"What time is it?"

"I don't know. Probably three or four o'clock."

"Someplace air-conditioned," Brendan said. "I'm not cut out for this heat."

"Really? I can't get enough of it. After growing up in Barrow, I never complain about weather like this. How about that movie?"

"No. A dark theater would make me fall asleep."

Trent put the truck into gear. "Your place?"

Brendan looked down at his hands. "We don't have to, Trent."

"Your place it is, then."

Trent pulled onto the road and headed back to central Austin. Once he shifted the truck into fifth gear, Brendan reached across the seat and took Trent's hand.

"I've been waiting a long time for someone to hold hands with," Brendan said.

"We'll never be able to do this in public, you know?"

"Never say never. The world is changing."

Trent signaled and then passed the car in front of him. "Maybe for other people, but not for major league baseball players."

"I thought we were going to table all that until tomorrow," Brendan said.

"Sorry, I forgot."

"No, I'm the one who should be sorry. I'm still worked up about those two white-trash assholes."

"Forget about it. You can't let guys like that get to you."

"Backing down isn't the answer either."

"It just as easily could've been one of them that pulled out the gun. Then what?"

"Then I guess I'd be dead."

"And what about me?" Trent asked. "Our third date and I'd already be going to your funeral?"

"What were the first two dates?"

"Today. And Bill's party last night."

"That was a date?"

"Sure. You pressed up against my knee under the table."

"I did no such thing."

Trent slapped the steering wheel with his free hand. "Are you seriously going to tell me you didn't do that on purpose?"

Brendan squeezed Trent's hand. "It was a small table. Besides, even if we did bump knees, that doesn't make it a date. There was no kiss at the end."

"That's the rule?" Trent said. "No kiss, no date?"

"That's the rule. You decided the virginity rules, so I get to decide the date rules."

"You're still riled up, aren't you?"

"I'm a control freak. I hate feeling powerless like that."

"It's silly."

Brendan pulled his hand away. "Don't call me silly."

"I didn't. I called the idea that you can control everything silly. On a good day, you *maybe* control 1 percent of your life. The sooner you surrender to that fact, the better."

"Never surrender. That's my motto."

They rode for a few minutes in silence, and then Trent asked, "Are you mad at me?"

"No." Brendan reached across the seat and took Trent's hand back. "Sorry."

"Don't let those assholes ruin our day."

"I won't. It's over."

"And stop apologizing."


WHEN THEY reached Brendan's apartment, Trent parked his truck on the street and they walked up the driveway. The doors of the Walsh house were closed, and Trent couldn't see any lights on inside.

"Bill and Grace must be out," Brendan said.

His apartment was over the garage, which wasn't attached to the house, but rather sat on its own at the end of the driveway. They climbed a set of stairs on the left that led to a door. Brendan unlocked it and Trent followed him inside. The living space was open and inviting, with windows on every wall. The furniture was sparse and eclectic, with a colorful Mexican rug in the middle of the hardwood floor. A sofa rested against the far wall, and a big, comfortable chair sat in one corner. Books were stacked everywhere—on the windowsills, on the cases made of milk crates, and even on an old steamer trunk in the opposite corner. And there was something about the light....

"You want a beer?"

"Sure," Trent said. "Can I use your bathroom?"

Brendan pointed to the left. "It's right there."

Trent went in and took a piss. After he washed his hands, he lifted his shirt and examined his ribs in the mirror. They were definitely getting better. When he returned to the living room, Brendan was sitting on the floor with two bottles of Shiner Bock and an ashtray. He held up what remained of the joint and said, "I thought we could finish this off."

Trent sat down on the floor a few feet from Brendan, with the bottles and ashtray between them, and propped himself up against the sofa. He took a swig of beer. Brendan lit the joint and inhaled. He passed it to Trent, who took a hit and rested his head on a cushion. He glanced to the side and saw a large poster hanging on the interior wall. In big bold letters, it read, *The Taming of the Shrew.*

"What's that?"

Brendan turned to look at the poster. "The play I saw when I visited Stratford, where Shakespeare was born."

"That in England?"

"Yep. It's a good day trip from London."

"How was the play?"

"Okay, I guess. I don't really understand why they call it a comedy. He seemed like an abusive prick to me."

"I've never seen it."

Trent handed the joint back to Brendan, who took a final hit and then stamped it out. They sat for a moment in silence. Trent rolled his head in a circular motion and let go of what little tension he still carried.

"You want a neck massage?" Brendan said. He stood up and moved the ashtray to the side. He sat down on the sofa with Trent still on the floor between his legs. Trent dropped his head back into Brendan's lap and Brendan started rubbing his shoulders.

"You're upside down," Trent said.

"How's your concussion?"

"I feel okay. Except for almost fainting yesterday."

"Does my touching you like this make you uncomfortable?"

"No, not at all."

"Should we keep going?"

Trent rubbed his cheek against Brendan's thigh. "Yeah, we should keep going. You know, there's something about this apartment that—"

"You feel it too?"

"Definitely."

"I think it's haunted," Brendan said.

"If you don't believe in souls, then you can't believe in ghosts."

"Maybe not, but I believe in ghost stories."

"So what happened?"

"I think they were lovers who died young, but not in a bad way. They're not angry."

"You mean there are *two* ghosts?"

"Of course. One would be too ordinary for me."

"Both guys?"

"Yes. I've already figured out you like stories about two guys. They're watching us right now."

"Really? Can you hear what they're saying?"

"I can barely make out…. One of them said, 'The redhead is really handsome.'"

"Well, I agree with that at least. What about the other one?"

Brendan paused and pretended like he was listening to somebody. Then he said, "He thinks I should kiss you."

# SEVEN

TRENT HAD dreamed of kissing a boy since seventh grade, when he had a crush on his best friend, Koda Patkotak. Koda was a full-blooded Inupiat and several years older than Trent. Everyone else called him Little Koda, even though he was three inches taller than all the other boys his age, because his father was Big Koda Patkotak. Trent, on the other hand, always called him Suuna, which was short for *suunaaga*, the Eskimo word for *friend*. Trent and Koda bonded one summer over Elvis Presley records and peanut butter by the spoonful. When he was young, Trent thought that certainly he would kiss Koda someday, but then he picked up a baseball bat and moved to Texas. He never saw his friend again, because a year later, Koda fell through the ice in a freak fishing accident and drowned.

Since then, Trent had dreamed of kissing other boys—his math tutor in high school, a shortstop who played for Stanford, and now a law student. Brendan must have interpreted Trent's silence as hesitancy, because the next thing he said was, "Wait a minute. The second ghost just changed his mind."

"What?"

"Yep. He said it's not time for the kiss yet."

Trent turned around. He was still sitting on the floor, facing Brendan on the couch. "What do you mean it's not time for the kiss yet?"

"Don't shoot the messenger."

"I've been waiting since seventh grade. Trust me, it's time."

"What was his name?"

"Who?"

"The guy in seventh grade. The one you wanted to kiss."

"I don't remember," Trent said.

"Bullshit. I told you Stanton's name. What was it?"

"Okay. It was Koda."

"Koda what?"

"Koda Patkotak."

"Is he an Eskimo too?"

"Was."

Brendan sat forward. "He's dead?"

"Yeah. But he would be happy for me. Happy I finally got here." Trent rose to his feet and said, "Stand up."

Brendan did as he was told, and they faced each other in the middle of the room. "Did you kiss Stanton…? What's his last name again?"

"Porter."

"Did you kiss Stanton Porter at the drive-in? When you were watching *Jaws* together?"

"No. Did you ever kiss Koda Patkotak?"

Trent shook his head.

"So this is kind of a big deal," Brendan said.

Trent nodded.

"Close your eyes, then."

"Why?" Trent asked.

"Just close them."

"Did the ghost change his mind again?"

"Something like that. Now close."

Trent did as instructed. Then, after a moment, he heard Brendan say, "One."

And he felt a kiss on his forehead.

"Two."

And a kiss on his left cheek.

"Three."

A kiss on his right cheek.

"Four."

"Why are you counting?" Trent said.

"Shh. You'll figure it out."

Brendan kissed him on one of his eyelids.

"Five."

Followed by the other.

"Six."

A kiss on the nose.

"Seven."

A lingering kiss on the chin, and then Trent could feel the moist rhythm of Brendan's breath. Even with his eyes closed, he knew Brendan's lips were less than an inch from his own, so when Brendan said the word, the number, Trent could taste it as much as hear it.

"Eight."

Trent's jersey number.

He fell into Brendan and their lips met. He wrapped his arms around Brendan's waist, tightened his grip, and then cried out in pain.

Brendan jumped back and said, "Jesus, I forgot again!"

Trent reached out and grabbed Brendan's arm to steady himself. He gasped and then groaned loudly. "Oh, man, that was stupid. Entirely my fault."

"Sit down." Brendan eased Trent onto the sofa and sat next to him. The pain subsided with each breath, and Trent felt more foolish than wounded. He looked at Brendan and saw the concern in his eyes.

"It's no big deal," Trent said. "I'm fine. Just not too bright."

"You should get some rest."

"No. It's too late for that."

Trent took Brendan's hand and laid it on his crotch.

Brendan squeezed and said, "You're hard."

"I want to keep going. We can work around my injury."

Brendan hesitated, but then lifted Trent's shirt and asked, "Where does it hurt?" Trent indicated his upper ribs on the right side of his body. Brendan leaned over and kissed them. "Feel better?" he said, and then he kissed them again.

"Much."

Brendan's tongue flickered over Trent's nipple, which just about made him jump out of his skin. So naturally, Brendan did it again, and then he lifted Trent's shirt up and over his head. Brendan bunched it into a ball, put it to his face, inhaled, and then threw it onto the floor.

"Tell me one of your fantasies."

"Now?" Trent said.

"Yes, now. I told you about Fred Lynn. Just give me one. Something you think about when you jack off. You do jack off, don't you?" Trent leaned forward and rubbed his nose against Brendan's. "Oh, no. You didn't just give me an Eskimo kiss. I refuse to be that adorable."

"Yes, I jack off."

Brendan traced the outline of Trent's pectoral muscles with his index finger. "What do you think about?"

Trent leaned his head back and enjoyed the sensation of Brendan's touch. "I order a pizza, and this really hot redhead shows up with an extra-large pie."

"The pizza boy, he delivers. A classic. Plain?"

"Pepperoni."

"How big is the pepperoni?"

"Big," Trent said.

"What happens?"

"What do you think happens?"

"Did you know people down here put pineapple on their pizza?"

Trent laughed. "You are so stoned. Yes, I know that."

"It's disgusting. We would never put pineapple on our pizza in the Midwest."

"Tell me another one of yours."

Brendan pulled off his shoes and tossed them aside. "I give you a blow job in the Astros clubhouse. After a game. While you're still in uniform."

"Do all your fantasies involve baseball players?" That's when it dawned on Trent. "Wait a minute. Are you saying you jacked off thinking about me, before we met?"

"That's what I'm saying. Public figures are fair game."

"Wow. I'm flattered. Really. I just hope I live up to myself."

"You already have."

"It's your turn now," Trent said as he sat up. "Off with that shirt." Brendan followed suit and threw his T-shirt onto the middle of the floor. Trent reached out and touched his shoulder. "You're in good shape."

Brendan ignored the compliment and said, "Of all the young major league players of your generation—I'm talking the rookies from this season and last season—who do you think will make it to the Hall of Fame?"

Trent shook his head. "What kind of question is that to be asking me now?"

"Sorry. I get chatty when I'm stoned. And horny. I just realized what an annoying combination that could be. But there are two really good ways to shut me up."

"Oh, yeah. What's the first?"

Brendan leaned over and kissed him, making sure not to crush his ribs. Trent closed his eyes and tasted the amazing Brendan Baxter, who had never once, since the moment Trent met him, felt like a stranger. Their tongues swirled together in a choreographed harmony that lasted for several minutes.

When they came up for air, Trent said, "Cal Ripken."

"A shortstop?"

Trent nodded and asked, "What's the second way to shut you up?"

"Voglio mettermi il tuo cazzo duro in bocca."

"Are you ever going to tell me what that means?"

"I want to put your hard cock into my mouth."

Trent felt himself turn red. "Which part is 'hard cock'?"

"Cazzo duro."

"*Cazzo*. That's Italian for cock?"

"Yep."

"So you want to suck on my *cazzo*?"

"Did that hooker give you a blow job?"

"She tried, but she used too much teeth."

"I bet I can do better," Brendan said.

"How do you even know you're going to like it?"

"Some things you just know are true. Even though you can't explain them."

Trent kicked off his shoes and got an idea. "Do you want to do something nice for me?"

"What?"

"Give me a foot massage."

"Are you kidding?"

"No. My feet are always sore. Please."

"I'm offering you a blow job and you're asking for a foot massage instead? No wonder we're both practically virgins. Between my incessant chattering and your need for podiatric stimulation, we're never going to get this thing off the ground."

"You got somewhere else you need to be?"

Brendan sighed. "No, I didn't say that. Okay, fine. Let's give you a foot rub. I'll sit here at the end and you lie down and put them in my lap."

Trent eased onto his back and propped up his feet.

"Well," Brendan said, "at least you have sexy feet." He started to rub them, and Trent melted into the sofa. "How's that?"

"Harder." Brendan ran his thumb up and down Trent's arch. "Yeah, just like that."

"This is going to permanently scar me, you know."

"How so?" Trent said.

"I'm sitting here with a hard-on, rubbing your feet. The juxtaposition will inevitably imprint itself onto my young and impressionable sexual psyche. For the rest of my life, whenever I see a hot guy's feet, I'll probably pop a boner."

"You've got some vocabulary, you know that? Juxtaposition and podia...."

"Podiatric."

"You got a good word for this?" Trent pressed his left foot against Brendan's erection.

"Big pepperoni."

Trent laughed and had to steady his ribcage with his hand. "That's two words."

"Does it hurt when you laugh?"

"A little. But it's worth it." Brendan continued to massage Trent's feet. "You're good at that."

"Glad I'm good at something."

"I bet you're going to make a great lawyer someday."

"I hope so. I'm thinking of starting out in a DA's office. If I go to a firm, they'll never take me seriously as a litigator."

"You should talk to Kieran's dad. He's a trial lawyer at one of the big firms here in town." Then Trent remembered. "Oh, sorry. I forgot you're moving to New York."

"We'll see. How would you even introduce me to Mr. Harrison?"

"I'm allowed to have friends," Trent said.

"It'll only raise suspicions."

"I thought we weren't going to talk about that today."

"Sorry," Brendan said. "It seems to keep popping up, doesn't it? 'There's no way we can ever be together.'"

"We just met yesterday."

"So?"

"Don't you think you're getting a little ahead of yourself?"

"I'm just saying, what's the point, if nothing can ever happen?"

"Do you want me to go?"

Brendan didn't reply, but when Trent tried to pull his feet away, Brendan stopped him.

"No, I don't want you to go."

Trent relaxed back into the sofa and stretched out his arms. "Come here," he said as he lifted his feet.

"No. I'll only crush your ribs."

"I'm sorry. I didn't mean to upset you."

"You didn't." Brendan ran his hand up Trent's leg and squeezed the bulge in his shorts. "You're still hard."

Trent knew he needed a bold move, so he reached down and undid his fly. He pulled out his erect cock and showed it to Brendan, who yanked the shorts off and tossed them onto the pile, leaving Trent naked and sprawled on the sofa. Still sitting at the end with Trent's feet on his lap, Brendan reached out and stroked it.

"Why don't you take your shorts off?" Trent said as he lifted his feet again.

Brendan got up and dropped the last piece of his clothing to the floor. He tossed his shorts aside and stood naked in front of Trent, his stiff dick jutting out. Trent sat up and Brendan knelt in front of him. He pushed Trent's legs apart and leaned forward. Trent watched in amazement as Brendan's tongue came into contact with his balls. Each time he licked them, Brendan went a little farther up the shaft until eventually his lips were teasing the tip. Then Trent's cock disappeared into Brendan's mouth. Trent closed his eyes and braced himself against the back of the sofa. He was certain he wouldn't last long if Brendan kept this up, so Trent pulled him off and leaned forward, bringing them face to face.

Trent kissed him and said, "We're going to have to take turns."

"Did I do okay?"

"You did great. Best blow job I've ever had."

"Is it okay to pull your foreskin back like that?"

"Yeah. My head is really sensitive, though."

Brendan put his mouth onto Trent's dick again and swirled his tongue around the tip. Trent cried out in exaltation. Then Brendan was kissing him.

"What's it like?" Trent asked.

Brendan kissed his neck. "It's hot. But I can only get half of it in my mouth before it hits the back of my throat. You want to try?"

"Yeah."

Brendan stood up, and Trent sat forward on the edge of the sofa. There it was, right in front of him—a real-life man's cock. He wrapped his left hand around it and stroked himself at the same time. Brendan was big without being too big. Trent looked up at him and then licked the head. Brendan arched his back and moaned. Trent opened his mouth and slid his lips onto the shaft. He, too, could only swallow half of it. He closed his eyes and saw a single white spot. He moved up and down Brendan's dick, tasting it with his tongue. Brendan took Trent's head into his hands and established a face-fucking rhythm, until Trent suddenly gagged and pulled away. With the back of his hand, he wiped off the spit dripping down his chin.

"Sorry," Brendan said.

But then Trent noticed the gagging made him harder than ever. He put his mouth back onto Brendan's cock until it rammed the back of his throat. He gagged again and almost came. He sat back on the sofa, his eyes watering and nose running. "Do you have a Kleenex?"

Brendan laughed and said, "Sure. I'll be right back." He disappeared around the corner and then returned a few moments later, with a box of tissues in his hand. "Here you go." He handed one to Trent.

"Thanks."

Trent blew his nose and looked around the room for a trash can.

"Just throw it on the floor with the clothes. We'll worry about it later."

Brendan sat on the sofa next to Trent. They reached out and grabbed each other's dicks. Trent tilted his head toward Brendan and kissed him.

"Did that turn you on?" Brendan said.

"Who knew gagging was the hottest part?"

"Are you close?"

"I could shoot yesterday."

"Me too."

"I'm sure we'll last longer the second time."

"I want to taste your come," Brendan said.

"We should suck each other off and come together."

"Sixty-nine?"

"Yeah."

"Let's go to the bed."

Brendan took Trent's hand and pulled him off the sofa. He led him to the bedroom, and they crawled onto the cool white sheets. They flipped in opposite directions, careful of Trent's ribs, and then settled into mutual blow jobs. Trent found the sensation overwhelming, balancing the pleasure of getting sucked with his hunger for blowing Brendan. He saw Brendan's balls tighten and felt his shaft swell between his lips. He tasted a bittersweet fluid and immediately began to ejaculate into Brendan's mouth. They grabbed each other and braced themselves against the onslaught of their orgasms. Semen filled Trent's mouth, and he pulled away from Brendan's cock, only to be confronted with spurts of come flying at his face. After the initial shock, Trent reveled in its smell and the way it tasted when he licked his lips. In the meantime Brendan had managed to swallow all of Trent's load.

Trent milked the last drops from Brendan's dick with his hand and then rolled onto his back. Brendan flipped around and laughed when he saw Trent's sperm-covered face.

"That was about half a gallon," Trent said.

Brendan licked a trail of come off Trent's cheek and kissed him. He then proceeded to clean Trent's entire face, after which they nestled together and fell asleep.

WHEN TRENT woke up, Brendan was gone. He sat up and looked around. It was still light outside, but just barely. He left the bedroom and found Brendan in the kitchen, still naked, making sandwiches. Trent put his arms around him from behind and rested his head against Brendan's back.

"Do you like turkey or roast beef?"

"Both," Trent said.

"Why do I ask such stupid questions? A club sandwich it is. You are hungry, right?"

"I'm a professional athlete. I'm always hungry. What time is it?"

"Eight thirty."

"I slept for two hours?"

"Sleep is how you heal, my young Jedi."

"Do you have any chips?"

"In the cupboard next to the fridge."

Trent turned and opened the slim door. On the middle shelf sat six or seven bags of chips, all of a different variety—Lays and Ruffles, barbeque, sour cream and onion, even a giant bag of Fritos.

"I guess that was a stupid question." Trent grabbed the bag of Ruffles and closed the door. He turned back to Brendan and asked, "Is there any kind of chips you don't like?"

"Unsalted. That's one of the drawbacks of being raised in the Midwest. Food is basically a delivery system for salt, sugar, and fat. I grew up thinking Miracle Whip was mayonnaise and margarine and butter were the same thing. News flash: they're not. I thought there were only three types of cheeses in the world: yellow, the kind with holes, and the stuff you put on pizza."

"You know how I feel about cheese."

"Damn, I forgot. Sex must make me stupid." Brendan had finished the sandwiches, but he opened them up, removed the slice of cheese from one, and added it to the other. "Did you have cheese in the house as a kid?"

Trent shook his head. "No. It costs a fortune to transport food like that to Barrow."

"That's why you don't like it, then. The lactose."

"What's lactose?"

"The sugar in milk. It can make you sick if you're not used to it. You like lettuce and tomato, right?"

"Yeah, that's fine."

"Mayonnaise *and* mustard?"

"No Miracle Whip?"

"Not in this house."

"Yeah," Trent answered. "I like both."

"Do you want to eat at the table, in the living room, or in bed?"

"In bed."

"Good answer. Grab two bottles of beer from the fridge and bring those chips."

Brendan took the plates with the sandwiches and led them back to the bedroom. Trent set the bottles of beer on the windowsill next to the bed and placed the open bag of chips between them. Trent took a bite of his sandwich. "Good job, chef. Thanks for feeding me again. I owe you a couple of meals."

"You don't owe me anything."

Brendan opened his sandwich and placed a layer of potato chips on top of the cheese. "You're putting chips on your sandwich?" Trent asked.

"You've never done that before? Man, you're missing half your life. Try it."

Trent opened his sandwich and piled on some chips. He reset the bread, took a bite, and nodded his approval. "Excellent," he said, his mouth half-full. He washed it down with a swig of beer.

They finished their sandwiches and then started kissing again. To Trent, the rest of the evening felt like a movie montage, complete with laughter, conversation, more making out, more sex, and a late-night pillow fight. It was as if someone or something had erected a force field around the garage apartment—a force field that protected them from the outside world. It was two in the morning before they finally turned off the lights and settled down. As Trent lay waiting to fall asleep, Brendan's words came back to him:

"There's no way we can ever be together."

In the piercing stillness of a summer night, Trent made a vow. He would find a way. Even if it was the last thing he ever did in his life, Trent would find a way to prove Brendan wrong.

# EIGHT

THE NEXT morning, the sun came streaming through the east window and right into Trent's eyes. He sat up and looked around the room. Brendan was spread out beside him, unconscious. Trent lowered himself and whispered into his ear, "Hey, sleepyhead."

Brendan, clearly not a morning person, shrugged him off without a reply. Trent backed away and decided not to wake him. He got out of bed, took a piss, and then went into the kitchen and poured himself a glass of orange juice. He needed to go home and check in with the front office, but he didn't want to disturb Brendan. He glanced around for a pad of paper, but all he found was the map of Travis County Bill had given them. He picked up the black magic marker and wrote on the front:

**I'M COMING BACK**

He put the map into the center of the counter, where Brendan would be sure to see it, then went into the living room and got dressed. He quietly closed the door and left the garage apartment. He managed to avoid an encounter with Bill Walsh on his way down the driveway, which was just as well, because Trent really didn't want to make up a story about why he'd spent the night at Brendan's place. He knew the lying would start soon enough.

When Trent got home, there were three messages on his answering machine. He listened to them one after the other, all from Kieran. The first was a casual check-in, the second a little concerned, and the third, which Kieran had left an hour ago, wondered where in the hell he was and why he hadn't called back.

Trent picked up the phone and dialed his number. Kieran's wife answered.

"Hey, Marcia. It's me."

"Where have you been? Kieran's going crazy. You know how he always thinks the worst. He convinced himself you were dead in a ditch somewhere."

"Can you calm him down for me before you put him on the phone?"

"I already tried and failed. Did you listen to the game last night?"

"Just the beginning."

"Lillis pulled him after three innings. Kieran doesn't like the way Ashby catches. My husband gave up fourteen hits and six runs."

"In three innings?"

"Is there any way you can come back early?"

"Not to play. I'm out for twenty-one days, no matter how fast I heal. You know that."

"It would help if you were here. Even if you weren't playing."

"Let me talk to him."

"Okay. Hold on a second."

Trent heard Marcia's muffled call, then a click as someone else picked up.

"Trent?"

"Yeah, it's me."

"Are you okay?"

"I'm fine."

"Marcia, get off the line, please."

Trent heard another click.

"Why haven't you called me back?" Kieran asked.

"Calm down. I just got your messages."

"Where have you been?"

"Nowhere. I forgot to check the machine. I've been sleeping a lot. That's what the doctors told me to do. These pills knock me out." The lying had begun, Trent noted.

"Oh," Kieran said. "Okay. Lillis told me you could come back."

"He did?"

"Yeah. I talked to him after last night's game."

"I don't think that's a good idea."

"Why not?"

"Because," Trent said. "My ribs are still sore, and I get these really bad headaches. It's better if I stay here and rest for another week."

"Another week? Are you crazy? You need to get back and be with the team."

"I hate when you start a sentence with, 'You need to....'"

"Do you know what happened last night?"

"Marcia told me."

"You weren't listening on the radio?"

"I slept through it. Sorry."

"Did you see the *Chronicle* this morning? 'Harrison Melts Down.' That's the headline on the front page of the sports section."

Trent didn't respond, and Kieran said, "Is something wrong?"

"No."

"You sound strange."

"It's the pills."

"Well, lay off them. You need to get out of bed and move around."

"The doctors said I should rest."

"What do they know? When Yogi Berra took a home-plate collision, he played the next day."

Trent sat down on one of the kitchen stools. "It wasn't my decision, Kieran."

"I know that. Will you call me tomorrow? Please."

"Yeah, I promise. I'm sorry I bit your head off. I'm just sick of not being healthy. Give me a week, and I'll be back. I can fix everything that's wrong with you. You'll come back stronger than ever, and everyone will forget about last night."

"Thanks, Trent. I love you, man."

"You too."

Trent hung up the phone and went into his bedroom. He lay down and considered never returning to the garage apartment, but the thought of not seeing Brendan again was too unbearable. Trent rolled onto his side and curled into a ball. He had gotten maybe five hours of sleep the night before. He thought about all the troubles ahead. He couldn't see himself keeping this from Kieran much longer, but how would he ever explain it? Before he closed his eyes, he decided not to think about it at all, and instead pretended he was back in Barrow, in the middle of a blizzard, completely surrounded by white, where no one could hurt or even touch him.

*TRENT SPOONED out some peanut butter and then handed the jar to Koda. They were lying on the floor of Trent's room, the one he shared with his brother, Mickey, who was sound asleep in his bed. It was three o'clock in the morning and still light outside. They were listening to* Almost in Love, *the Elvis Presley album from 1970. Koda liked it because it had "A Little Less Conversation" on it, but Trent preferred the last song, "Stay Away Joe." Trent kept the volume down so it didn't wake Mickey, even though he knew his brother could sleep through anything. Koda mumbled the lyrics because of the peanut butter in his mouth. They shifted their weight to the rhythm of the music.*

*Someone knocked on the door and opened it. Trent's father poked his head in. "What's going on, you two? It's time to turn that record player off and hit the sack."*

*"Come on, Dad,"* Trent said. *"It's summer vacation. We're allowed to stay up as late as we want."*

*"Hmm,"* Trent's father said as he stepped into the room. *"Which one are you listening to?"*

*"Almost in Love,"* Koda whispered.

*"Oh, I like that one too. Especially 'Rubberneckin.' Okay, but don't wake up your brother."*

*"That's not even possible,"* Trent said.

*His father left the room and closed the door behind him.*

*"Are you tired, Nuka?"* Koda asked. *He always called Trent "Nuka," which was short for* nukaaluga, *the Eskimo word for "my little brother," because Trent was the closest thing Koda had to a sibling.*

*"No. Are you?"*

*"No. What do you want to listen to next?"*

*"Double Trouble,"* Trent said. *"I like that last song."*

*"Yeah, me too."*

*Koda sat up and changed the records, but instead of starting at the beginning, he positioned the needle over the final track. He lay back down next to Trent, and together they softly sang the lyrics to "What Now, What Next, Where To."*

FROM THE bedroom Trent could hear someone knocking on the back door. He sat up and looked around in a daze. It took him several moments to realize he'd fallen asleep. He looked at the clock. Two in the afternoon. Then he heard another round of knocking. He jumped out of bed and went into the kitchen. He opened the door and found his lawn boy, Patrick, standing on the porch.

"Hi, Mr. Days. I saw your truck in the driveway, so I figured you might be home. Is everything okay with the lawn? My dad showed me how to put fertilizer on last week. Would you like me to put some on your grass? I can water it too, if you want. In addition to the mowing, I mean. Since it's July, we won't be getting much rain for a while. It's already starting to brown on the tips."

Trent wiped his face with the palm of his hand in an attempt to wake up. "That's fine. I'll pay you extra."

"No need, Mr. Days. I don't mind doing it for free. My dad and I are coming to Houston next month to see you play."

"Really? Did he buy tickets already?"

"Yeah. They're in the nosebleed section, but he said we couldn't afford anything closer, the price of gas being what it is and all. I told him I didn't mind, just as long as I got to see the Eskimo Slugger hit a home run in the Astrodome. Is it true the whole thing is air-conditioned?"

"Yeah, it's true. You tell your dad to write down when you're coming and put it in my mailbox. I'll get you some seats behind home plate."

Patrick's eyes widened. "For real, Mr. Days?"

"For real. I need to do something to pay for all the extra work."

"Holy crap, Mr. Days. Thank you! I'll tell my dad. And I'll come over tonight and lay on some fertilizer. And water too. Is that okay?"

"Sure," Trent said. "I'll probably be gone, though."

Patrick looked disappointed. "Okay. Well, I know where all the stuff is. Do you have a sprinkler?"

"There should be a few of them in the garage."

"Okay. How's your injury, if you don't mind me asking?"

Trent touched his ribs. "A lot better today, thanks."

"Fantastic. I can't wait to see you back on the diamond, Mr. Days. You have a good afternoon, now."

"You too."

Patrick turned, ran across the yard, and escaped out the back gate. Trent closed the door and stood alone in his kitchen. He needed to see Brendan, but they hadn't exchanged phone numbers. He took a shower and got dressed. He drove north back to the Walsh house, but when he knocked on Brendan's door, no one answered.

"He's at work."

Trent looked down and saw Bill standing at the foot of the stairs. "Ah, okay. I was just dropping by to say hi."

"How was the fishing yesterday?"

Trent descended the stairs. "We had a great time. That was an amazing spot, thank you."

"You're welcome. You should stop by the store. Brendan was complaining the other day about how slow it can be in the summer. He would probably enjoy the company."

"I think I'll do that." Bill shook his hand and grinned, as if he'd figured out what was going on. "I'll probably see you later."

"I hope so," Bill said.

Trent drove to West Campus and parked his truck in the same spot as Monday. He walked to Inner Sanctum Records and the bell sounded above his head when he entered.

"I'll be right out," Brendan called from the rear of the store.

"What do you do back there, anyway?"

"Trent?"

"Yeah, it's me."

Brendan appeared from the other room and stood behind the counter. They were alone in the store.

"Where did you go this morning?"

"I had to call Kieran. Didn't you get my message?"

"Yes, but it didn't explain where you went, or when you were coming back. Our first night together and I woke up alone?"

"I'm sorry." Trent turned his head to make sure no one was coming through the door, and then he leaned across the counter to give Brendan a kiss. "Forgive me?"

"Of course I forgive you. I'm just…."

"What's wrong?"

"I… I did something that maybe wasn't so smart."

"What could you have done in a couple of hours?"

Brendan put his hands on the edge of the counter and braced himself. "I called Stanton."

"Stanton Porter? The guy who gave you the blow job?"

"Yes."

Trent shook his head in disbelief. "Why would you do that?"

"Because I woke up this morning and you were gone. I freaked out. I told you I would freak out at some point. I have no one to talk to."

"Well, neither do I."

"I know that, but the blow job kept coming up yesterday, and telling you about Stanton reminded me that he's a really good guy. He understands where I come from, so I took a chance. I know it was impulsive, but—"

"How did you even find him?"

"I called his mom."

"Did you tell him I'm gay?"

Brendan didn't reply. Trent turned his back and thought he might throw up.

"It gets worse," Brendan said.

Trent spun around. "Worse? How could it get any worse?"

"His lover knows too. And they're coming to visit. On Friday."

Anxiety surged through Trent's body. His knees buckled. He grabbed his ribcage and fell to the floor. Brendan flew around the counter and tried to help him up, but Trent pushed him away. He sat on the floor and covered his head with his arms. The next thing he heard was the bell above the door, and then voices, several voices.

"Fuck," Brendan said as he stood up. Trent heard him talking to the voices and telling them the store needed to close for an hour. A girl said, "What the fuck?" and a guy asked, "Why is he sitting on the floor?" Brendan didn't reply, but he herded the voices back out the door and locked it behind them.

"Come on, Trent. Stand up. Or at least look at me." Trent didn't move or speak. "I'm sorry, but please trust me. I know it's a huge leap of faith. I understand that. But Stanton would never tell anyone, and we can't do this on our own. He's gay. He's out of the closet. We need someone like that to talk to. At least I need someone like that. I'm not asking you to tell the whole world. Two people, Trent. We have to be able to trust at least two people."

He tried to listen to Brendan, but all he could think about was the scandal that would end his career. Finally, Trent uncovered his head and stood up. "How could you do this to me?"

Brendan's face went white. "I didn't—"

"Do you have any idea what will happen if this gets out?"

"But it won't. I know I should have talked to you first, but you weren't there, and I didn't have your number."

"Do you want to have sex with him again?"

"Oh, Jesus." Brendan put his hands over his face. "Do you honestly think that's what this is about?"

"I don't know what I think. I leave you alone for a few hours, and you're calling high-school buddies and telling them I'm gay. And why on earth did you invite them to visit?"

"That wasn't my idea. Stanton suggested it."

"Did it ever occur to you that he suggested it in order to meet me?"

"No. He suggested it because I asked him for help. Get over yourself, man. Not everything's about you." Then Brendan's whole manner changed, and an angry defiance tinged his voice. "You know, you're right. It was a stupid idea. So get out of here and don't come back. I'll tell Stanton I made the whole thing up. I never met you. Problem solved. Just say the word and I'll disappear. Poof. *Magic.*"

Trent didn't like the sound of that at all. He wanted to run, but his feet refused to budge. "I can't do that, and you know it."

"Then stop acting like I called the *National Enquirer*. We're on the same side, remember? I would never do anything to jeopardize your career."

Trent bowed his head and began to calm down. "Okay. I talked to Kieran, by the way. Lillis pulled him last night after three innings. He gave up fourteen hits and six runs."

"In three innings?"

"I know. It's ridiculous."

"I take it you didn't tell him about me?"

"No. But I wanted to."

Brendan took a pause. "Clearly, yesterday is over."

"I'm sorry I pushed you away. It was just a reflex."

"It's okay. I'm sorry I called Stanton without saying something first. I've been dreading telling you all day. At least now it's over, and you're still standing here. You are still standing here, aren't you?"

Trent glanced at the counter and saw a pad of paper. He grabbed a pencil, wrote down his phone number, and handed it to Brendan.

"Does this mean we're going steady?"

"I don't know what it means," Trent said. "All I know is, I'm not ready to say good-bye to you yet."

"It would make your life a lot easier if you did."

"Will you put up with me for a little while longer, until I figure things out?"

"Will you meet Stanton and his lover on Friday?"

"You're answering a question with a question."

"Sorry," Brendan said. "It's a bad law-school habit. Yes, I'll put up with you."

"Then I'll meet Stanton and his lover. But no more blow jobs from either one of them."

"Only from you. I promise." Brendan kissed him and said, "Do you know who Wallace Simpson is?"

"No. Does he play baseball?"

"I don't think so. Stanton said I would become someone named Wallace Simpson. I bet Bill knows who it is."

"I just saw him before I came over here."

"Bill?" Brendan said. "You went to my apartment first?"

"Yeah. Do you think he knows?"

"Hell, no. He doesn't look at two guys going fishing together and think, 'Ah, they must be cocksuckers.'"

Trent laughed, which relaxed him even more. "How late are you working?"

"Ten. I have to close."

"Can I pick you up? Let's spend the night at my place. That way I'll be there in case Kieran calls. Otherwise I'll have to lie about why I'm not at home."

"Sounds like a plan. I'd like to see your house, anyway."

Trent kissed Brendan. "You can unlock the door now. My meltdown is over. I'll see you at ten."


TRENT PASSED the evening helping Patrick fertilize the grass, which seemed to thrill the boy to no end, and arrived back at the store shortly before ten o'clock. It was dark by the time they got back to Trent's house, and he doubted any of the neighbors saw them arrive together.

They immediately hit the bedroom, tore off each other's clothes, and settled into a sixty-nine position. After a vigorous round of oral sex, Trent ordered a pizza, which was followed by another round of sex—this one less frenzied and more relaxed. At one point they took a shower together, and then Brendan suggested a walk.

Trent looked at his watch. "Can you believe it's already three o'clock in the morning?"

"Which is why it's a perfect time to take a walk. No one will see us."

Trent agreed, so they got dressed and strolled the slumberous streets of Travis Heights. When they hit a particularly dark patch of sidewalk, Brendan said, "We should hold hands."

"It's too risky. We don't have eyes in the back of our heads."

"Eight seconds. It's completely dark right here. Look around. No one can see us. Let's hold hands for eight seconds. It may be the only chance we'll ever get to do this in public."

Trent felt a rush of adrenaline. He reached out and took Brendan's hand. They intertwined their fingers and counted to eight. Then they let go and didn't speak until they returned to the house and were back in bed.

"One more round before we go to sleep?" Brendan said. Trent responded by sucking Brendan's cock until he blew an only slightly diminished load, after which they both promptly passed out.

TRENT WOKE up to someone knocking on the back door. Patrick again, no doubt. Brendan lay on his stomach, dead to the world. Trent got dressed and shuffled into the kitchen. He would need to get rid of Patrick as quickly as possible.

He opened the door.

"Do you know what time it is? Don't tell me you're still sleeping. It's eleven o'clock."

It was Kieran.

# NINE

"WHAT ARE you doing here?" Trent asked. He tried to keep his voice calm.

"I came to see how you're doing. It's not even a three-hour drive, and I'm not pitching tonight. Are you going to let me in?"

Trent didn't answer. He couldn't focus on anything except Brendan asleep in the bedroom. He needed an excuse to get back there.

"I need to piss," Trent said. "Come on in." He turned and bolted out of the kitchen. He closed and locked the bedroom door behind him, then sprang on the bed and rolled Brendan over.

"What the—"

Trent straddled him and covered Brendan's mouth with his hand. They made direct eye contact. Trent mouthed the words, *Kieran's here*. Brendan's eyes widened in panic, and he nodded, so Trent removed his hand.

"What are we going to do?" Brendan whispered. "Can you get rid of him?"

"He drove in from Houston. He's not going to turn around five minutes later and drive back. He'll be here for a few hours, at least."

"What time is it?"

"Eleven."

"What am I going to do for a few hours? Hide in the bathroom?"

Trent rolled away and onto his back. "I don't know what to do."

Brendan sat up. "It's okay. I can handle this. You're a major league baseball player. That comes first. You have another bathroom, right?"

"Yeah, down the hall."

"Just keep him out of this one. Leave your bedroom door open, though, so he doesn't get suspicious. What does he think you're doing?"

"Taking a piss."

"Then go. Get back out there. I'll be fine."

Brendan got out of bed, grabbed his clothes, and went into the bathroom. He closed and locked the door without saying another word. Trent went into the kitchen, but Kieran had moved to the living room. He was looking at the New Order record on the turntable.

"Why are you listening to this faggy shit?" Kieran asked.

Trent sat down in the rocking chair. "You drove all this way just to criticize my taste in music?"

Kieran took a seat on the sofa. "How are you feeling?"

"Better. I'll be completely healed by next week. I'm going to see my grandma this weekend."

"That old witch is still alive?"

"Kieran—"

"Shit, you know it's true. She's the meanest woman I've ever met. Where are we going for lunch?"

"Why didn't you call first?"

Kieran looked confused. "Since when do I need to call first? You have other plans or something?"

"I might."

"Oh, yeah. With who?" Trent didn't answer. "Go put some shoes on, and let's get some grub. I like that Magnolia Cafe a few blocks from here."

Trent went into the bedroom and put on his shoes. Why was he doing this? Did he believe Kieran would betray him? He took a few steps and knocked softly on the bathroom door. He heard the lock being undone, and then the door cracked open. Brendan peered through. His eyes were red, and his nose was running.

"You've been crying," Trent said.

"It's just allergies. I'm fine."

There were many things Trent could deal with, but being the cause of Brendan's tears was not one of them. "This ends now. Come with me. There's someone I want you to meet."

Brendan almost smiled, but then he stopped and said, "No. You can't do that."

"You were allowed to tell someone, so now it's my turn. Follow me." He pushed open the door and Brendan stepped into the room. Trent gave him a kiss and then led him into the living room.

Kieran stood up. "Who's this? What's going on?"

"This is Brendan Baxter. Brendan, this is Kieran Harrison."

Brendan reached out his hand and Kieran shook it in a daze. "Where did you come from?"

"Sit down," Trent said. "There's something I need to tell you." He sat next to Kieran on the sofa, and Brendan took a seat in the rocking chair.

"I knew something was going on," Kieran said. "I could hear it in your voice. Is it drugs? Is this your dealer?"

"No."

"Do you have cancer? You're not going to be the Brian Piccolo of baseball, are you? Shit, would that make me Gale Sayers? Why do I have to be the black guy? Not that I'm a racist or anything, it's just that—"

"I'm gay."

Kieran looked at Brendan, then at Trent, and then back at Brendan. He opened his mouth, but no words came out. He stood up and sat down. He glanced back and forth between them again.

"You're joking, right?"

"No. I'm not joking."

Then, after a long pause, Kieran said, "I'd rather it have been cancer."

Trent recoiled. He turned to Brendan and saw a look of horror on his face.

"Are you fucking my best friend in the ass?" Kieran said to Brendan. "Or is he fucking you?"

Trent stood up. "Get out of here."

Kieran remained seated. "You can't be serious. Who is this guy? When did you meet him?"

"A couple of days ago."

"A couple of days ago? And now you're suddenly gay?" Kieran turned back to Brendan. "What did you do to him?" He lunged toward the rocking chair, and Brendan jumped up. Trent got stuck in the middle and threw Kieran back onto the sofa.

"I need to get out of here," Brendan said. "He's going to kill me."

"You got that right, faggot."

Trent grabbed Kieran by the arm and pulled him to his feet. "You and me are going out to the backyard. Brendan, don't leave. Please. Just give me five minutes." He shoved Kieran across the room, into the kitchen, and out the back door. He realized anyone walking by could hear them, so he pointed toward the garage and they went inside.

Trent closed the door and said, "I hate you right now."

"I only have one question. What in the fuck happened?"

"What do you mean, what happened? I met someone. Can't you see that?"

"You *met* someone? And now you're a fucking fag?"

"Would you stop using that word?"

"What word? Fag? Fag, fag, fag. Did he drug you or something?"

"Don't be an idiot."

"Are you saying you've always been this way?"

"Don't tell me you've never suspected. Are you really that blind? I've never dated a single girl the whole time you've known me."

Kieran sat down on the weight bench in the middle of the cement floor. He put his head in his hands and said, "Fuck. Anything but this, Trent. Anything but this."

"You'd rather I was dead."

"Who else knows?"

"No one." Trent didn't see any point in telling him about Stanton Porter.

"So it's not too late," Kieran said.

"Too late for what?"

"To stop this. We can pay him off and find you a girlfriend. No one needs to know. There are ways to deal with this."

Trent felt sick again. "I'm not going to do that."

Kieran stood up. "What in the fuck is the alternative? You can't be a cocksucker and play major league baseball. Am I the only one who gets that?"

"I'm not saying anyone else needs to know. But *you* needed to know."

"Why? What could possibly be gained by me knowing? What's the upside? Are Marcia and I supposed to go on a double date with you and your butt buddy? Do you think you can have a relationship with him? You're out of your fucking mind."

"I've had enough of this. You're supposed to be my best friend. Maybe I thought the upside was that I wouldn't have to lie to you anymore, or that you'd at least support me in private. But clearly this is a game changer for you, so go home. As long as you feel this way, you're no longer welcome in my house, and for an Eskimo to say those words is a very big deal." He turned toward the door. "I need to check on Brendan."

"You're choosing a stranger over me?"

Trent stopped for a moment, but then realized he had nothing to say except, "Tell Lillis I'll be back next week, as scheduled." He left the garage and went into the house. He found Brendan on the sofa, staring down at his hands. He heard Kieran's truck start up and peel away.

"That went well," Brendan said.

Trent sat next to him. "He's never talked to me that way before. I thought he would at least listen to—"

"I want to go home."

Trent nodded. "Okay. I understand."

HE DROVE Brendan back to the Walsh house in silence. When they pulled into the driveway, Trent left the engine running and said, "You got my number?"

Brendan looked confused. "You're not coming in?"

"I didn't think—"

"I'm not mad at you, Trent. How could I be? If anything, I'm a little overwhelmed. Why did you risk everything for me back there?"

"I don't know. It seemed like the kind of thing my father would do."

"Well, now we're really in this together, so you might as well turn off the engine and come inside."

Trent followed Brendan up the stairs and into the living room of the garage apartment. They sat down on the floor, side by side, with their backs against the sofa.

"What is it about this place?" Trent said.

"You feel better too?"

"Yeah. Just walking through the door."

"Maybe it's built on top of some ancient Indian temple." Brendan leaned over and kissed him. "You want a foot massage?"

Trent laughed. "I'll never say no to that."

They moved to the sofa and Trent propped his feet on Brendan's lap. Brendan removed Trent's shoes and then bent over and kissed his bare toes. He ran his thumb up and down the arch.

"Sorry I didn't handle things very well," Brendan said. "I needed to get out of there before he came back and beat me up."

"I don't blame you. It's just the way he was raised. This is Texas, after all."

"I get it. That's the way I was raised too. Texas, Ohio, Alaska—it's all the same when it comes to queers. Did you expect him to hug you or something?"

"I don't know what I expected. I didn't have time to think it through. But I knew I couldn't leave you in that bathroom and I couldn't keep lying to him. That feels really good, by the way. You can do it harder, though."

Brendan dug deeper into the sole. "What did he say when you guys went outside?"

"More of the same. I tried to tell him I wasn't planning on announcing it to the world."

"What was his response?"

"Do you think you can have a relationship with him?"

Brendan kneaded Trent's toes between his fingers and said nothing.

"What?" Trent asked.

"That's what Stanton said too."

"What do you mean?"

"He said, 'You can't just date Trent Days. He'd have to leave the sport, and you'd become the Wallace Simpson of baseball.' That's why I asked if you knew who Wallace Simpson was."

"There's got to be another option."

"How are your ribs?"

"A lot better."

"Then you'll be going back to Houston next week, and we'll probably never see each other again. That's the only option. I know that yesterday I said, 'What's the point if we can never be together?' But I've changed my mind. We can make the next few days matter, and that's enough."

"What if it's not enough for me?"

"It'll have to be. We both know you're not going to quit baseball. You're one of the greatest players the game has ever seen, and there's no way I'd ever get in the way of that. You need to be selfish right now."

Trent closed his eyes and wondered for the umpteenth time how his life had become such a mess.

"Do you think he'll tell anyone?" Brendan said.

"He'll tell Marcia, his wife."

"Any of the other players?"

"No way."

"How can you be sure?"

"Think about it. If it gets out I'm gay, what is everyone going to say about him?"

Brendan laughed to himself and patted Trent's feet. "That you guys are secretly lovers. That would be some sweet karmic justice right there. Kieran the Great labeled a fag. What an asshole."

"He's not an asshole."

Brendan turned his head and looked straight at Trent. "Come on. You're not going to defend the way he reacted, are you?"

"That doesn't make him an asshole."

"Right. You keep telling yourself that. Forget that he almost physically assaulted me."

"Can we put Kieran off-limits please? I don't want to spend any of our time fighting."

"Fine. But I'm not going back to your house."

"Can I stay here, then?" Trent asked.

"You already know the answer to that."

"Where are Stanton and his lover going to sleep?"

"I haven't really thought it through yet. In here, I suppose. I hope they don't mind sleeping on the floor."

"What are you going to tell Bill and Grace?"

"That I'm hosting a gay sex orgy. I don't know. Why do I have to tell them anything? I have a high-school friend visiting. It doesn't exactly smack of a homosexual conspiracy."

"I feel like people are going to know, just by looking at me."

"That's ridiculous," Brendan said. "You're being paranoid."

"Wouldn't you be?"

"I would probably think the whole thing was exciting if I were you."

"You're crazy."

"No, I'm actually pretty sad. I have the right temperament for the spotlight, but none of the talent to get into it. If I were you, everything would come second to baseball."

"I don't believe that."

"There's nothing wrong with wanting to be the best at something, but you need to be single-minded about it. I'm just a distraction."

Trent covered his face with his hands. "Don't talk that way."

"Why not? You're taking everything wrong. I'm glad I'm the distraction. This will probably be one of the most exciting chapters of my life, but that's where it ends. We're not a book, Trent. We're a short story, and a bittersweet one at that. We might as well embrace it."

"Will it bother you if I don't embrace it quite yet?"

"No, it won't bother me. Rail against the inevitable. It won't change the way I feel about you, but it also won't change the outcome."

"You feel something for me?"

"Yes, I feel a growing bulge in my shorts. You want to have sex?"

"It does seem like the perfect distraction right now, doesn't it?" Trent jumped off the sofa and headed toward the bedroom. "You coming?" he said over his shoulder. "My cock isn't going to suck itself."

Brendan raced after him and tore off his T-shirt. "I have to be at work at two."

Trent pulled him into the room and looked at the alarm clock. "That gives us thirty minutes."

They fell onto the bed and started kissing. Trent honestly didn't understand how he could ever be expected to give Brendan up, but he didn't dare speak that thought out loud. After a quick round of blow jobs, they got dressed, and Trent drove them to West Campus. He parked his truck, which prompted Brendan to ask what he was doing.

"I thought I'd drop into Les Amis and get something to eat."

"Without me?"

Trent turned off the engine and rolled up his window. "Is that a problem? It's not my fault you have to work."

"Quincy's going to talk your ear off the whole time. You know that, right?"

"So what? I like him." Brendan glared at Trent as they got out of the truck. "Okay, so I may have thought he was a little weird at first, but he grew on me."

"I don't get off until ten."

Trent fell into step with him, and they walked toward Inner Sanctum. "Then I'll be on your doorstep no later than nine fifty-five."

"You promise?"

Trent made a slicing gesture over his chest. "Cross my heart and hope to die."

TO HIS surprise, Trent ended up spending the rest of the day and evening inside Les Amis. Quincy introduced him to an endless stream of people, most of whom were graduate students in things like anthropology and feminist studies. He got to see the wheel spin twice. One of the girls he met even knew who he was and asked him to autograph a paper napkin for her brother. When Tony Atwood discovered he'd returned, he brought out one dish after another for Trent to sample, so their table was always filled with food. Brendan stopped by on his break and commented on the ease with which Trent had adapted to cafe life. When he went to the bathroom, Trent found the walls covered with quotes from philosophers and other famous people. As he took a piss, his eyes landed on one in particular, by a guy named André Gide. Someone had scrawled,

"In hell there is no other punishment than to begin over and over again the tasks left unfinished in your lifetime."

In the evening, he and Quincy got into a long conversation about Inupiat culture, and the adjustments Trent had to make when he moved to Texas. They also discussed the gold sparks again. Quincy was a good listener, and much calmer when he stepped out of his master-of-ceremonies role.

Around nine, a pregnant redhead came through the door and eased herself into a nearby booth. A few minutes later, Tony exited the kitchen without his apron. He walked over and kissed her.

"Is that Tony's wife?" Trent asked Quincy.

"Not yet. They're supposed to get married after the baby comes. I love Tony, don't get me wrong, but he's going to make a terrible father."

"What an awful thing to say about a man."

"I know. I'm evil that way. Sometimes the truth is an awful thing. But he's a child. Responsibility just isn't in his DNA. Why do you think he fits in so well here?"

"You don't believe in responsibility?"

"I believe in helping people walk the path they came here to walk. Sometimes that means hanging out in a cafe, talking about Foucault and Derrida. For years. But just because I cater to slackers doesn't mean I think they should be raising children. That kid will end up taking care of them, not the other way around."

"Maybe that's the path the kid is coming here to walk." Quincy looked exasperated, and Trent said, "You can't have it both ways."

"You're right. That doesn't mean I don't have my judgments."

"Do they live together?"

"Yes, up in Round Rock, with her mother. She drives him in and picks him up every day. Sure, they're in love now, but in five or ten years? Forget it. That's a white-trash nightmare waiting to happen."

Trent laughed, but at least he felt bad about it. "I think you have to let people try. Even if they fail, you have to give them a chance to be good parents."

"Hopefully their son will have a similarly forgiving heart."

Shortly before ten, Trent thanked Quincy and the staff, and headed next door to pick up Brendan. On the drive home, Brendan told him all about his day.

"I talked to Stanton again."

"You called him from work?" Trent said.

"Yes. You think I'm going to pay for the long distance? We call distributors in New York all the time. It will blend right in on the phone bill."

"What did he say?"

"They're flying in tomorrow afternoon. I gave him the address and told him I'd be there, but then Fiona asked me to cover for her. Her mother's in the hospital, so I couldn't exactly say no."

"What are you going to do?"

"I don't know. I haven't figured it out yet."

When they arrived at the Walsh house, Trent parked the truck on the street, and they walked up the driveway. The porch light cast a long shadow across the backyard. Trent stopped Brendan at the foot of the stairs and kissed him.

"Don't do that out here," Brendan said.

Trent felt giddy. "Come on. It's dark, no one can see us. It's a beautiful night. The moon is almost full. Give me a kiss."

"This is crazy, especially after what happened with Kieran."

"I don't care. Kiss me."

Brendan wrapped his arms around Trent's waist and pulled him close, but not close enough to crush his ribs. "You think I won't."

"I don't know. I'm still waiting. You chickenshit or what?"

Trent shut his eyes and felt the tender pressure of Brendan's lips. He opened his mouth and swooned at the familiar taste. He put his arms around Brendan's neck and kissed him deeper. The world and all its problems melted away. Then Trent heard the sound of tires on gravel. A car and headlights. It all happened so quickly he didn't have time to react. Brendan jumped away, but it was too late.

Bill and Grace Walsh had seen everything.

# TEN

THE ENGINE shut down, and the lights went dark. Trent heard a door open and then slam shut. Grace walked into the house without saying a word. Bill climbed out of his truck and came around to the front. "Go upstairs," he said to Brendan and Trent. "Everything's going to be fine. Just let me talk to her."

Trent followed Brendan up the stairs and into the garage apartment. They sat on the edge of the sofa, like two kids waiting for the principal to chew them out. For some reason, Brendan thought it was a good time to quote Pete Rose. "This is some kind of game, ain't it?" Trent sneered at him. "Oh, sorry. I forgot you hate the Reds."

"It was my fault," Trent said. "I should have listened to you."

Brendan sat back and relaxed. "I don't think they'll say anything."

"In the last twenty-four hours, we've gone from zero people knowing about my sexual orientation to five. At this rate all of Texas will know by Sunday."

"I think Quincy suspects."

"Me too. He didn't say anything the whole time we were talking, but I know he saw the way I lit up when you came in for your break."

"Nothing gets past him. What did you two talk about?"

"We didn't at first," Trent said. "People kept coming and going, and they did most of the talking. I can't say much of it interested me, but it was good to be around people who don't think baseball is the center of the universe. I used to be one of those people. Eventually, though, everyone else moved on and he asked me a bunch of questions about the North Slope and Eskimo culture. Then I asked him if he'd figured out what the gold sparks mean yet. He said, 'Not exactly.' He's seen the sparks before, and seems to think they're memories from a previous life, but the sparks are always the color of the auras. Or a mixture of the colors. He's never seen the gold before, and that's what's got him stumped. He's certain this is our first go-around."

"Which begs the question...."

"How can we have memories if we don't have a past together?"

"Ah," Brendan said. "The idiotic conundrums of New Age spirituality."

"Have you ever seen the quote about hell on the bathroom wall?"

"The one by Gide?"

"Yeah."

"It's one of my favorites. Gotta love the French. Did you get to see someone spin the wheel?"

Trent nodded. "Twice."

"What did it land on?"

"Russian Literature and the Irish Diaspora."

"How depressing."

"Are they always the same topics?"

"No, they change them every day, except for one."

"Which one is that?"

"*The Theory of Love.*" Brendan took Trent by the hand and kissed him. "It felt really good walking in there today and seeing you light up that way. I didn't know if you were thinking about me as much as I was thinking about you."

"I was. I am."

"But we've got to be more careful."

They were startled by a knock. Brendan crossed to the door and opened it. Trent heard Bill say, "Can I interest you?"

"Absolutely," Brendan replied. He stepped aside, and Bill entered with a joint. Brendan got an ashtray and a lighter. They sat in the living room and passed it around, with Trent and Brendan on the sofa and Bill in the corner chair. When they finished and Brendan had snuffed out the roach, Trent sat back and wished he could prop his feet onto Brendan's lap. The pot was a perfect way to unwind, and he continued to believe that nothing bad could happen to him inside the garage apartment.

"How's Grace?" Brendan asked.

"In shock, but she'll live. She needs time to process it, that's all."

"How are you?" Trent said.

Bill reached back and repositioned one of the pillows behind him. "I already knew."

Trent elbowed Brendan. "See? I told you."

"Are you okay with it?" Brendan asked. "You understand if this gets out, Trent's career will be over."

"I get it, and Grace gets it too. I'm finding out she has a lot of judgments about homosexuality that I don't share, but she would never intentionally cause someone harm. I'm not going to put a word to what's going on between you two, but it's written all over your faces. And it's a beautiful thing. I didn't come up here to lecture you. I came to offer my help."

Brendan looked at Trent and said, "Can I tell him about Stanton?"

"Yeah, might as well. The cat's out of the bag."

"A friend of mine from high school is coming to visit this weekend. Tomorrow, actually. And he's bringing his lover."

"His male lover," Trent said.

"We don't know any other gay people, and I really need to talk to someone who has a little experience with this. Now that you know, at least we don't have to tiptoe around you all weekend."

"Where are they sleeping?" Bill asked.

"On the floor, I guess."

"Horseshit. They can stay in the house. There are two bedrooms upstairs, and they'll have their own bathroom. That way you two can still have some privacy."

Trent sat forward and put his elbows on his knees. "You would do that?"

"Why wouldn't I?"

"You must have some Eskimo in you," Trent said.

"Where are they coming from?" Bill asked.

"New York City."

The excitement on Bill's face was unmistakable. "Are you working tomorrow?"

"Yes," Brendan said. "If you want to help, can you meet them for me? I won't be here when they arrive."

"Don't worry about it. I'll take care of everything."

"I work until four, so I'll be home shortly after that."

"I'll pick you up," Trent said, which made Brendan smile. "What about Grace?"

"We'll need to strike a compromise. Look, I know my wife. She doesn't want to be confronted with it, that's all. If you keep things platonic around her, she'll suspend what she knows and treat you like two really good friends who don't sleep in the same bed. She has a powerful sense of denial."

"Did you talk about it at all with her?" Brendan asked.

"No. Now's not the time. I asked her to put everything aside and just tell me she understood what would happen if she told anyone about what she saw."

"Thank you," Trent said.

"What time do your friends get in tomorrow?" Bill asked Brendan.

"Around three. They'll take a taxi from the airport."

"I'll be sure to be here. And don't worry about Grace. I can handle her."

Together, Trent and Brendan broke out laughing.

"Okay, you two. Very funny. Ha-ha. So I don't exactly wear the pants in the house. She's worth it."

"Look," Trent said. "I've never liked girls that way, but I can certainly see why you married her."

Brendan nodded. "She's so beautiful. Your kids are going to be gorgeous."

Trent nudged Brendan again. "Do you want to ask him about that Simpson guy?"

"Oh, yeah," Brendan said. "Do you know who Wallace Simpson is?"

"The woman King Edward abdicated the throne for."

"It's a woman?" Trent asked.

"Yes. Edward was the king of England for less than a year, in 1936. He fell in love with a woman named Wallis Simpson. W-a-l-l-i-s. She was an American with one ex-husband and a second on the way. The prime minister basically told him he couldn't marry a twice-divorced woman without destroying the country, so he gave up the throne rather than live without her. As far as the grand romantic gesture goes, it doesn't get much grander than that."

"Stanton told me I can't date Trent unless he leaves the sport, and then I would become the Wallis Simpson of baseball."

"So that makes me the king of England?" Trent said. "I think he's exaggerating things just a tad."

"Stanton always was prone to hyperbole."

Bill sat forward in his chair. "Have you thought about what you're going to do?"

Trent shook his head. "No. It feels like the only options are bad ones."

"Hmm," Bill said. "Muddy waters."

"What does that mean?" Brendan asked.

"Sometimes we look into a river, and we can't see the bottom because the water is muddy. Think of the river as your problem, and the bottom as your solution. The more you kick about and make a fuss, the muddier the water gets, and the farther away the solution seems. But that's an illusion. The riverbed hasn't gone anywhere. It's as solid as ever, waiting for you, just beyond the muddy water. So instead of making it worse, try sitting still. Let the water clear up. Decide what's important, and I promise you, the answer will reveal itself." Bill stood up. "In other words, try to focus on the here and now. You hear me?"

"We hear you," Brendan said. "Thanks for the advice. And the weed."

"I'll slip you another one tomorrow to share with your friends."

Bill gave them each a strong hug and then returned to the house. As soon as he left and they sat back down on the sofa, Trent propped his feet onto Brendan's lap and grinned.

"You've been dying to do that since we got up here, haven't you?"

"Please," Trent pleaded.

"How about you give me a blow job first and then I'll rub your feet. Quid pro quo."

"Sounds fair enough. Have you thought about...? You know. The other stuff."

"What other stuff?"

"The Hershey highway."

"Oh. Sure, I've thought about fucking you."

"I'm glad to hear that. Have you thought about me fucking you?"

Brendan laughed. "No. That one may take some time."

Trent moved to the floor and knelt in front of Brendan. He undid his shorts, pulled out his cock, and stroked it. "Time's the one thing we don't have."

"I'm still enjoying the blow jobs, aren't you?"

"Yeah. I just thought I'd bring it up. For future consideration. Hopefully near future."

Brendan leaned down and kissed him. "Duly noted. Now suck my dick."


THE NEXT morning Trent drove Brendan to work and confirmed that he would pick him up at four. He went home and found two messages on his machine, one from Lillis and the other from the front office.

Trent called the Astrodome. "Good morning, Sandra. It's Trent Days. Can I speak to Bob, please?"

"Why, yes indeed, Trent. How are you feeling?"

"Better. I'll be back next week."

"Oh, that's good to hear. We miss you. Okay, hon, one sec. I'll put you through to Bob's office. I just saw him head down that way."

The line clicked and then clicked again. "Trent?"

"Hi, Coach."

"What in the hell did you say to Harrison? He was sulking around the dugout last night, cursing anyone who got in his way. I may have to pull him out of the rotation, the way he's fucking up."

"Please, Coach. Don't do that yet. Wait until I get back."

"Your twenty-one days isn't up until the thirtieth. Today's the fifteenth. That's two weeks away, kid."

"I can come back to Houston next week. I can help him then, even if I can't play."

"You know you can come back now, don't you? I just thought it'd be a good idea, getting away from it all. You looked like you needed a break from the whole Eskimo Slugger circus."

"You were right. It was a good idea. I needed some perspective. So I'm going to take a few more days, if that's okay."

"I want you back here no later than the twentieth. That's next Wednesday. You'll need at least ten days of reconditioning."

"You got it, Coach."

"Get some rest and check in with the front office on Monday. Just to let them know you're alive."

"I'll do that. Thanks, Coach."

Trent hung up the phone and thought about calling Kieran, but decided against it. He called his father instead.

"Hello?"

"Hey, Dad, it's me."

"Trent? How are you doing, son?"

"It's a mixed bag right now. How's Barrow?"

"Oh, you know. It's summer, so Stephen's home from college, and Jeffrey's getting ready for his freshman year at Anchorage. Mickey has a girlfriend. Now that he's sixteen, he thinks he doesn't have to listen to his father anymore."

"Is Mom there?"

"No, she's over at your Naga's. Are you okay? You sound like you're in trouble."

"I can't get into it, Dad. Not right now."

"Are you going to jail?"

"No, sir. Nothing like that. We'll have a long talk once I figure things out. I just wanted to hear your voice."

"Okay, son. If it ever gets to be too much, you can always come home. You know that, don't you?"

"Yeah, I know that. Thanks. It helps a lot. Don't say anything to Mom, okay? She'll only worry."

"I can't stop your mother from worrying."

"I know. Just tell her I'm fine and I'll call her next week. Is Mickey there?"

"Hold on a second."

"Wait. I love you, Dad."

"Thanks, son. I miss hearing that. I love you too."

Trent heard his father call for his youngest brother, who moments later took the phone and said, "What?"

"Don't give Dad a hard time."

"Why do you care? You're never here."

On top of everything else, Trent hated the fact that he was on the verge of becoming a stranger to his three brothers. "I care. You're coming to visit next month. I'll see you then."

"He doesn't trust me."

"Who? Dad?"

"Yeah."

"Is he listening now?" Trent said.

"No, he went into the other room. He thinks I'm boning Jerica Qutuq."

"Are you boning Jerica Qutuq?"

"Yeah, but I'm using a rubber."

"He probably thinks you're too young, rubber or not."

"There's nothing else to do in this frozen hellhole. And next year Jeffrey's leaving too."

"It'll be your turn soon enough."

"I don't know what Mom's going to do when Jeffrey's gone. We both know he's her favorite. How's your injury?"

"I'm fine," Trent said. "I'm going to visit Grandma this weekend."

"I hope she remembers who you are. Otherwise, she'll mow you down with her shotgun."

"Will you go easy on Dad? Listen to him every once in a while, even if you're just pretending. It'll make him feel better."

"I'm not going to stop boning Jerica Qutuq."

"Fine. But be careful. He doesn't want you to get her pregnant and ruin your life."

"And you think *I* want to get her pregnant and ruin my life? Never mind. Thanks for the advice, big brother. How's your sex life?"

"None of your business."

"But mine is yours? What kind of double standard is that?"

"The older-brother double standard."

"Do you even have a sex life?"

"Yeah, but that's all I'm saying."

"What's her name?"

Trent hesitated, but then said, "Brenda."

"Big tits?"

"We're not talking about her tits."

"She go down on you? Jerica goes down on me."

"I need to hang up now. Tell Stephen and Jeffrey I said hello."

"Yeah, I'll tell them. I miss you, Trent."

"I miss you too, Mickey."

They said good-bye and hung up. Trent spent the rest of the day listening to music and trying not to think about how nervous he was to meet Stanton Porter and his lover. He arrived at Inner Sanctum just before four, and Brendan called Bill to let him know they were on their way.

"Are they here?"

"Yep," Brendan said. "They're sitting in the kitchen right now with Bill and Grace."

"I wonder if she's going to make them sleep in separate bedrooms."

"Jesus, I hope not. How embarrassing would that be? She can't treat them like they're twelve."

"Her roof, her rules."

"Well, it's Bill's roof too. That's not going to fly with him."

"Isn't it weird, the way everything we do has this ripple effect?"

"It does seem like a lot of drama over something that shouldn't be a big deal. You ready to head home and face the music?"

"Yeah," Trent said. "Are you excited to see Stanton again?"

"Yes, but I realized today I haven't seen him since he was sixteen. He's all grown up now and graduated from college."

"Speaking of sixteen, I talked to my little brother this morning. He asked about my sex life. You're Brenda now."

"Gee, thanks. Just castrate my 'n' like that."

"I talked to my father too. He asked if I was going to jail."

"Drugs, cancer, jail. What is it with these people? They act like it's 1963 instead of 1983. Steven Carrington is gay, for Christ's sake."

"Who's Steven Carrington?"

"Blake Carrington's son on *Dynasty*."

"Never watched it."

"The point is, he's there, on television. Gay. We're not living in the Stone Age. This whole business should be getting easier."

"I think you're naïve, but I don't want to argue about it. Let's get out of here."

When they got to the Walsh house, Trent followed Brendan through the back door and into the kitchen. Bill and Grace were sitting at the table with the two guests. Everyone stood up, and the dark-haired guy reached his hand out to Brendan. Trent assumed that was Stanton. The blond one smiled at Trent and offered his hand.

"I'm Hutch."

"Trent Days."

"Yeah, I know."

They weren't what Trent expected at all. He would never have guessed they were gay, except maybe they were a little too good-looking. Both of them.

"Trent," Brendan said. "This is Stanton."

"Nice to meet you," Stanton said as he shook Trent's hand.

"You too."

"Are you guys all settled upstairs?" Brendan asked.

"Yes, we are," Stanton said.

Trent looked over at Grace and mouthed, *Thank you.* She seemed a little overwhelmed, and he couldn't really blame her.

"Y'all are on your own tonight," Bill said. "But tomorrow we're having you in for dinner, and I won't take no for an answer."

"Thanks, Bill," Brendan said. He turned to Stanton and Hutch. "Let me show you guys my apartment. We can hang out for a while and then maybe head over to Les Amis."

"Sounds good," Stanton said as he looked at Trent. "Lord knows, we have a lot of catching up to do."

THE ESKIMO SLUGGER | 123

# Eleven

TRENT STEPPED aside and allowed the other three to file out the back door as he brought up the rear. The four men climbed the steps to the garage apartment, and Trent wished he could see Hutch and Stanton's expressions as they entered. Once he got inside, they were turning around and taking in the room with a familiar look of awe on their faces.

"It's like a tree house," Stanton said.

"Very groovy," Hutch hummed.

They took a seat on the sofa while Brendan went into the kitchen. Trent sat down in the corner chair, and a few moments later, Brendan returned with four bottles of beer.

"Everyone stand up," Brendan said. They all stood and took a bottle. Brendan raised his in a toast. "Here's to old and new friends. Welcome to Texas."

They clinked the necks of their bottles together and drank to the weekend ahead. Stanton and Hutch returned to the sofa, and Trent to the corner chair. Brendan sat on the floor in front of him.

After a long silence, Stanton said, "Are we allowed to have a fan moment?"

Brendan turned his head, as if to pass the question to Trent, who said, "Go ahead. Brendan got to have his."

"I was really into baseball when I was a kid," Stanton said. "Then I started playing football in junior high and lost interest. You brought me back to baseball. I kid you not."

"I never left," Hutch said. "I've followed the Yankees my whole life. But you—the way you attack the game. And your swing belongs in a museum."

"Thank you. I didn't expect gay guys to be into sports."

"You'd be surprised," Stanton said. "I make a terrible homosexual half the time. I got the impression from something Bill said that you'd rather we not make a big fuss."

"I'm very uncomfortable with a big fuss."

Stanton nodded. "Understood."

"What did Bill say?" Brendan asked.

Hutch grinned. "Stanton wanted to change his shirt before he met you, and Bill said you'd make fun of us if we dressed up."

"I would have."

Stanton pointed to his plain white T-shirt. "Obviously, I took his advice. But let's move on to more important things, like what in the fuck is going on with you two?"

Everyone laughed, and Hutch said, "You'll have to excuse my boyfriend. He has a very direct manner sometimes."

"You want to be treated like a regular guy? This is how I talk to our friends. So, how did you two meet?"

"I work at a record store, and Trent came in to buy an album."

"Which album?" Stanton and Hutch asked simultaneously.

"*Power, Corruption & Lies*," Brendan said.

Stanton made a face like he had eaten something bitter. "New Order? Ugh. How disappointing."

Trent didn't know quite what that meant. "It was actually the twelve inch of 'Blue Monday' that brought us together. When I got home, I took a couple of painkillers and lay down to listen to it. Halfway through, it skipped. I grabbed the record and jumped into my truck, but forgot all about the painkillers."

"He almost fainted when he got back to the store."

"I didn't almost faint. I was a little light-headed, that's all."

"So I took him to the cafe next door, and we got something to eat. He gave me a ride home afterward, and when we got here, we ran into Bill, and he invited us to his birthday party that night."

"How old is he?" Stanton asked.

"Thirty."

"I guessed late twenties. Sorry, go on."

"Well," Brendan continued. "It wasn't exactly a party. More like dinner with a few guests. And a cake. Anyway, after that Trent asked me if I wanted to go fishing the next day."

"Fishing?" Stanton said.

"Yes. Did your dad ever take you fishing?"

"Every summer. My family spent a week up in Michigan. Five o'clock in the morning. My brothers hated it, but I didn't mind. Did you catch anything?"

"We caught a buzz," Trent said, "but no fish."

Hutch sat up. "You guys smoke weed?"

"Oh my God," Brendan said. "Bill keeps giving us joints. I feel like such a pothead. When I moved in here, there was one taped to my door."

Hutch rolled his eyes. "What a Mrs. Madrigal rip-off."

"Do you know what book that's from?" Brendan asked.

"Yeah, don't you?"

Stanton took Hutch's hand and said, "They just acknowledged their homosexuality four days ago. They haven't had time to read *Tales of the City* yet."

"Is that the name of the book?" Trent asked.

"Yes," Hutch said. "Armistead Maupin. Mrs. Madrigal is the landlady at 28 Barbary Lane, and she tapes joints to the door when new tenants move in."

"It was on the required reading list Hutch's friends gave me a few weeks after I met them," Stanton said. "I was woefully uneducated about all things gay, so they made a list of books and movies."

"Do you still have it?" Brendan asked.

"The list, you mean?"

"Yeah."

"I'll mail you a copy."

"Thanks, man. Yes, Hutch, we smoke weed. I'm sure Bill will slip us something later. But we're not supposed to talk about it in front of Grace."

"And we're not supposed to hold hands or make out in front of her either," Trent said.

"Sounds like my mom," Stanton said. "She just wants to pretend I'm not gay."

"Did something happen?" Brendan asked. "She was so nice to me on the phone."

"That's because you're not her son. My parents basically disowned me last week. I wrote them a letter and told them everything. They wrote back and said I couldn't bring Hutch home for Christmas."

"So that's what I have to look forward to?" Brendan said.

Hutch put his arm around Stanton. "You have a family." Then he turned back to Trent and Brendan and said, "What were we talking about?"

"Fishing," Trent said.

Brendan nudged his leg. "We had fun, didn't we?"

"I had a blast."

"My dad never took me fishing," Brendan continued. "But Bill gave us directions to this secluded cove on Lake Travis. We got stoned and went skinny-dipping."

"Then we almost got beat up by a couple of rednecks," Trent said.

"That was definitely a highlight."

"While we were swimming, Brendan asked me if we were on a date."

"Whoa," Stanton said. "That took some balls."

Brendan nestled between Trent's legs. "It paid off. When we got back here, one thing led to another, and the next thing you know.... Well, here we are."

"Here we are," Trent repeated.

"You two are glowing," Hutch said, and then he leaned into Stanton. "Do you remember the weekend we met?"

Stanton kissed him. "How could I forget? I got a ring and tickets to see Bruce Springsteen."

"Who else knows about you guys?" Hutch asked. "Besides Bill and Grace. And us."

"Just Kieran," Trent said.

Hutch's eyes popped. "Has he known you're gay this whole time?"

"No. No one has. He drove in from Houston yesterday and dropped by my house."

"While we were asleep," Brendan added. "In bed. Together."

Stanton gasped. "He caught you having sex?"

Hutch rubbed his back and said, "Calm down there, Starsky."

Trent shook his head. "No, he didn't catch us having sex. But I couldn't let Brendan hide in the bathroom, so I introduced them to each other."

"At least you didn't ask him to hide in the closet," Stanton said. "Is Kieran cool with it? I can't believe I'm calling Kieran Harrison by his first name."

"Not at all," Brendan said. "He almost beat me up."

Stanton grimaced. "Oh. I'm sorry to hear that. Was it knock-down-drag-out bad?"

Trent nodded. "We both said some ugly things, but I think he'll come around once the shock wears off. At least I hope he will. He's my best friend in the whole world. I can't believe he'd cut me out of his life."

"Why did you tell your landlord?" Hutch asked. "Not that he isn't totally cool. And hot, by the way."

"We didn't tell him," Brendan said.

"They drove into the driveway last night while we were making out at the foot of the stairs."

Stanton laughed and said, "You two have had some shitty luck, haven't you? Okay, final burning question. Why in the hell did you call me?"

"Does Hutch know about...?" Brendan asked.

Hutch looked around, as if to emphasize that he was still in the room, and said, "The blow job?" He looked at Trent. "Do you know about the blow job? I hope you know about the blow job."

"Yeah, I know about the blow job."

"Good," Hutch continued with a chuckle. "So it's out in the open. We all know about the blow job."

"Thanks for establishing that," Brendan said. "By the way, Stanton, I'm sorry I was such an asshole afterward."

"What are you talking about?"

"I avoided you and never called again."

"Did I call you?" Stanton said.

"No, but—"

"Exactly. I avoided you too, so an apology is completely unnecessary. Unless you want me to apologize too, and then we can cancel each other out. We did the best we could, Brendan. But how is our trip to the drive-in connected to why you called me two days ago?"

Hutch turned to Stanton. "You didn't tell me it was at a drive-in."

"I didn't think the details were important."

"What movie did you see?"

Trent answered for him.

"*Jaws*?" Hutch exclaimed. "That's priceless."

"Anyway," Brendan said, "you kept coming up in the conversation on Tuesday, because you're the only other guy I've ever... you know. Done it with."

Stanton turned to Hutch. "Can I say it?"

"I'd rather you didn't."

"Say what?" Trent asked.

"Stanton still revels in the humor of teenage boys."

Trent started to laugh. "You weren't going to say something about—"

"The Eskimo Slugger is eating my sloppy seconds. Sorry, but we were all thinking it."

Brendan groaned. "Can we make a sacred pact never to speak of that again?"

"Agreed," Stanton said.

"What was I talking about, anyway?"

Hutch took a swig of beer. "Stanton coming up in the conversation because he's the only other guy you've ever done it with."

"Right. So that night, Trent slept here. First time ever. Morning arrived. I woke up. No Trent. I panicked."

Trent sat up. "Do I get to say something here?"

"Go ahead."

"Brendan is not a morning person. I tried to wake him up and got shoved to the other side of the bed. I needed to go home and check my messages."

"Did you leave a note?" Stanton asked.

"Yes."

Brendan shook his head. "The note was cryptic at best."

"Then it's a minor offense," Hutch said. "Though not really a princely move on your first morning together."

"That's fair," Trent said.

"Anyway," Brendan continued, "like I said, I panicked. I needed to talk to somebody and I had mentioned you, Stanton, the day before. I figured I had about a fifty-fifty chance you had come out of the closet, and if you hadn't, I knew you'd at least be nice to me. It was an impulse call."

Trent ruffled Brendan's hair. "An unauthorized impulse call."

"You didn't know he told us?" Hutch asked.

"Nope."

"Trent had a little meltdown in the store," Brendan said. "After I told him."

Trent considered protesting, but then thought better of it. "That's fair too. It all hit me at once. I just don't know what I'm going to do."

"You can trust us," Hutch said. "We didn't breathe a word of this to anyone. And we never will."

Trent believed him. "Thanks. That means a lot. You both seem like good guys. And Brendan was right—it's nice to have someone to talk to. It makes me feel like we're not so alone."

"You're not," Stanton said. "But have you thought about what's next? Are you going to keep seeing each other after you come off the DL?"

Brendan leaned against Trent's leg. "We haven't crossed that bridge yet."

"Wow," Stanton said as he relaxed into the sofa. "That would be a very deep closet, guys. Deep and inescapable."

Hutch sat forward. "I don't agree. Have you considered coming out?"

"No," Brendan said. "He'd have to quit baseball."

"Why?" Hutch pressed.

Stanton slapped him on the arm. "Come on, get real. There's no way an openly gay man could ever play in the major leagues."

"Why not?" Hutch said. "There was a time, not too long ago, when people said the same thing about a black man. Someone had to be the first, and you're one of the best players in the game, Trent. You could be the gay Jackie Robinson."

Trent didn't like that idea one bit. He knew the story of Jackie Robinson, including the near torture he endured. "It would never work."

But Hutch wouldn't take no for an answer. "I think it would. Didn't you hear about that episode of *Cheers* last winter? The one where Sam's old teammate writes a book and comes out to him? Sam accepted him in the end, and they were baseball players."

Stanton huffed. "There's a reason they call that fiction."

"What about Glenn Burke?" Hutch said. "He never hid it. Did you see the interview with Bryant Gumbel? He was dating Tommy Lasorda's son, for Christ's sake."

"And they ran him out of baseball because of it," Trent said.

"They would never do that to you."

"What's going to stop them?"

"Winning. If you're helping them win, they won't run you out."

"It wouldn't be enough," Trent insisted. "Robinson didn't integrate baseball—Branch Rickey did. I would need a Branch Rickey, and trust me when I say this—the Houston Astros don't have anyone like that. This isn't a battle they want to take on."

"But you could write yourself into *two* history books," Hutch said. "Baseball and the gay rights movement."

Brendan laughed. "Telling Trent that something will make him even more famous is not the way to convince him of anything."

Trent shook his head. "I'm no Jackie Robinson. I wouldn't last two seconds in that firestorm."

"Why don't we just chill out for a while?" Stanton suggested. "And talk about something else. Like, what are our plans for the weekend?"

"I thought we could go to Les Amis for dinner tonight."

"How can we go out in public?" Hutch asked.

"Well," Brendan said, "obviously we'll need to be discreet, but no one recognizes Trent at Les Amis. It's all tortured academics and starving musicians."

Hutch lit up. "Let's go, then!"

"I have to visit my grandmother tomorrow," Trent said.

Brendan turned around and looked up at him. "You have to do that tomorrow?"

"Yeah. It'll give you guys a chance to catch up. I'll be back in time for dinner."

Hutch raised his hand and said, "You can't leave me here alone with them. I'm begging you, show a little mercy. They're going to talk about high school the whole time. Please, can't you take me with you?"

Trent couldn't think of a reason to say no. Besides, he liked Hutch. "She lives in the middle of nowhere. You'll be bored out of your mind."

"No, I won't," Hutch said. "I would love to see Small Town, Texas. Please. I promise not to press you about the gay Jackie Robinson thing. We can talk about baseball. Or music. Or nothing at all."

"Okay," Trent said. "I guess I wouldn't mind the company."

"Groovy," Hutch said. "What's the name of this town, anyway?"

Trent took a long drink from his bottle of beer and then said, "Dime Box."

# TWELVE

THEY LEFT the garage apartment and walked down the driveway to the street.

"Can all four of us fit in the front seat?" Brendan asked.

When Hutch saw Trent's pickup truck, he jumped and asked, "Can we sit in the back?"

"Really?" Brendan said.

"I've never ridden in the back of a truck before."

Stanton looked skeptical. "Is it legal?"

"Yes," Trent said. "At least in Texas."

"Then let's ride in the back," Stanton said.

"Is it okay if I join them?" Brendan asked Trent.

"Suit yourself. I don't mind playing chauffeur."

They climbed into the bed of the truck, and Trent headed toward West Campus. He popped in one of his Hank Williams cassettes and turned it up to add to the atmosphere. He looked in the rearview mirror and saw the three of them laughing like kids. Trent found Hutch's enthusiasm infectious. It dawned on him that, outside of Kieran, he'd never really made many friends after he moved to Texas. Sure, he always had teammates, but no one he could ever be himself around. Stanton and Hutch lived their lives in the open, something Trent had never thought possible. More and more he was beginning to see the high price tag attached to being a professional baseball player.

Brendan had told Quincy some friends were visiting for the weekend, so when they walked into Les Amis, Monica pointed to an empty corner booth and said, "I saved you a table." Then she stuck her head into Quincy's office, probably to let him know they had arrived.

"They know you here?" Stanton asked Brendan.

"Yeah. The record store I work at is in the house next door. I'm a regular."

Tony emerged from the kitchen and strolled right up to Trent. He shook his hand and said, "I heard you were coming in today, so I picked up some salmon at the market. I thought I'd steam it with a little oil and ginger. Maybe a touch of soy and lemon too. How does that sound?"

"Can't wait to try it, Tony."

"Hot damn. How are those ribs?"

"Almost healed. I should be good to go by next week."

"Fantastic," Tony said, ignoring the others. "I'll get back in the kitchen and start prepping."

Tony turned to go as Quincy came out of his office. He approached them with outstretched arms. "Welcome to Les Amis. Are these your friends from New York, Brendan?"

"Yes. This is Stanton and Hutch. Guys, this is Quincy. He owns the place."

Hutch stepped forward and shook his hand. "It's groovy to meet you, Quincy."

"Are you Stanton or Hutch?"

"I'm Hutch."

"Well, Hutch, it's groovy to meet you too." Quincy shook Stanton's hand and gave Trent a hug.

"Hey," Brendan said. "What about me?"

Quincy put his arm around Brendan. "Are you feeling neglected?"

"No. Well, maybe a little."

"I have the perfect antidote for that." Quincy turned around. "Monica, will you please bring these boys two plates of Tony's deep-fried potato skins?"

"One with extra cheese and one with no cheese," Brendan added.

"Coming right up."

Quincy grabbed four menus and led them to their booth, where Brendan and Trent sat together on one side and Stanton and Hutch on the other. Quincy distributed the menus and said, "I'll let you get settled before I butt in and dominate the conversation."

Trent laughed. "You're not going to join us?"

Quincy winked at him. "Later. We'll spin the wheel after dinner. I hate watching people talk with their mouths full."

He returned to his office, and Stanton asked, "What's the wheel?"

Brendan pointed to the far wall. "Did you see what they did, Trent?"

Trent turned around and glanced at the wheel. All the topics were baseball related: The Mechanics of Pitching, Best Post-Season Players, Cheating in Baseball, Race and the American Pastime, The Art of Hitting, Great Shortstops, and so on. Monica arrived at the table with the potato skins, and Trent asked, "Did you do that for me?"

"We did," she said as she placed the plates on the table. "It was Quincy's idea, but Tony helped, since frankly we didn't know enough about baseball to come up with eleven topics."

"That is the nicest thing. Thank you."

"You're more than welcome."

She left the table, and Brendan picked up one of the potato skins. He took a bite and then said to Stanton, "It's a wheel of topics. You spin it, and Monica gives you a discussion question. The topics are usually academic, but they knew Trent would be here tonight, so... I saw it this morning when I dropped in to grab a coffee."

Hutch leaned into Stanton. "Robert would love this place."

"You're right. He could run the whole wheel, especially if the topics were about music. What's good to eat here?"

"The lasagna," Trent said as he bit into one of the cheeseless potato skins.

"Then why are you having salmon?"

"Because I don't like cheese. Brendan swears by the lasagna, though."

Hutch looked up from his menu and smiled at Trent. "You guys already have history."

Stanton had a puzzled look on his face. "I don't see the salmon on the menu."

"He's making that special for Trent," Brendan said.

"I autographed his apron the other day."

"Star treatment, eh?" Stanton said. "Must be nice. Hutch grilled salmon for our first dinner together. Do you remember that?"

"It was also the first time you and Marvin played the greatest game."

"Who's Marvin?" Brendan asked.

"My roommate at NYU," Stanton said. "Also my best friend. Does the lasagna come with garlic bread?"

Brendan nodded. "And a salad, if you want one. I usually don't. I break out if I eat too much green stuff."

Monica returned and took their orders. Brendan and Stanton both got the lasagna. Hutch decided on a Cobb salad with extra chicken.

"Let's do twenty-second recaps of our lives," Brendan said to Stanton.

"Okay, I made first-string when I was a senior, finished high school, went to college at NYU, came out of the closet. Marvin and I met Hutch and his friends—best thing that ever happened to me—graduated from college. And now I'm starting a career as a music journalist with the *Village Voice*. That may have been twenty-five seconds."

Brendan took a deep breath. "Moved to Houston, went to college at Rice, didn't come out of the closet—except for one friend. Backpacked across Europe—changed my life. And now I'm starting my second year of law school at UT in September. Oh, and I'm sleeping with the Eskimo Slugger."

"How did you two meet?" Trent asked.

Stanton remained silent and allowed Hutch to answer. "I was tending bar on Fire Island two summers ago. We met on July 3rd. Stanton walked onto the deck of the Blue Whale and it was love at first sight, for me at least. He played hard to get."

"Only a little."

"Only a little?" Hutch said. "You made me practically beg for that first walk on the beach." He turned back to Brendan and Trent. "I gave him a ring, won over Marvin, wined and dined him, introduced him to my friends, threw a little dancing in there, and even took him to Jersey for a Bruce Springsteen concert."

"That's when I finally gave in," Stanton said.

"We did it on the train back to the city."

"But not like there was anyone else around," Stanton clarified. "It was late at night, and we found an empty car."

"I could never imagine being that free," Trent said.

"Is this the first for both of you?" Stanton asked.

"Pretty much," Brendan said. "Except for the drive-in."

"You just broke our sacred pact."

"Sorry. There was also a hooker Trent had to sleep with for some team excursion up in Cape Cod."

Stanton took a bite of potato skin. "Yum. My father would love these, if he was speaking to me. Honestly, I didn't deal with the whole coming out thing well at all, and I'm not even talking about telling people. I mean with myself. It took me a long time to be able to say 'I'm gay' out loud."

"I'm not really having that problem," Brendan said.

"Me neither," Trent added. "I feel like, no matter what happens down the road, Brendan and I are doing this part together."

"That would make a huge difference," Stanton said. "I felt so alone."

Hutch forgot about their need for discretion and kissed Stanton on the lips. Trent couldn't bring himself to object. His closet belonged to him and nobody else. If he wanted to, he could get up and walk away and never look back. He could protect himself from any kind of scandal. But he didn't do those things. Instead, Trent accepted the risk. He accepted that Hutch wanted to comfort Stanton, and Trent shouldn't do anything to stop it. He accepted that if Brendan was a mistake, then he would gladly make it, over and over again. There was something reckless about Trent's behavior, and that was the point.

After dinner, Quincy pulled a chair up to their booth and asked Trent if he wanted to spin the wheel. He couldn't resist the offer, so he went over and gave it a go. It landed on *The Art of Hitting*. Trent returned to the table and Monica joined them.

She read from a piece of paper, "In your opinion, which major league batter most elevated hitting to an art form? Discuss among yourselves."

Monica walked away, and Stanton said, "Babe Ruth."

Brendan nodded. "I agree, though I know Trent doesn't."

"You two clearly know nothing about great hitters," Hutch said.

Trent slapped his hand down on the table. "Anyone who's really serious about baseball knows the answer is Ted Williams."

"Thank you," Hutch said.

Stanton turned to him. "How can you say that Babe Ruth is not the greatest hitter of all time?"

"That wasn't the question, Starsky."

"Williams's average is higher," Trent said.

"By a razor-thin margin," Stanton protested. "If I recall correctly, .344 to .342. Ruth beats him in every other category, careerwise."

Trent held up his hand. "You're not taking into account the five years Williams lost to the wars. The question was very specific. Sure, Ruth hit better when it came to power, but power isn't art. His at bats were never a thing of beauty. Williams had a relationship with the ball that no man has ever been able to duplicate."

"A relationship with the ball?" Brendan said. "Jesus, he wasn't fucking it. I think you have to take into consideration what Ruth did for the sport overall. He was a showman. More than any other player, he told a story, and that made him an artist. And I'm sorry to break this to you, but Williams has been forgotten by the masses. If you walk up to ten people at random on the street and ask if they know who Babe Ruth is, all of them will say yes. If you do the same with Ted Williams, half of them will think he's the guy who wrote *A Streetcar Named Desire*. Babe Ruth is Mr. Baseball."

Trent turned to Quincy. "What do you think?"

"You're not going to like my answer."

"Don't tell me you've never heard of Ted Williams."

"I'm afraid I haven't, so I'm siding with Brendan and Stanton on this one."

Hutch pounded his fist on the table. "This is a travesty of justice."

"Then why don't you spin the wheel, Hutch?"

He needed no further encouragement. Hutch jumped up and gave it a vigorous twirl. It landed on *The Theory of Love*. He looked confused. "What does that have to do with baseball?"

"It's the one topic that never changes," Quincy said.

"Oh. Groovy. Let's have at it, then."

He returned to the booth and waited for Monica. She walked over and read, "In four words or less, describe the most effective strategy for attracting love."

"Four words?" Stanton said.

"That's what makes it fun." Monica tore the paper into pieces, threw them into the air, and walked away.

The five men sat in silence for almost a minute. Then Stanton said, "Do unto others."

Quincy nodded. "That's good. Expound."

"What's the point of using four words or less if we get to expound?" Hutch asked.

"Life is a continuous seesaw between distillation and dilution. Stanton?"

"The only way to attract love is to be the kind of person other people want to be around, and the most effective way to demonstrate that is to treat them like you want to be treated."

Quincy nodded. "Brendan?"

"I'm thinking. Okay, I can do it in two words: be genuine."

"I like that," Hutch said.

Brendan continued: "As a lawyer, I notice right off the bat—note the baseball reference—that the question leaves some room for interpretation. Are we talking about romantic love or the deeper, longer-lasting kind? Because the most effective strategy for attracting the latter is to be genuine, warts and all. Do we want to pretend to be something we're not just so someone will fall in love with us?"

"To thine own self be true," Quincy quoted. "You're a true Renaissance thinker, Brendan. How about you, Hutch?"

"Those are both really good answers, but I think I can name that tune in one note: music."

"Of course," Stanton said. "I agree completely."

"If you want to attract love," Hutch continued, "play music. Sing a song. Join a choir. There are so many different ways to express yourself with music, but I promise that if you do, love will follow."

"Brilliant," Quincy said.

Everyone looked at Trent. He wasn't used to this kind of thing at all and mumbled, "Hell if I know."

That got a laugh at first, but then Quincy said, "Four words exactly. The only true wisdom is the acknowledgment that we know nothing. Trent, are you saying love is a mystery that can neither be quantified nor qualified by strategies and philosophies?"

Trent smiled. "Yeah, that's what I'm saying."

"Equally brilliant."

"But if I had to take a more serious crack at it, I'd say, be grateful. I think people focus way too much on what they don't have, and not enough on what's right in front of them. Before we try to attract more, maybe we should take better care of the love we already have."

"I am digging this table tonight," Quincy said.

"Don't you have an answer?" Hutch asked.

Brendan laughed. "Quincy? An opinion? Never."

Quincy sat with his elbows on the table, like he might be praying. He waited for several moments before he spoke, but finally he said, "Resist separation. Embrace visibility."

A silence fell over the table.

"You certainly got the most bang out of your four words," Brendan said. "Expound."

"Think about what Trent said. Don't look elsewhere; look to what you have. And what we have is each other. Always. I know we live our lives as individuals. I can look out into the world and see that. I'm not an idiot. But I also know that thirteen billion years ago, there was no 'we.' There was only an 'I.' Everything that exists now existed then. Everyone who exists now existed then. *There is only one of us.* And that, Brendan, is not New Age bullshit. That's physics. To our detriment, we emphasize our individual spirits and journeys over our collective spirit and journey. We teach our children that life is a process of learning, but if we've been around since the beginning of time, what could there possibly be left to learn? We only need to remember what we already know. Our struggles are not born of ignorance, but of forgetfulness. If you want to attract love, the first step is to embrace the idea that we are all connected to each other."

"You mean empathy," Hutch said.

"Yes, but not occasional empathy. I'm talking about a sustained and perpetual empathy, uninterrupted by ego. John, chapter ten, verse thirty: 'I and my father are one.' What do you think Jesus meant there?"

"That he was God," Stanton said.

"No. I think he meant the human and the divine are one. Literally. Flesh becomes spirit, and spirit becomes flesh. There's no separation between you and me, and there's no separation between us and God, because—"

"There is only one of us," Hutch said.

Stanton shook his head. "That's just downright anti-American. We live in a country founded on the individual. What you're talking about is communism."

"Communism is an economic theory," Quincy said. "What I'm talking about goes well beyond economics. It addresses the very purpose of why we are here."

"Which is?" Brendan asked.

"To manifest the divine."

"My head hurts," Trent said. "What about the second part?"

"Embrace visibility. Naturally, I'm expanding on Brendan's answer, because for me, it's not enough to be genuine. In order to attract love, we must be visible. An enlightened person lives openly and honestly, without shame or the capitulation to fear. This is one of the hallmarks of all the great masters, regardless of religious orientation. Look at who attracted love and devotion by the millions—Jesus, the Buddha, Krishna, Gandhi. They all embraced visibility. So I ask myself, 'Is my life an open book? Could I publish the details on the front page of the newspaper? And if not, then *why am I behaving that way?*'"

"So there's no place for privacy in the world?" Brendan asked.

"Privacy is the veil we pull over our shame."

Stanton shook his head. "That's an impossible ideal to live up to."

"Ideals aren't meant to be easy. They're meant to be the pinnacle of our achievement. Cling to your privacy for as long as it serves you, but someday, and it may be many lifetimes down the road, you will find that it doesn't serve you anymore."

"You believe in reincarnation?" Hutch asked.

"Yes," Quincy said. "It's the only spiritual philosophy that makes any sense to me. I have no doubt that the entire spectrum of experience is available to all of us, equally, as many times as we wish. We are all choosing, in every moment, where we'll go next. Even from one lifetime to the next."

Hutch pressed on. "Do you think we come back and find the same people, over and over again?"

"I think many people do. Like you and Stanton. Can you see their colors, Trent?"

"Excuse me?" Stanton said.

"Aura color," Brendan explained. "Reds are movers and shakers, greens are creative, and blues are negotiators. Quincy can see them, and now it looks like he's teaching Trent."

Trent looked them over. "Stanton is a red and Hutch is a green."

"Very good," Quincy said. "Can you see the yellow sparks flying everywhere?"

"Yes."

"Bullshit," Brendan protested.

Trent leaned into him. "You don't see the sparks between them?"

"Yes, but they are of no particular color, and you know it."

"Ours are gold," Trent said to Hutch.

"Your auras?"

"No, our sparks. Brendan and I are both blues, but our sparks are gold. Quincy hasn't figured out what that means yet."

Stanton laughed. "It means those were the colors of our high school football team. I'm sorry, but this is a ridiculous conversation."

"Come on, Starsky. Don't be an asshole."

"I said I was sorry. I didn't mean to offend you, Quincy."

"I've heard much worse from Brendan. It must be something in the water up there in Ohio."

"You're not buying any of this either?" Stanton asked Brendan.

"Not a word. I see the point about being connected, and visibility is an obvious virtue, but I can't make the leap to reincarnation. When we die, that's it. I'll entertain the possibility that we're all incarnations of a single intelligence, but not that my individual soul will be magically reborn as someone else when I die. And why destroy an otherwise compelling argument with the aura business? You almost had me hooked until you jumped into the deep end of the batshit-crazy pool."

"See what I mean?" Quincy said.

Stanton grinned. "Sorry, it's too *Jonathan Livingston Seagull* for us Midwestern boys."

AFTER MIDNIGHT they thanked the staff of Les Amis and returned to the Walsh house.

"Let's meet for breakfast at nine," Brendan said as they stood in the driveway.

Trent turned to Hutch. "We can head out around ten or ten thirty."

"Sounds good," Hutch replied. "Do you think we can go downtown tomorrow night after dinner to see some live music?"

"Sure," Trent said, setting caution aside. "I don't think anyone will recognize me in a crowd, and even if they did, Austin is a cool place. As long as we aren't kissing or holding hands, we're just four friends having fun."

"So much for embracing visibility," Stanton mumbled. Hutch elbowed him. "What was that for? You're the one who kissed me in the middle of dinner. If we're going to hang out with a major league baseball player in public, you've got to cool it with the PDA."

"I'm sorry. It won't happen again."

"Lucinda Williams is playing at Liberty Lunch tomorrow night," Brendan said. "She has a very Austin sound."

"Can we go?" Hutch asked. "I promise to behave myself."

"I'll call tomorrow and see if they have any tickets left."

"Groovy. Good night, then. We'd better be quiet going in. We don't want to wake Bill and Grace."

Stanton took his hand. "Something tells me Grace isn't sleeping much these days, with all that baby she's schlepping around. I hope she doesn't feel too uncomfortable with two gay guys in the house."

"I'm going to win her over," Hutch said. "I have an idea. Let's get up early and make breakfast for them. For everybody." He turned to Brendan and Trent. "You guys just meet us in the kitchen at nine."

"You don't have to do that," Brendan said.

Stanton laughed. "Try and stop him."

"Okay, good night, then. I hope you're making pancakes."

"You can count on it," Hutch said.

They disappeared through the back door, and Trent followed Brendan up the stairs to the garage apartment. Trent waited until Brendan sat down before he lay on the sofa and propped his feet on Brendan's lap.

Brendan took off Trent's shoes and started rubbing his feet. "What did you think of them?"

"You were right," Trent said. "We needed to see what it's like to hang out with other gay guys. They're the first people to really understand us. But I feel like shit asking them to change who they are around me."

"I don't think they mind."

"That's not the point."

"Stanton has definitely come out of his shell since he was sixteen. He was always kind of a smartass, but I really like him."

"Hutch seems nice too. Tomorrow should be fun." Trent sat up and jumped onto Brendan's lap. He faced him and straddled his legs. "I've been wanting to do this all night." He kissed Brendan with the force of a fastball. Trent loved the way he tasted. He loved the way their tongues swirled and probed and retreated. He stood up on the sofa and tore open his fly. He pulled out his cock, and Brendan pounced on it with his mouth. Trent closed his eyes and put one hand on the back of Brendan's head and the other against the wall behind him. He raised his foot and placed it on the arm of the sofa. Brendan unzipped his own fly and released his dick. He started stroking himself with one hand and caressing the inside of Trent's thigh with the other. Then Trent felt Brendan's fingers rise until they slipped under the fabric of his shorts, past his balls, and into the crack of his ass. An index finger pressed against Trent's sphincter, and his cock jumped. Brendan quickly withdrew and paused his blow job to liberally coat his fingers with spit. Then they were rubbing Trent's hole again, this time in a circular motion, and Trent moaned. Brendan's warm lips wrapped around his dick, and the tip of his finger forced open the tight butt muscle. The finger entered him, and Trent's moan became a gasp. Brendan was touching something that felt like the base of his cock.

"There," Trent whispered. "Right there."

Brendan pressed against the hardening gland, and a wave of pleasure surged through Trent's body. The more Brendan massaged the spot, the closer he got to coming. Brendan increased the pace of his sucking and slipped in a second finger, which pushed Trent over the edge. He pulled his cock out of Brendan's mouth and shot all over his face. Brendan beat his dick until come started flying everywhere. The first spurts reached as far up as Brendan's chin, and the rest landed on his T-shirt, soaking it with semen. Trent stepped off the sofa and let his shorts drop to the floor.

"I'm covered in come," Brendan said. He carefully peeled off his shirt and then wiped his face with one of the dry sleeves. "Did we find one of your erogenous zones or something?"

"I don't know, but whatever you were doing back there, I definitely liked it."

"Let's take a shower before bed. I'll even wash your back."

Trent took off his shirt and stood naked in front of Brendan. "I'm ready for anything."

They jumped into the shower and positioned themselves under the stream of cool water. Even though they had just come, Brendan's dick got hard again, and Trent squatted down to suck on it. Brendan leaned against the porcelain tiles, and Trent worked his cock over, focusing special attention on the sensitive head. When Brendan came for the second time, Trent swallowed it all. He stood up and kissed Brendan. He wanted to say something. He wanted to acknowledge this thing between them, but he didn't know which words to use.

They finished their shower and dried off, then crawled into bed. They both lay on their right sides. Brendan wrapped his arms around Trent from behind. He pulled Trent close, and said, "Thank you."

"For what?" Trent asked.

"Everything. Your answer tonight was 'be grateful.' So that's what I'm doing. I'm being grateful. Thank you."

"I've been wanting to say something. I... I just didn't know how."

"But you did say something," Brendan said. "When you told Stanton and Hutch that whatever happens down the road, we're doing this part together. That pretty much says it all."

Brendan kissed Trent on the neck and relaxed into the pillow. Trent took one last look at the bright moon outside the window and then closed his eyes. Every day he spent with Brendan was making it harder to walk away. He knew that. But what was he supposed to do? Give up baseball? He pulled Brendan's arms tighter around himself and tried to wish his troubles away. An eerie silence settled over the garage apartment, punctuated only by the cadence of Brendan's breathing. Then Trent reluctantly fell asleep.

# THIRTEEN

*TRENT HEARD the crack of leather against wood. Like a slow-motion instant replay, he saw a ball coming toward him. Why was he playing second base? He caught the ball, but then didn't know what to do with it. Kieran was standing on the mound yelling at him. "Get your shit together or get off the field." A second ball hit the baseline and popped Trent square on the forehead. Like an astronaut in outer space, he floated backward from the force of the blow. Everything stopped for a moment, and then gravity exerted itself and Trent crashed onto the AstroTurf. He stared up in awe at the vast dome above him.*

*He saw snow falling from the ceiling and said, "It's true. The whole thing is air-conditioned."*

"HEY. WAKE up."

Trent felt someone nudging him. He opened his eyes and bolted upright in bed. "What happened?"

"Nothing," Brendan said. "You were having a nightmare."

Trent rubbed his eyes and tried to shake it off. "It was terrible."

"Come here. Lay back and tell me about it."

He fell onto the pillow and nestled himself into the crook of Brendan's arm. "I was in the Dome for a game, but I was playing second base, and it was snowing."

"Second base?"

"I know. That alone is a nightmare. The batters kept hitting the ball to me, and I didn't know what to do with it. Kieran was yelling at me. Then a ground ball slammed me in the face, and it started to snow. That's when you woke me up."

"It's a baseball version of the actor's nightmare."

"What's that?"

"When actors dream they're on stage, but they don't remember their lines or even what play they're in. It's pretty common. Christopher Durang even wrote a play about it."

"Someone wrote a play about being in a play?"

"Yep."

"What do you think it means?"

"The play or your dream?"

Trent kissed him. "My dream. Share your wisdom with me, Obi-Wan."

"Dream interpretation Jedi-style, eh? Hmm, let's see. Do you remember that part of *The Empire Strikes Back*, when Yoda lifts Luke's ship out of the bog using nothing but the Force? Luke says, 'I don't believe it!' And Yoda says—"

"That is why you failed."

"Exactly. I think that's what your dream is about. The injury has shaken your confidence."

"But why second base?"

"Who's the most famous second baseman of all time?" Brendan asked.

"Jackie Ro—Oh. You're good, Jedi Master."

"Forget about what Hutch said. No one expects you to come out publicly, especially not me."

"These past few days, it's like we're living in a bubble."

"And you know what happens to bubbles, don't you?"

"I'd rather not think about it."

"Which is why you're having nightmares."

Trent knew Brendan was right. "What time is it?

"Eight thirty. We should jump in the shower."

"Can I borrow a fresh shirt?"

"Sure. What's mine is yours. There's a bunch of them in the second drawer from the bottom."

They took a shower and started to get dressed. Trent chose a blue T-shirt with *Findlay High School Football* printed in gold letters. On the back was Brendan's last name.

And the number eight.

"Your jersey number as a quarterback was eight too?"

"Yes," Brendan said.

"Why didn't you tell me that?"

"I don't know. I didn't want to be like every other dickhead who comes up and tells you their jersey number was eight in high school."

"You're hardly every other dickhead."

"It's just a coincidence."

Trent shook his head. "Wait until I tell Quincy about this."

They finished dressing and went over to the house. In the Walsh kitchen, Stanton and Bill were sitting at the corner table while Hutch and Grace finished making breakfast. Grace was laughing, and it appeared to Trent that she had warmed to Hutch considerably. They discussed their plans for the day over pancakes and omelets. Brendan told them he and Stanton were going to spend the morning catching up.

Grace shifted around in an attempt to find a comfortable position. "Bill, I'm gonna love this child, but right now I just want to strangle him. He's kicking up a storm."

"Only a few more days," Bill said.

"Have you guys picked out names yet?" Brendan asked.

Hutch chuckled. "Haven't you heard? Bill's going to name all his children after the Compson siblings in *The Sound and the Fury*."

"I love that book," Brendan said. "So that means Benjy if it's a boy and Caddy if it's a girl?"

Trent took a bite of bacon. "My dad made me read it. Went right over my head."

Grace nodded in agreement. "You and me both. Though I'm certain this one's a boy, and I do like the name Ben." Then she raised a finger to Bill and added, "Though no one will be calling him Benjy, you hear me?"

"I hear you, honey."

"I don't want anyone thinking he's named after some damn movie mutt."

"Actually," Stanton said, "the character's name in the book is spelled B-e-n-j-y, and the dog's is spelled B-e-n-j-i."

"Ignore him," Hutch said. "What if you have four boys?"

"We'll improvise," Bill said. "After Ben, there's Quentin. There is both a male and female Quentin in the book, so that gives me some wiggle room. Jason comes next, which could become Jase for a girl, and Caddy could become Cade for a boy."

"Enough of this nonsense," Grace said as she gestured to Brendan and Stanton. "Bill, why don't you drive these boys around the city this afternoon? Grab some barbeque for lunch and maybe take them up to Mount Bonnell."

Bill looked at them over a forkful of pancake. "You interested?"

"I'd love a tour," Stanton said. "Really, I would. But right now you'll have to excuse me for a minute. I need to go upstairs."

"Where are you two heading?" Bill asked Trent as Stanton left the kitchen.

"To grandmother's house we go," Hutch said. "I'm seeing Small Town, Texas today. As you can tell, I'm more than a little excited."

Bill chewed the bite of pancake and swallowed. "Where does she live, Trent?"

"About seventy miles east of here. A tiny fork in the road called Dime Box."

"Really?" Grace said. "Well, I'll be damned. I grew up in Caldwell and used to go to the Dime Box rodeo when I was in high school. Imagine that. So the story the other night, the one where you learned to play baseball in a field next to your grandmother's house? That was in Dime Box?"

"Yes, it was."

"But you never lived there, right?" Grace asked.

"No, I never did. When I moved to Texas, I lived with the Harrison family, here in Austin. My father was raised in Dime Box, though. He moved to Alaska when he was eighteen and pretty much never looked back. When I was in high school and college, I used to drive out and visit my grandma at least once a month, so I'm familiar with the place."

"When did you see her last?" Bill asked.

"Christmas."

"Oh," Grace said. "I'm sure she'll be excited, then."

"We'll see about that."

After breakfast, Brendan and Stanton retired to the garage apartment, and Bill helped Grace into the living room. Trent and Hutch cleaned up and washed the dishes, then climbed into Trent's pickup and headed out of town. Once they were on the road, Hutch asked him how long the drive was.

"Just under an hour and a half," Trent said.

"That's not bad. Tell me about your grandmother. And who are we going to say I am? I figured I could be a friend from high school who went to college at Columbia. That way at least half of the story is true. I'm in town for the weekend and crashing at your place."

"You don't have to lie for me."

"So you plan to tell her we know each other because our boyfriends were blow buddies in high school?"

Trent groaned. "Okay. Maybe your story is better. Do you mind?"

"Not at all. The whens and hows of coming out are your decision. I don't think a harmless white lie about where I'm from will damn my soul."

"Do you think it's okay that we left Brendan and Stanton alone together?"

"Why? Are you afraid they're going to have sex?"

"I can't say the thought hasn't crossed my mind."

"Well, let me put it at ease, then. I know Stanton comes off as abrasive sometimes, but he's the most loyal person I know. He would never cheat on me, or do that to you. Besides, what they're doing right now is…. Stanton would hate me for saying this, but gay guys call it 'girl talk.'"

"What's that?"

"Being gay isn't just about fucking other guys. It's also about the friendships, and sometimes those friendships can get a little girly. That's one of the things Stanton hates about being gay, but that's his hang-up. I guarantee you, right now, he and Brendan are dishing about us like two teenagers."

"Really?"

"Brendan only has eyes for you. Everyone can see that, and you should be able to see it too. You've got nothing to worry about."

"You and Stanton seem well-suited to each other."

"We are. He's a handful, but he's my handful. Though I'm a little scared about the future."

"Why's that?"

"I've been trying to break into the music industry for about five years now, and it just isn't happening. So when we get back to New York, I'm starting a new job with my brother."

"What kind of work?"

"Real estate."

"I bet you're going to be good at it."

Hutch turned his head and smiled. "That's not much comfort. I worry that I'm making a huge mistake. I have no idea what's going to happen to me when I give up my music. By the way, what was that we were listening to last night?"

"Hank Williams."

"Can you play some more?"

"Sure." Trent reached down and pushed the cassette back into its slot. Hank started to sing "I'm So Lonesome I Could Cry."

"Stanton is so vulnerable right now," Hutch continued. "He needs me to be solid after his parents wrote him those horrible letters. I don't understand how they can treat their own son that way."

"Sounds like you're going through a big transition."

"On pretty much every front. We're moving into a new apartment, and we're both starting new jobs. It's scary."

"Play the long game," Trent said.

"What do you mean?"

"Focus on the big picture. In fifty years, when you and Stanton are sitting on the porch of the old-folks home, you'll look back on this time and think.... What? Probably that it was the beginning of an amazing adventure. That's how I deal with my fear when we're down 4-0 in the bottom of the second. I've got seven more innings to play, and now I'm fired up, and they're overconfident. That's the perfect recipe for success."

"You give good pep talks. Did you know that?"

"Then why do I feel like such a mess?"

"You're going through a transition too," Hutch said.

"Or I'm avoiding one."

"Well, it's good advice, regardless. You're doing the best you can, Trent. Cut yourself some slack."

"You think I should come out of the closet and try to play."

"I promised I wouldn't bring that up."

"And you didn't. But that's what you think."

"It's an opportunity for greatness," Hutch said. "And I don't understand how you can pass on something like that."

"Not everyone's cut out for that kind of greatness."

"That's what Stanton said. He's like you. The idea of fame makes him sick to his stomach. He also says greatness comes in a lot of different forms. So I hear you, but I'm the total opposite. I would be jumping at the chance to make history."

Trent stared out over the hilly pastures lined with grazing cows. "I guess the world needs both kinds."

"It sucks to want it without the talent to back it up, though."

"You sound like Brendan. He wants to be a great lawyer, but he's afraid he didn't get into the right school and isn't good enough."

"Which is something you can't exactly relate to."

"My situation comes with its own problems. The snow is always whiter on the other side of the fence. That's my Eskimo wisdom for the day."

"Do people actually say that in Alaska?"

"No, just me. We don't have grass in Barrow."

"What's your grandmother's name?" Hutch asked.

"Gertrude. But everyone calls her Gertie."

"Like Hamlet's mother. Except no one called her Gertie. What's she like?"

"All bark and no bite. Don't take anything she says personally."

"Sounds like a challenge."

"Do you want everyone to like you?"

"Sure. Stanton thinks it's irrational to pursue a goal that's statistically impossible, but what if I'm the first person to pull it off? As far as I know, there's not a single person in the world who hates me."

Trent swerved to avoid a pothole. "As far as you know. That's a big qualifier. I'm sure there are plenty of guys who hate how good-looking you are."

"That has nothing to do with me, so it doesn't count. And you should talk. Do you have any other cassettes?"

"Check the glove box."

Hutch opened the compartment and rummaged through the scattered tapes. "Elvis Presley. Elvis Presley. Buck Owens. Elvis Presley. Who's your favorite singer, Trent?" Then he gasped and raised a cassette in triumph. "Ah, here we are."

"What?"

"Evidence that you are a certified homosexual. Patsy Cline!"

Hutch stopped Hank Williams and replaced him with the new cassette. When Patsy started singing "I Fall to Pieces," both Hutch and Trent joined her. With the windows down, singing at the top of their lungs, they spent the rest of the trip cycling through "Walkin' After Midnight," "Crazy," "She's Got You," and other Patsy Cline favorites. Finally, as "Sweet Dreams" finished, Trent turned onto Route 141, and they pulled into the center of Dime Box, Texas.

"THIS IS like something out of a movie," Hutch said as he stared out the window. They passed the bank, the lumberyard, and Dime Box Automotive before crossing the railroad tracks. Trent turned left onto a dirt road with no outlet and pulled into the gravel driveway of the last house.

Hutch pointed to the open space beyond the garage. "Is that the field? Where you learned how to play baseball, I mean?"

"That's it."

"Man, this is so groovy. I can't believe I didn't bring a camera."

"This is top secret, remember?"

"Oh, right. Sorry. I was never here."

Suddenly, someone kicked the door open and Grandma Gertie stepped onto the front porch wearing an old flannel nightgown and a pair of house slippers. Her long white hair hung loose and fell to her waist. As Mickey had warned him, she quickly aimed her Winchester Model 12 at the truck.

"Holy fuck," Hutch said.

"You best get off my property, roughnecks!" she shouted. "I ain't got no diamonds to steal and I shoots to kill."

Trent stuck his head out the window. "It's me, Grandma. Trent."

"Trent? You mean Carson's oldest boy?"

"That's the one."

"Who's in the truck with you?"

"Just a friend."

"Another Eskimo? I never did trust those damn Eskimos."

Trent heard Hutch laugh. "No, Grandma. Someone I went to high school with. He's just visiting for the weekend, so I brought him along. Why don't you put the gun down and invite us in?"

"I ain't dressed proper for callers. What do y'all mean, sneaking up on old Gertie so early in the morn?"

"It's almost noon, Grandma."

"Don't get smart with me, boy. You ain't too old for a licking." She slowly lowered her weapon. "You wait right there while I get dressed."

She disappeared into the house and Trent relaxed into his seat. "Sorry about that. I guess I should have warned you."

"Is she for real?" Hutch asked.

"Oh, yeah. She's old-school Texas. You know, shoot first and ask questions later."

"You could have gotten us killed."

Trent laughed. "Relax, I'm joking with you. The gun's not even loaded. I told you she's all bark and no bite."

"Why didn't you call ahead and tell her we were coming?"

"She doesn't have a phone. Your heart racing a little?"

"Man, oh man, is it ever."

"Nothing wrong with that. Gets your blood pumping." Trent glanced at the house next door. Someone was peeking through the curtains and watching them. "She makes the best biscuits and gravy I've ever had in my life. Just watch. As soon as we get inside, she'll start cooking."

"What if she doesn't like me?"

"Well, she hates Kieran, so…. But you said you were up for a challenge."

"She hates Kieran Harrison?"

"Yeah, but in her defense, he was kind of an asshole the day I brought him out here. He can be a real prick sometimes."

"Does she know you're famous now?"

"No idea. I'm sure one of my uncles has told her about me, but I doubt it even registered. She doesn't pay attention to much outside of Dime Box. She's lived in that house her whole life."

"Any advice?"

"Just be yourself and you'll do fine."

Grandma Gertie reappeared on the porch, this time wearing a floral-print house dress and a white apron. Her hair was pulled into a bun, and she had powered her face—which did more to accent her wrinkles than hide them. "Get on in here," she said with a wave. "I ain't gonna bite."

Trent and Hutch got out of the truck and walked to the porch to greet her. Trent bent down and gave her a hug. "It's good to see you, Grandma."

She released him and stepped back. "Let me look at you. You're still a runt of a boy, ain't you? Never did grow tall like your daddy. All that Eskimo blood's stunted your growth. Who's this?"

Hutch reached out his hand and introduced himself. "It's a pleasure to meet you, ma'am."

"Where you from, boy?"

"I live in New York."

"New York City?"

"Yes, ma'am."

She turned back to Trent. "Your Uncle Clay went to New York City last year. Said it was nothing but panhandlers and porno shops. And foreigners. Lots of foreigners. Said he tried to hire a taxi, and the driver couldn't talk a lick of American. Wouldn't catch me dead there, no sir. You boys hungry?"

"I'm always hungry, Grandma."

"Come on in, then. I made some fresh biscuits earlier and can stir up some gravy. You like fried chicken, Hutch?"

"Oh, yes, ma'am, I do."

"You ain't had real fried chicken until you've had old Gertie's. Ain't that right, Trent?"

"That's right, Grandma. I was just telling him your biscuits and gravy are the best I've ever had."

She reached up and patted him on the cheek. "You little brownnoser you. Let's get inside before that busybody next door comes sniffing around."

They followed her through the house and into the kitchen, which was dominated by a tall wooden table surrounded by stools. Trent and Hutch took a seat while Gertie began to work at the counter.

"You got new neighbors?" Trent asked.

"Yes. A young couple with a little girl. The damn woman won't leave me alone. Just as chipper as a canary. Always stopping by and asking if she can help out, like I'm crippled instead of old."

Trent laughed. "Sounds like a real pain in the ass."

"There's that smart mouth of yours again. I've a mind to take you over my knee, and don't think I won't. Damn Eskimos never did teach you no manners."

He winked at Hutch. "Now, Gertie, you know I'm your favorite grandson."

"Don't be trying to sweet talk me, boy. I ain't never played favorites with any of you, so stop your clowning and catch me up. Clay says you're playing baseball down in Houston."

"That's right."

"Don't know why you couldn't of taken up a real sport, like football."

Hutch burst out laughing, and Trent smiled at him. "You too?" They heard a knock on the front door.

"There she is," Gertie said. "Already come a-knocking. Damn busybody. Can't have a couple of callers without everyone stopping by to snoop. Ain't no such thing as privacy in this town. You best go answer it, Trent. She's nothing if not persistent."

Trent crossed back through the living room and opened the front door. A young woman stood on the porch with a little girl in her arms.

"Oh my," she said. "It is you."

"Can I help you?"

"I'm sorry. I live next door and saw you pull up in your truck. My husband's out of town today, and I know he'd shoot me if I didn't at least try and get an autograph. I promise not to intrude."

"It's fine. My grandma's making fried chicken. You want to come in and join us?"

Her face lit up. "Really? Are you sure it's okay with Gertie? She can be a little short with me sometimes."

"Don't worry about that. Come on in."

Trent stepped aside and then closed the door behind her. He led them back to the kitchen. "Look who's here, Grandma. It's your next-door neighbor, asking for an autograph."

Gertie turned around. "Autograph? Whose autograph?"

"Mine," Trent said.

"Yours? What in the hell does she want with yours?"

The woman shifted the little girl from one arm to the other. "Why, Gertie, don't you know your grandson is a famous baseball player?"

Grandma Gertie waved her flour-covered hands. "What kind of nonsense are you talking, Marilyn? I swear, I'm the old woman but you're the senile one."

Trent offered his hand. "Your name is Marilyn?"

"Oh my," she said. "What's happened to my manners? Meeting a famous person has gotten me all discombobulated." She shook his hand. "Yes, I'm Marilyn. Marilyn Manning. And this is my daughter, Trisha."

The little girl immediately spread her arms out toward Hutch, who stood up and introduced himself.

"She seems to like you," Marilyn said.

"Can I hold her?"

"You can try, but she's never let anyone else do that before." Hutch reached out and the little girl slipped effortlessly into his arms. She cooed with delight and buried her face in his shirt. Marilyn looked on in shock. "Well, I never."

Gertie returned to her fried chicken and mumbled, "It's a fucking miracle."

"Grandma, not in front of the child."

"Don't matter one lick. The kid's stone-cold deaf. Ain't that right, Marilyn?"

"It's true. My husband and I have been driving to College Station twice a week to learn sign language."

"How old is she?" Hutch asked.

"Thirteen months."

"Y'all have a seat while I finish up this chicken. Trent, fetch some lemonade from the ice box. Pour everyone a glass, now, you hear?"

Trent went to the cupboard and pulled down four tall glasses and a smaller one for Trisha. He filled them with ice and then lemonade. He left one on the counter for Gertie and carried the others to the table.

"Do you play baseball with Trent?" Marilyn asked Hutch.

"No, we're friends from high school. I live in New York now."

"New York City?"

"Yes."

"My, how sophisticated. I can only imagine how countrified little old Dime Box must seem to someone such as yourself."

"I actually like it here. A lot."

"What kind of name is Hutch, if you don't mind me asking?"

"It's a nickname. I picked it up in college."

"What's his real name, Trent?" Marilyn asked.

She caught him with a mouthful of lemonade, which gave Hutch an excuse to answer.

"Christopher."

Marilyn clutched her hand to her chest. "That is my favorite boy name. We're trying for another, and if it's a he, we're going to name him Christopher."

Trent couldn't help but notice the way Hutch instantly bonded with Marilyn and her daughter. They continued talking all through the meal, and Hutch kept commenting on the delicious food. For dessert, Grandma Gertie served up homemade peach pie with vanilla ice cream. She gave Hutch an extra scoop, which was her way of telling Trent that she liked his friend.

After they finished their pie and cleared the dishes, Hutch said, "Is that a Martin guitar I saw in the living room?"

"It sure as hell is," Gertie said. "Do you play?"

"Yes, I do."

Gertie went into the living room and returned with the beautiful, natural-wood guitar. She handed it to Hutch. "This belonged to my second husband. Play us a tune."

Hutch handed Trisha back to her mother and took the guitar. He slipped the strap over his head and gave it a strum. He retuned a few of the strings and then began to sing "Amazing Grace." Although he had heard Hutch singing along to Patsy Cline in the truck, Trent wasn't prepared for the beauty of his voice. Even Grandma Gertie was visibly moved. When he finished, Marilyn clapped her hands and said a simple, "Oh my."

Hutch followed that with a soulful rendition of "Danny Boy," which led Gertie to exclaim, "That's some set of pipes you got on you, boy."

"Do you know any Emmylou Harris?" Marilyn asked.

"I'm afraid I don't."

Gertie lit up. "Give us a round of 'The Eyes of Texas.'"

Hutch threw a panicked look in Trent's direction. Trent quickly sang the first line a cappella and Hutch repeated it. Trent could only hope he'd figure out the tune was the same as "I've Been Working on the Railroad." Hutch smiled in understanding and strummed some chords. Trent continued the song and Gertie joined him. Hutch did his best to fake it and no one seemed to notice. Finally, Marilyn added her voice for the rousing finish.

*"The Eyes of Texas are upon you*
*'Till Gabriel blows his horn."*

"That is so groovy," Hutch said. "Let's do it again. By the way, I've always wondered, who's Gabriel and why is he blowing his horn?"

Trent balked. "You don't know who the angel Gabriel is?"

"Oh, they mean *that* Gabriel?"

"Hell, yes," Gertie said. "When he blows his horn, that's the signal that Jesus is coming back to Earth. What's wrong with you, boy? Weren't you raised with proper religion?"

Hutch strummed the guitar. "I guess not. So when Jesus returns, his first stop is going to be Texas?"

"That's right. You know what Davy Crockett said, don't you?"

"No, what?"

"You can all go to hell, I'm going to Texas," she quoted.

Hutch strummed again. "I thought Davy Crockett was from Tennessee."

"Would you quit your yapping and sing the damn song!"


AROUND FOUR o'clock, Trent told his grandmother they needed to hit the road and head back to Austin. Gertie gave them both big hugs and told Hutch he was welcome anytime. Marilyn walked them to Trent's truck, and Hutch reluctantly handed Trisha over to her mother. Trent had an extra jersey stored behind his seat, which he autographed and handed to Marilyn.

"Tell your husband I'm sorry we missed him."

"Oh, he's gonna be beside himself when he sees this. Thank you, it was such a pleasure to meet you both."

"I'm never going to forget this," Hutch said. "Never."

"Will you come back and see us sometime?"

"Yes, I promise."

Trisha reached out for Hutch again. "No," Marilyn said to her, "he has to go, sweetie. Y'all have a safe trip now, you hear?"

"Thanks for keeping an eye on Gertie," Trent said. "I know my dad worries about her a lot, being so far away. I'll tell him she has someone watching out for her."

"Oh, it's no trouble. Next time you visit, make sure to give us a knock and say howdy."

"I'll do that."

They climbed into the truck and headed west toward Austin. Trent felt a little queasy at first, but then he realized what was wrong and grinned. He wasn't sick—he just missed Brendan.

# FOURTEEN

HUTCH STARED out the window and didn't say anything for a long while.

"You okay?" Trent asked.

"Yeah. Where I come from is just so different. My family only cares about money and influence. Going to a place like that makes me feel like I missed out big-time."

"You made quite an impression. Gertie never takes a shine to anyone that quickly."

"Mrs. Manning is just so...."

"What?"

"I don't know." Hutch pushed the Patsy Cline tape back into the slot and hit play. "Everything my mother isn't."

"Well," Trent said, "maybe you'll come back and visit someday. Now, explain to me why you're giving up on music with a voice like that."

"You sound like Stanton. A voice is nothing if all I'm doing is singing other people's songs. That doesn't interest me."

"Still, don't ever say you're not great at something."

"Fine. I told you I don't know if I'm doing the right thing."

Trent reached up and adjusted his rearview mirror as Patsy started singing again. After spending the afternoon with Hutch, he felt comfortable enough to bring up something that had been on his mind for several days. He turned the volume down and said, "Can I ask you a personal question?"

"What kind of personal question?"

"Well, it involves... I don't know how to say this, really.... Brendan and I are both new to things. In the bedroom."

"You want to ask me about sex?"

Trent felt himself blushing. "Never mind. I just thought that maybe—"

"Whoa, wait a minute. I wasn't saying no. You definitely came to the right place. Go ahead. Ask me anything."

"We've only joked about it."

"Joked about what?"

"The Hershey highway."

"You mean fucking?"

"Yeah," Trent said.

"So you haven't done that yet?"

"No. But I want to."

"You've blown each other, right?"

"Yeah. We both like that a lot. But when I mentioned the Hershey high—"

"Okay, first of all, stop calling it that. You can't do it if you can't say it. Use the word. Fucking. Come on, let me hear you say it."

"Okay, sorry. When I mentioned *fucking* to Brendan, he seemed a little reluctant."

"I get it," Hutch said. "Putting a cock in your asshole can be a scary thing at first, but it's totally worth it. Trust me when I say that."

"Do you and Stanton...?"

"Say it."

"Fuck?"

"All the time."

"How do you decide who's going to do what?"

"Well, I don't give Stanton much of a choice. I love to get fucked, and he's got an amazing dick. Huge and perfect."

"Do you ever fuck him?" Trent asked.

"Never. I can't get off that way and don't have any interest in it. I was pretty upfront with him when we first met."

"Is he okay with that?"

"I think so. At least he never complains."

"Are most gay guys one way or the other?"

"No," Hutch said. "I'd say most guys do both, though there are certainly plenty of men like me around. When you said you want to, did you mean fuck Brendan or vice versa?"

"Well, I thought maybe both, but he wasn't too keen on the idea of being the catcher."

"A lot of guys are uptight about it. They think it makes them the woman, which is so stupid. How do you feel about being the catcher? It should come naturally to you."

"Very funny. I want to try it. That's why I brought it up. But is it going to hurt?"

"Oh, baby, it's going to hurt so good."

Trent laughed. "I'm serious."

"Yes, it's going to hurt, but only at first. The more you do it, the better it'll feel. And once you have your first orgasm with a dick in your ass, your whole life will change. Be prepared for the floodgates to open."

"What about shit?"

"Ah, yes. The great gay hazard. If you're fucking all the time, like Stanton and me, shit's going to happen at some point. But there are ways to prepare if you're worried about it."

"What ways?"

"You probably don't know this, but your local drug store carries something called a disposable enema. They're, like, two bucks."

"They make them for gay guys?"

"No, they make them for old people. They're sold as a constipation aid, but they work just as well for what we're talking about. It's a bottle of soft plastic filled with saline water. There's a long tip on the cap. You stick that up your ass and squeeze. Then you sit on the john and shit it out, along with any poop you got up there. Take a shower afterward and you're good to go."

"I'd be too scared to buy one."

"Well, luckily you brought me along. We'll stop at a drug store when we get back to town. You can even wait in the truck if you want."

"When I brought it up, why do you think Brendan didn't want to try it, even after I offered to be the catcher?"

"Because he's just like you. He doesn't know what he's doing and he's scared. Fortunately, he and Stanton are having the exact same conversation today."

"Really?"

"Oh, yes. I know guys, and I know my boyfriend. If you've mentioned it to Brendan, then he's asking Stanton for advice—and Stanton *loves* giving advice. The good news is, I've trained him very well. Brendan's going to get some good tips."

"What about me? Can I get some tips too?"

"I thought you'd never ask. First, stop eating two or three hours beforehand. That way, when you clean out, there won't be any crap right behind it. Tell Brendan you're going to take a shower. Do your enema thing and make sure to give your asshole a good soaping. Your butt needs to be clean enough to eat off. Literally."

"What does that mean?"

"You've never heard of rimming?"

"No."

"Have you at least seen a gay porno?"

"Hell, no. Where would I have seen something like that?"

"The Adonis on Eighth Avenue. Never mind. Anyway, after some time with Stanton, Brendan will know everything about rimming."

"What is it?"

"When Brendan licks your asshole." Trent was so taken aback by Hutch's answer, he almost drove off the road. "Careful, man. You're going to get us killed."

"You're kidding, right?"

"I promise you I'm not kidding. Rimming is a crucial part of fucking. It chills you out, turns you on, and lubes you up, all at the same time. Stanton and I both agree—a good pitcher must eat ass. You'd better start getting over your hang-ups now, because I guarantee the next time you two get into bed, Brendan's going to do just that."

"Lick my asshole?" Just the thought of it made Trent shiver with excitement. "Does it feel good?"

"Oh my God. It feels amazing, so when he does it, let him know you're having a good time. Reach behind and pull his face in deeper. Throw him down on his back and sit on his face, then suck his cock while he eats you out. It's sex, man. Don't be afraid to get nasty. Guys want a gentleman in the streets and a pig in the sheets."

"I've never had a conversation like this."

"That's because you've never hung out with me or my friends. Come to New York in the off-season. We'll teach you a thing or two."

"I bet that would be an eye-opener."

"You have no idea. So after he's rimmed you for a while and his dick is good and wet from your blow job, get on your back and guide his cock toward your butt. I'll pick you up some K-Y as well, but don't overuse it. He'll probably fumble around the first time, trying to find your asshole, but when he does, the head will pop right in, and you'll scream out like a little girl."

"Then why am I even doing it?"

"Let me finish. This next part is really important. Don't push him out. Yell and curse if you have to, but then bear down and just count to ten or something."

"Why ten?"

"I don't know. It's a nice round number."

"Can I use eight?"

"Sure. Eight, ten, twelve, somewhere in that ballpark. The point is, if you leave his dick in until the pain passes, you'll enjoy it more. If you push him out, you'll only have to start all over again. Since he's getting tips from Stanton, he'll know to take it slow at first. Now I don't need that, but you're not quite ready for the major leagues when it comes to fucking."

"Maybe someday."

"Here's the thing you need to know. Everyone thinks the pitcher is in charge. That is so not true. The catcher controls the pace. Tell him if you want to go faster or slower. Make out with him. Feel what's happening. He's literally inside of you. Once you start to open up, wrap your legs around his waist and pull him in deeper. Don't be passive. There's nothing worse than a limp noodle in bed. Then, when it looks like he might be ready to come, pull him in close and whisper the pièce de résistance into his ear."

"What's that?"

"Say the thing that's better than 'I love you.' Four words that will reduce him to putty in your hands."

"Four words? What are they?"

Hutch turned his head and grinned wide.

"My ass is yours."

"Really?"

"When Brendan hears that, game over. He's going to come so hard, it'll make his head spin. That's when you should jack yourself off and come too. And be prepared, because you're going to find out why you went through all that pain in the first place."

"Intense?"

"When I come with Stanton inside me, I sometimes feel like I'm going to blackout."

"Last night Brendan stuck a finger up there and hit some kind of supersex spot."

"That's your prostate. It's a gland just inside your asshole, behind your balls. It's very sensitive, and when Brendan's dick starts rubbing against it, watch out. Keep trying different positions until you find the perfect angle. When you hit on it, you'll know. Gay people like the same positions as straight people—missionary, doggie, cowgirl, reverse cowgirl. Try them all."

Trent wiped his forehead. "Damn, I'm sweating."

"Look at you, all nervous and excited. I wish it was me, getting fucked for the first time. I wish it had been with Stanton. I hope you know how lucky you are."

"I never thought of it that way."

"You know he's falling in love with you, don't you? Brendan, I mean."

"How do you know that?"

"He told Stanton. On the phone, when he called. Brendan said he thinks he's falling in love with you."

Trent had never been happier to hear anything in his life.

"I probably shouldn't have told you that," Hutch continued. "Oops. Consider it a little bonding between blood brothers. Besides, take it for what it is. He met you five days ago. It's the hormones talking. I only waited two weeks before I told Stanton I loved him."

"I'm not upset by the news."

"You guys haven't used the L word yet, though, have you?"

"No. Not even close. I've wanted to say something, but…. No. I'm okay with saying, 'My ass is yours,' though. I think that'll get the message across."

"Trust me, it will. Once I picked Stanton, he never really had a chance. He was going to fall in love with me, one way or another."

"How did you know for certain?"

"The same way you did. I see how you look at Brendan. Do you have any doubt that you two belong together?"

"No, none."

"Listen to that, and don't let anyone tell you it's not real. You and I, we're the same. We were both born to love one man. My advice? Just surrender to it, 'cause it ain't gonna change."

"Listen to you, sounding like Gertie."

"I love the way she talks. After today I swear I should have been born in Texas."

AFTER STOPPING at a drug store on the way into town, Trent and Hutch arrived at the Walsh house just before dinner. Bill grilled some steaks and fish, and Stanton took a cue from Hutch and helped Grace in the kitchen. She had relaxed considerably since the day before, no doubt aided by the fact that they never mentioned the word "gay" again. During the meal Trent occasionally reached under the table and took Brendan's hand, careful to be discreet (a word he had already grown to despise). He only had one thought on his mind, and he kept saying it to himself, over and over again:

*He loves me.*

Afterward Bill offered up his car for the trip downtown to the Lucinda Williams concert at Liberty Lunch, so no one would have to ride in the back of Trent's pickup. Brendan decided he should drive, of course, and they made their way to the open-air venue on Second Street. Hutch loved her blend of folk, rock, and country, although Stanton thought she needed to develop more as a songwriter.

"Does she live here?" Hutch asked.

"No," Brendan said. "Not anymore. She used to about ten years ago, but she lives in LA now. She just comes back for a show every once in a while."

When she finished her set, around one in the morning, they walked to Antone's on Sixth Street because Brendan had heard Stevie Ray Vaughan was in town and might be making a surprise appearance. Sure enough, shortly after two, SRV and Double Trouble took the stage and played their special brand of blues for forty-five minutes. Hutch was in heaven and moved as close as he could to better see Stevie's finger work on the guitar. A couple of guys recognized Trent throughout the night, but no one made a fuss or caused a scene.

When they returned home around three thirty in the morning, Bill met them in the driveway with two joints in his hand.

"What are you doing up this late?" Brendan asked.

"I'm a natural night owl. Drives Grace crazy, but I can't help it. Especially in the summer. It's the only time when you can sit outside and be comfortable." He held up the blunts. "Can I interest you?"

"Yes, Mrs. Madrigal," Hutch said.

Bill laughed. "Did Brendan tell you about the joint I taped to his door?"

"Copycat," Stanton said.

"I know, but I couldn't resist when I became a landlord. I love those books. Made me want to live in San Francisco, but I suppose Austin is the next best thing."

They sat down around the patio table in the backyard and smoked Bill's weed. They told him about the concert and Stevie Ray Vaughan's impromptu set at Antone's. Trent sat back and realized the pot was making him horny, so he wasn't upset when Bill, Stanton, and Hutch quickly retired to the house. As he and Brendan moved toward the stairs of the garage apartment, Trent said, "I need to get something from the truck."

"What something?"

"None of your business. You tired?"

"Not at all," Brendan said.

"Good." Trent retrieved the brown bag of items Hutch had bought for him. When they got inside, he told Brendan he wanted to take a shower before bed.

"Should I join you?"

"Not this time," Trent said, and Brendan didn't press him any further.

"Suit yourself. I'll be waiting for you in the bedroom."

"Don't fall asleep."

"There's absolutely no chance of that happening."

Trent went into the bathroom and took off his clothes. He removed the disposable enema and the tube of K-Y from their boxes. He rubbed some of the jelly onto the long tip and then around his asshole. He put his foot on the toilet seat, gently inserted the tip, and squeezed. The sensation made his cock thicken a little. He waited a few seconds and then lifted the seat and sat down. It was easy and painless, and best of all, he felt clean.

He jumped into the shower and soaped up his ass, sticking his finger in and out of his hole to relax. He was still buzzed from the weed and thought about Brendan's cock inside him. He stroked himself until he was hard, but then rinsed and turned off the water before he got carried away. He buffed his hair and skin dry with a towel and then walked naked into the bedroom.

Brendan lay on his back with his cock in his hand. In no time, Trent jumped on the bed and swallowed it. He licked and slurped and sucked until Brendan sat up and demanded to change places with him.

"I want to try something," he said as he took Trent's dick in his hand. He started to suck it as usual, but then he paused when it hit the back of his throat. Every other time that would have been the point where he pulled off. This time, though, Brendan didn't retreat. Instead, he relaxed and forced the head of Trent's cock all the way down his throat.

Trent looked down in amazement. His cock had completely disappeared into Brendan's mouth. After a few seconds, Brendan sat up and took a fast, deep breath.

"How did you do that?" Trent asked.

"I suppressed my gag reflex. Stanton told me how to do it. It's called deep-throating."

"So that's what the movie title means?"

"I guess so. I've never seen it, but makes sense for a porn flick."

"Let me try," Trent said. Brendan traded places with him again, and Trent started sucking. The tip of Brendan's dick hit the sticking point, but wouldn't go any further.

Brendan ran his fingers through Trent's hair. "Relax. It'll feel like you're going to throw up, but just ignore that feeling for a few seconds and keep going."

With a little help from the weed, Trent released the tension in his muscles and slid Brendan's dick all the way in. He buried his nose in Brendan's red pubic hair and closed his watering eyes. He reached down and stroked his stiff cock. Finally, he pulled off and inhaled, then collapsed on top of Brendan and kissed him.

"Who knew that was even possible?" Trent said. "Let's try doing it at the same time." He flipped around, and they rolled onto their sides. They each sucked the other's cock until they both reached the sticking point. Trent relaxed and pushed past it, which brought his nose into direct contact with Brendan's nutsack. When they came up for air, Trent licked Brendan's balls, and Brendan returned the favor. Then Brendan's fingers traced a line up Trent's thigh and into his butt crack. Trent lifted his leg and Brendan's tongue darted over his asshole. Trent responded by reaching down and pushing Brendan's face into his ass.

Trent had never experienced anything like rimming. He rolled Brendan onto his back and stood up on the bed. Then Trent squatted down and sat on his face. Brendan's tongue opened him up and penetrated his hole. He leaned forward and sucked Brendan's cock. After a few minutes, Trent was afraid they might come, so he jumped off the bed and hurried into the bathroom. He dabbed a little of the K-Y onto his fingers and then applied it to his asshole. He returned to the bedroom and squeezed a little more onto Brendan's dick.

"Hey, that's cold."

"Sorry."

"It's okay. I just wasn't expecting it. Feels good, though. Nice and slippery."

Trent stroked Brendan's cock to distribute the jelly. He set the tube on the nightstand, and Brendan rose to his knees. Trent kissed him and lay down on his back. "Come here."

Brendan knelt between Trent's open legs and leaned in. "I would ask if you're sure about this, but you clearly know what you're doing."

"Hutch and I had a little talk too."

Brendan laughed. "Remind me to send them a gift basket next week."

"Or maybe some Yankees tickets." Trent reached down and stroked Brendan's wet dick. He guided it between his legs and took a deep breath. Brendan kissed him and rubbed the tip of his cock against Trent's hole. Suddenly it popped in, and Trent yelped in pain. When Brendan tried to withdraw, Trent gripped Brendan's asscheeks, stopped him, and said, "Don't." Trent gritted his teeth. "One-one thousand, two-one thousand, three-one thousand, four—"

"Why are you counting?"

"Shh. Five-one thousand, six-one thousand, seven-one thousand, eight." He took another deep breath, and the pain began to subside. He wrapped his legs around Brendan's waist and kissed him.

"Are you okay?"

Trent nodded. "I think so."

"How does it feel?"

"Weird. A little tingly. But it doesn't hurt anymore."

Brendan didn't even try to move for several minutes. They lay there while Trent got used to the sensation of having a dick up his butt.

"You're inside of me," Trent said. "Can you believe it?"

"I know. It's really turning me on. How are your ribs?"

"Fine." After another breath, Trent announced, "Okay, I'm ready. You can fuck me now."

Brendan pulled his dick out and then pushed it back in. Trent moaned and lifted his legs until the soles of his feet were planted against Brendan's chest. Brendan rubbed the tops and then lifted one foot to his face. He sucked on the toes and Trent gripped the sheets.

"Damn, that feels good. Go faster."

Their rhythm increased, and Trent could feel Brendan's cock massaging his prostate. He wasn't even jacking himself off, but Trent swore he was on the verge of an orgasm. Brendan's strokes became long and deep, and Trent could feel Brendan's cock swelling and getting harder.

He lowered his legs, pulled Brendan in close, and whispered, "My ass is yours."

A shudder ran through Brendan's body as he pounded Trent's hole. "Fuck. I'm going to come."

"Me too."

Trent had no idea he could get off without touching himself, but that's exactly what happened. Brendan lifted up, and Trent shot so hard that the first spurts landed on his chin. Brendan licked them off, kissed him, and kept fucking. More come shot out of Trent's dick with each thrust, and then Brendan ended with several staccato slams. Trent watched Brendan's face as it went through a series of contortions. He'd never seen someone come before, and it was mesmerizing. Brendan kept trying to go deeper, as if being inside Trent wasn't enough. Finally after depositing the last of his seed, Brendan collapsed into his arms. Trent lay staring at the ceiling with Brendan on top of him. Trent believed that for as long as he might live, nothing would ever exceed the happiness he felt in that moment.

Brendan rolled onto his back and pulled Trent close. "I'm yours. I don't know what's going to happen tomorrow, but tonight I'm yours."

Trent nestled into Brendan's arms and caught their reflection in the windowpane. As his eyelids grew heavy, the soft light of morning appeared, and he drifted off to sleep.

TRENT WOKE up with Brendan's erection pressed against his asscheeks. He felt something running down his leg and wiped it off. He smelled his fingers. Brendan's come was dripping out of his butt.

*Natural lube*, he thought.

He rolled onto his back and stroked Brendan's dick. Brendan made a muffled sound in his throat and opened his eyes. Trent kissed him.

"Do I have morning breath?" Brendan asked.

"No. Do I?"

"I wouldn't care if you did."

They kissed again, and Trent propped himself up on his elbow. He threw his leg over Brendan's stomach and ground his hardening cock against his torso. He caressed Brendan's balls and tried to climb on top, but Brendan had other plans. He rolled Trent onto his back and knelt over him. He licked one of his nipples and then worked his way down Trent's abdomen. When Brendan started sucking him, Trent arched his back and raised his arms above his head. As he slurped on Trent's cock, Brendan straddled one of Trent's legs while Trent instinctively lifted the other into the air, giving Brendan access to his asshole. Brendan fingered the opening as he continued to suck Trent's dick.

Brendan lifted up and spit onto his fingers. He smeared the saliva onto Trent's hole and then leaned forward to kiss him. The tip of Brendan's cock teased Trent's butt.

"Stick it in," Trent pleaded.

"Not yet. This is my show now."

Brendan continued to rub the head of his dick against Trent's ass without entering him. He wrapped his arms around Trent and kissed him on the neck. Trent lifted his legs, but still Brendan wouldn't fuck him. Then Brendan pulled up and pushed Trent's knees to his ears, which left his ass raised and exposed. Brendan dove in and ravaged the hole. He spit on it, fingered it, and lapped at it with his tongue, shaking his head from side to side. Trent clutched his ankles and spread his legs wider.

"Is that my come I taste?"

Trent grinned. "You like it?"

"Fuck yeah, I love it."

Brendan rose up and smacked his stiff cock against Trent's butt. He rubbed the entire length against the hole and then went back to his rim job. He spread Trent's cheeks apart and speared the slit over and over again with his tongue. He slapped Trent's ass and then teased it some more with his cock.

"Give it to me!"

Brendan ignored him and instead worked his finger and tongue in tandem around the rim. Then he stuck two fingers into his mouth, coated them with spit, and pushed them into Trent's asshole. Brendan kissed Trent's buttcheeks as he opened him up, then rubbed his cock against the crevice while his fingers were still inside. He removed his fingers and leaned over to suck Trent's hard prick, then worked his tongue down across the balls and returned to his hole. He did that several times, back and forth between sucking dick and eating ass, until Trent was driven to distraction. He lowered his legs, and Brendan took Trent's cock all the way to the base, careful to concentrate on the suppression of his gag reflex. He switched to a sucking/stroking combination and then deep-throated Trent again. Trent played with his nipples as he watched Brendan work on his nob. He caressed the top of Brendan's head as he brought Trent to the edge, only to slow down and back off before Trent got too close.

Brendan licked his way up Trent's torso and kissed him full on the mouth. Their tongues met and swirled together as Brendan pressed their cocks against each other. Then his mouth was on Trent's dick again, down to the base—only this time he let Trent literally fuck the back of his throat.

Finally, Brendan relinquished his hold on Trent's cock and pulled him into a sitting position. Brendan lay down on his back with his feet at the headboard, and Trent crawled on top of him. He licked Brendan's chest and then kissed him, while Brendan cupped the cheeks of Trent's ass. Then Brendan moved his right hand away and placed his index finger in Trent's mouth.

"Get it wet for me."

Trent covered the finger with spit, and Brendan inserted it into Trent's ass. They kissed until Brendan put two fingers into Trent's mouth, then into his own, and then back into Trent's. Brendan pressed the spit-soaked digits into Trent's open hole. He shivered and moaned.

Trent inched down and darted his tongue over each of Brendan's nipples until they stiffened. He kissed his way across Brendan's abdomen and then licked his cock from base to tip. Trent took Brendan's dick into his mouth and sucked it with as much gusto as he could muster. He slapped the stiff dick against his lips and tongue. Brendan moaned and grasped the back of Trent's head. He forced his cock down Trent's throat until he gagged, which only turned him on more. Trent licked Brendan's nutsack and took one of his balls into his mouth. He swirled his tongue around it and then did the same with the other before he returned to sucking Brendan's cock. Trent pulled up and let a string of spit drop slowly from his mouth to the tip of Brendan's dick, then devoured it whole. In the meantime Brendan was tweaking Trent's nipples and rubbing against his asshole with his big toe.

When it came to getting a blow job, Brendan was anything but passive. With one hand on the back of Trent's neck and the other under his chin, Brendan raised his hips like a bull rider. He lifted Trent's face and kissed him, then returned Trent's mouth to his cock. He latched on to Trent's ears and fucked his face. He repositioned Trent so that he was straddling Brendan's stomach, then reached around and once again slapped his cock against Trent's hole.

"You ready?" Brendan asked.

"Yes!"

"You sure? You want it?"

"I want it."

"Tell me."

"I want you to stick your cock in my ass."

"And whose ass is it?"

"Yours. My ass is yours."

Brendan inserted two fingers from each hand into Trent's asshole and gently pulled him open. Trent felt a stream of Brendan's come trickle out, and could hear Brendan coating his cock with the semen. Then Brendan removed his fingers and Trent sat down on his dick—all the way to the base.

"You are one talented catcher," Brendan said.

It was an exhilarating moment. Trent swallowed the pain and Brendan counted, "One Mississippi, two Mississippi, three Mississippi…," until he got to eight. Then Trent collapsed forward and buried his face in Brendan's neck. In a muffled voice, he asked, "What position is this?"

"I think they call it 'cowgirl' in Texas, because you're riding me like a horse."

"Can we call it 'cowboy' instead?"

"We can call it 'pineapple' if you want."

Trent lifted himself upright. "What's 'reverse cowgirl' then? Or 'reverse cowboy'?"

"Same thing, only you turn around and face my feet."

Brendan bent his knees and arched his legs so that Trent could lean back and brace himself against Brendan's thighs. Trent pressed down until it felt like Brendan's dick was in his throat, then he started to ride him, and Brendan reached down to stroke Trent's cock.

"Not yet," Trent said as he removed Brendan's hand. "I'll come soon enough without that."

Brendan pulled him down and kissed him, then cupped Trent's ass in his hands and pounded him from below. The angle made Trent's prostate sing and he panted with each thrust. In a surprisingly acrobatic move, Brendan sat up, repositioned Trent's legs so that they were around his waist, and then rolled Trent onto his back, the whole time keeping his dick firmly planted in Trent's ass. With Trent's feet to the ceiling, Brendan laced his fingers behind Trent's neck and fucked him relentlessly.

"There's one more position I want to try," Trent said.

Without further instruction, Brendan pulled out, grabbed one of Trent's ankles, and rolled him onto his stomach. Trent rose onto all fours, and Brendan rammed his cock back in. Trent stretched his arms above his head and pushed back against Brendan's anal assault.

"Harder," Trent said.

Brendan seized him by the hips and laid into him with a mighty force. That hit the spot, and Trent soon felt himself spraying the sheets with his spunk. Brendan pulled out, flipped Trent onto his back, and then straddled his chest. Trent furiously jacked him off until a spurt of come smacked against the headboard, followed by several more that landed on Trent's face.

As Brendan leaned over to lick it off, Trent heard a banging on the door of the garage apartment. Brendan looked at the clock. "Holy shit. It's one thirty." He jumped off the bed, threw on a pair of gym shorts, and left the bedroom. Trent could hear him talking to Stanton. Then he yelled, "Get dressed. They're heading to the airport."

Trent didn't see a towel, so he tore a pillowcase off one of the pillows and wiped his face clean. He put on his shorts and T-shirt, then checked himself in the mirror. No come in his hair, at least. He picked Brendan's shirt off the floor and handed it to him when he got to the door.

"I can give you a ride," Trent said to the back of Stanton's head as they followed him down the stairs.

"No, that's okay. Bill already called us a taxi. We just wanted to say good-bye."

Since they were both barefoot, Brendan and Trent carefully made their way to the end of the gravel driveway, where Hutch was waiting with the luggage and a knowing grin. "You two smell like you've been fucking all night." The taxi pulled up in front of the house, and the driver got out and loaded the bags into the trunk. "Give us two seconds," Hutch said to the driver, who got back into the cab and waited.

Stanton wrapped his arms around Brendan. "This has been spectacular." He released Brendan and turned to Trent. "I really hope you guys can work things out."

Trent nodded. "Me too."

Hutch hugged Brendan and then smiled at Trent, who stepped forward and embraced his new friend.

"Thank you for inviting us," Hutch said. He pulled away, and Trent noticed his eyes were a little misty. "I can't tell you how much I am in love with Texas now. I feel like I'm leaving a piece of my soul behind."

Brendan laughed. "It has a way of grabbing you, doesn't it?"

"It sure does."

Trent didn't want them to go. He felt as if Hutch and Stanton were a lifeline to his real self. Somehow they represented what he and Brendan could become someday. Stanton must have mistaken his sadness for concern, because he said, "We're not going to talk about this with anyone. We promise."

That was the least of Trent's worries.

Hutch nodded. "I can't imagine what it's like to be you, Trent. We're here for you guys, no matter what you decide."

"Thanks," Trent said. "Don't forget what I told you, Hutch."

"I won't forget." Stanton got into the cab, and before he joined him, Hutch turned around and waved goodbye. "Y'all have a good evening."

The taxi pulled away from the Walsh house, and Brendan turned to Trent. "What did you do to that boy yesterday?"

"When you meet Grandma Gertie, you'll understand."

"He's obsessed with Texas now."

"Well, there are worse things in life."

Brendan looked around to make sure no one was watching, and then he kissed Trent. "I guess we slept through breakfast."

"And fucked through lunch. Maybe Bill will make us something."

"Should we ask him?"

As if someone had cued his entrance, Bill Walsh stepped out of the front door and onto the porch. "You boys hungry?"

"Are you a mind reader on top of everything else?" Brendan said.

"Come on into the house. I'll whip you up some migas."

# FIFTEEN

THEY SPENT the rest of Sunday afternoon in the Walsh living room, watching the Yankees pound the Red Sox into submission. They drank lots of beer, and Bill made a variety of snacks. Grace spent the day in bed reading, and Bill assured them it was nothing personal. When the game ended, Brendan and Trent returned to the garage apartment and Brendan's bed.

On Monday morning, Trent dropped Brendan off at work and went home to check his messages. There were three from Marcia Harrison, Kieran's wife, expressing support and asking that Trent please call her. Before he did that, though, he checked in with the front office and told them he would be in Houston on Wednesday. Sandra asked him to hold. When she came back on the phone, she said, "Trent, Bob wanted to know if you could come back tomorrow. Is that possible?"

"Well, I—"

"He wants you here for the start of the series with the Dodgers. We're having a morale problem, and he thinks you can help, even if you're not playing."

How could he say no?

"Okay. What time's the game?"

"Seven."

"Tell him I'll be at the Dome by five."

"Thanks, hon. You have a safe trip now. No speeding tickets, 'kay?"

Trent hesitated to call Kieran's number for fear he might answer, but he went ahead anyway. Thankfully, Marcia picked up instead.

"Hello?"

"Hi, Marcia. It's me."

"Oh, Trent. Are you okay? I can only imagine what you must be going through."

"It's a mixed bag right now. So Kieran told you?"

"Yes, but it's not like I didn't already know. My husband may be blind, but I'm not. You haven't dated a single girl the whole time I've known you. I figured you must be either gay or dead."

"Well, I'm definitely not dead. Has he calmed down any?"

"I'm working on it. If only he knew at least one other gay person."

"Do you?"

"Oh my God, Trent, of course I do. My hairdresser is gay."

"Right. I'm sure we'd have a lot in common."

"You might be surprised. He's a big baseball fan."

"I take it Kieran hasn't told anyone else."

"Of course not. Who would he tell? He's not about to go blabbing it to the rest of the team, or the press, for that matter. Your secret's safe with us."

"That's comforting. Now all I need to do is figure out how to live the rest of my life with that secret."

"Kieran said you met someone. What's his name?"

"Brendan. Brendan Baxter."

"Is he nice?"

Trent choked up. "He's the best."

"When are you coming back to Houston?"

"Tomorrow."

"You should talk to Kieran before then."

"Is he there now?"

"No, but he'll be back tonight. They were in Atlanta over the weekend for a three-game series."

"That's right. I don't know, Marcia. I'm not too keen on him at the moment. He tried to beat Brendan up."

"Temporary insanity. Please, Trent, give him a chance. You two have been best friends since you were fifteen. You can't just throw all that away."

"I'm not the one doing the throwing."

"I know that. I'll talk to him again when he gets back."

"Thanks, Marcia. He's lucky to have someone like you."

She laughed. "You think I don't know that?"

After he hung up the phone, Trent checked the fridge and realized he didn't have anything in the house for lunch. It had been days since he'd slept in his own bed. Since he didn't see the point of stocking up, he took a shower and headed back north to Les Amis. He knew it was time to make some decisions, and for some reason, he felt like Quincy could help him sort it all out.

WHEN TRENT entered the cafe, Quincy was sitting alone in his usual booth. Monica greeted him with a hug and told him Tony had bought some red snapper that morning.

"That sounds delicious," Trent said. "Can you ask him to grill up some more of those vegetables too?"

"Will do. You joining Q?"

"Yeah."

"I'll bring it right out."

Trent crossed to the booth and sat down opposite Quincy. The owner looked up from a pile of invoices and smiled. "Well, I didn't expect to see you again so soon. Aren't you supposed to be heading back to Houston?"

"Tomorrow. I didn't have anything in the house for lunch, and I've gotten used to eating Tony's fish."

"I swear that boy would do anything for you. Did you know he framed that apron you signed and hung it up in the kitchen?"

"Really? I'll have to send him a couple of tickets. Maybe box seats."

"Oh, he'd love that." Quincy paused. "What's wrong, Trent? You look like you're about to burst into tears."

"Is it that obvious?"

"It is to me, but then I like to think of myself as slightly more observant than the average homo sapien."

"I don't know who else to talk to, and you seem like a pretty wise fellow."

Monica appeared at the booth with a glass of water. She set it down in front of Trent and said, "He's an old soul. Sorry, I didn't mean to eavesdrop. Your fish will be right out, and probably Tony with it."

"Thanks," Trent said.

Monica walked away, and Quincy asked, "Is this about Brendan?"

"In a way. But in a way not. I don't know how to talk about it without spilling some beans. Brendan should be allowed to tell things at his own pace."

"Then let me guess. You and Brendan have been having a love affair for the past week."

Trent smiled. "We thought maybe you'd already figured it out."

"Oh, my dear boy, we've all figured it out. Well, probably not Tony. But Monica and the rest of the staff, yes. You do know we won't say anything, right? Your secret's safe with us."

"I wish people would stop saying that. The last thing I ever wanted in life was to be that guy with a big secret. I heard what you said the other night. *Embrace visibility.* I'm struggling with how to do that. I feel like such a coward."

"Why?"

"Because Hutch thinks I should come out of the closet and be the gay Jackie Robinson. But whenever I think about what he went through, it makes me want to throw up. I hate the Eskimo Slugger circus as it is. If I try to tell people I'm gay, chances are I'll be run out of baseball for good. I don't want to be a coward. I want to live my life with at least a little bit of honesty. But I don't think I would survive that ordeal."

"That's because you imagine going through it alone."

Tony appeared with Trent's plate of fish and vegetables. "Howdy, Trent. I had a dream last night that Suzie had our baby, and it was a boy. And guess what? You were there in the hospital with me. And when I woke up from the dream, I said to her, 'Suzie,' I said, 'I bet Trent Days is coming in for lunch today. I'd better pick up some—'"

"Tony," Quincy said, "not now, please. Can't you see we're in the middle of a conversation? Just leave the snapper."

Tony's whole manner deflated. "Sorry. I just thought Trent would get a kick out of—"

"Thank you," Trent said. "I did get a kick out of it. When is she due?"

"This week sometime. Could be any day now, in fact. Ain't nothing scarier than becoming a father, let me tell you. I hardly knew mine, so I got nothing to go on. I don't even know how to change a diaper."

"Have you picked out names yet?" Trent asked.

Tony Atwood nodded. "Travis."

"What if it's a girl?" Quincy said.

"Travis."

Quincy shook his head, and Trent said, "I'll tell you what. When the baby gets here, tell Brendan, and I'll have all the Astros sign a ball for him. Or her."

Tony lit up with joy. "Hot dog! I ain't never gonna forget you." He laid the plate of fish in front of Trent and walked away.

"That boy's a mess," Quincy said. "Travis for a girl. Whoever heard of such a thing?"

"I guess he really likes the name Travis." Trent took a bite of the snapper. "And he sure knows how to cook fish. It's been perfect every time. I hope he passes that on to his son, at least."

"So, let's go back to your gay-Jackie-Robinson dilemma. I hope you understand that embracing visibility doesn't mean making yourself miserable. You get that, don't you?"

"I don't know what I get anymore. All I know is I want Brendan in my life, but that doesn't seem very compatible with playing major league baseball."

"Have you talked to Brendan about this?"

"Not really. He says he would never get in the way of my career. He thinks playing ball should be my number one priority."

"And what do you think?"

"I love the game, don't get me wrong. It's done a lot for me. But I loved it more when no one paid attention to what I was doing. Since I started in the majors, I have fans and reporters in my face every day. I'm on the cover of *Sports Illustrated*, and people I've never even met know my whole life story. Kids and grown men wear jerseys with my name on the back. It's not anything I ever wanted. I didn't even grow up with baseball."

"Let me ask you a question. Do you feel obligated to play?"

Trent chewed on some vegetables and thought it over. "Yeah, I guess so. My family made huge sacrifices so I could move to Texas. My high school coach told my dad that I have more raw talent than any player he's ever seen and that it'd be a sin not to develop it. And before my injury, I was on track to be the National League Rookie of the Year. I could still do it if I come back strong. My team depends on me, so no matter what I do, I'm going to let someone down."

"Every choice you make is bound to disappoint. Take it from me. There are days when I think I'm nothing more than one big disappointment machine. My parents, my professors, my children, women, men...."

"Men? Are you—"

"I'm bisexual," Quincy said. "I was married once upon a time and proved to be a huge disappointment to my wife. I have two daughters who are embarrassed because I own a run-down cafe that barely breaks even. My last relationship, though, was with a man."

"What happened?"

"He killed himself. He had what they call manic depressive disorder—wonderful highs followed by terrible lows. Lithium could have saved his life, but none of the doctors around here had heard of it. Texas is hardly on the cutting edge when it comes to mental healthcare. Still, I could have done more. I failed him too."

"How did you deal with it?"

"Who says I did? Or even could? I try to look at the big picture. I try to resist the idea that I'm separate from him, or any of the people I've disappointed. As for the rest, I take a certain amount of comfort in the great karmic balance. It would be one thing if I fucked people over and made a profit off it, but I've lost too much for that to be true. I've paid a price for every bad thing I've ever done. So if my life hasn't been good, at least it's been fair. That's how I sleep at night."

"Are you seeing anyone now?"

"No. I don't have the patience for that. All relationships come with a certain amount of drama, but after Timothy, I'm all tapped out. Friends are what I value, hence the name of my cafe."

"Brendan had to translate it for me."

"You two complement each other beautifully. But I'm disturbed by something. It sounds as though you believe baseball defines you."

"Well, yeah, of course it does. Why would that disturb you? I can hardly remember a time when I didn't play baseball."

Quincy smiled. "Maybe that's part of the problem. You think a person is defined by what he does. Do you think I'm defined by the fact that I own a cafe? Do you think Monica is defined by being a waitress, or Tony by being a cook? God doesn't care what you do, Trent. The only thing she cares about is what kind of person you are while you're doing it. The question is, how do you measure the success of your life? Is it the number of home runs you hit or how many bases you steal? Or is it the lives you touch and the people who love you?"

"So I should give up baseball?"

"I didn't say that. You came in here because you wanted to talk about your future, and I understand your confusion. Really, I do. But I don't have answers for you. Where you are right now, the crossroads where you stand, is the very point of life. You're about to decide who you are, and I wouldn't step in and make that choice for you even if you let me. I'm not here to judge, which, I might add, is not at all characteristic of me. There's no right or wrong answer. There's only the answer that says to the world, 'This is who Trent Days is. This is what's important to him. This is what he values.' What do you value? Once you decide that, the rest will follow—and pretty effortlessly, I might add. It may not be easy or comfortable or make sense to anyone else. It doesn't have to. It only has to make sense to you. I will say this, though...."

"What?"

"You aren't obligated to do anything. Talent doesn't come with a clause that says you have to develop it. Talent is random. It strikes the worthy and the unworthy equally. Look at Ty Cobb."

"You know who Ty Cobb is?"

"I've been reading a little bit since I met you. He was a monster. A terrible excuse for a human being—hateful, sadistic, and full of spite. He assaulted a crippled fan because the man called him a 'half-nigger.' But he's also considered one of the greatest baseball players to ever live. Am I right?"

"Yes, you're right. His career average of .367 is still the highest in the game."

"If you ask me, he would have been better off if he had never picked up a bat. His talent was big, but his ego was even bigger, and that turned out to be a terrible thing. He probably came back as a slug in his next life."

"Why does everything have to be so difficult?"

"That's your choice too."

"Excuse me?"

"Why do you think we reincarnate over and over again through a series of lifetimes?"

"I suppose it's to gather different experiences."

"Yes, but to what end? It's not random. We're trying to evolve, Trent. Take a figure skater, for example."

"A figure skater? That's not even a sport!"

"Hear me out. What happens when a figure skater masters a single jump?"

"She moves onto a double, I suppose."

"Exactly. As your soul evolves, it increases the degree of difficulty. First a single, then a double, then a triple. And one day, some little girl from the Soviet Union is going to step onto the ice and do a quadruple jump. This choice in front of you, which you see as a problem, is actually an opportunity."

"What kind of opportunity?"

"To decide and demonstrate who you really are."

"So you think I intentionally made things hard? That's insane."

"When two souls meet for the first time, it's a sign."

"Why can't I have a peaceful life in the country?"

"Because those days are over. You and Brendan are increasing the degree of difficulty, and you're doing it consciously. Together. That's what the gold sparks mean."

"You figured it out?"

"I don't know why it took me so long. Here I am, the person who complains that no one understands time, and I was trapped by it myself. As I've always said, the sparks are memories."

"But how can we have memories if we don't have a past together?"

"Because time isn't linear. Like the poets tell us, the past, present, and future exist simultaneously in every moment. Your memories with Brendan aren't from the past. They're from the future."

"What? How can you—Geez, my head hurts again. Did you know his jersey number as a high school quarterback was eight too?"

"So?"

"That's *my* jersey number."

"Just another sign that I'm right. This is only the beginning, Trent. Come out or don't come out. Play baseball or don't play baseball. God doesn't care. All roads lead to the same destination for you, and the name of that destination is Brendan Baxter."

"But how can you say that? We just met a week ago. We hardly know each other."

"Those are someone else's doubts, not yours."

Trent finished the last of his meal and took a drink of water. "I still don't know what I'm going to do."

"Talk to Brendan. Ask for help. I envy you, because it's a big moment. Whatever you decide, we both know it's going to change your life forever. You need to prepare yourself."

Trent took a long pause. Then he said, "I'm scared."

"I know. I can't do anything about that. But fear is just like baseball in one sense—it doesn't define you."

Trent wiped his mouth with a napkin and stood up. Quincy did the same, and Trent embraced him.

"Good-bye," Trent said. "I hope to see you again soon."

"I'm an easy man to find."

Trent said farewell to Monica and Tony, then headed next door to the record shop.

"Hey, you," Brendan said from behind the counter. "What's up? You're early. I don't get off for another hour."

"I know," Trent said. "I was next door and wanted to see you."

"How was the snapper?"

"Fantastic." Trent hesitated, but then he said, "I talked to the front office this morning. They want me back tomorrow."

# SIXTEEN

BRENDAN'S FACE went white. "Tomorrow? I thought we had until Wednesday?"

"So did I, but it didn't work out that way. Lillis thinks me being there for the start of the Dodgers series will help with morale. My team's losing, and they need me."

"Of course. I totally understand. So the bubble is about to burst."

"We should probably talk about what we're going to do."

"I know. But not here." Brendan sat down on a stool. "Hard to believe it was just a week ago you walked in looking for a copy of 'Blue Monday.' Seems like we've known each other for months."

"I feel the same way."

Brendan nodded. "We got some stock in, so I have to finish the inventory check and then shelve everything. You're welcome to hang out and listen to some records if you want."

"No, that's okay. I'm going to take a walk around campus. I used to do that sometimes when I needed to think."

"Okay. See you in an hour, then?"

"I'll be here." Trent put on his sunglasses and walked down the Drag a few blocks. He cut through the courtyard of the architecture building to the South Mall, and then took a seat on the grass. Even after talking to Quincy, he still didn't know what to do. He wondered what Brendan was thinking. He wondered how much he could ask of him.

Trent stretched out on his back and closed his eyes. He figured it must be at least a hundred degrees, but he never complained about the heat.

His thoughts turned to the first time Kieran brought him to this place, shortly after Trent moved to Austin. They were only freshmen in high school, but they already dreamed of playing for UT, and someday in the major leagues. Kieran told him the students called the South Mall the "six pack," because of the six similarly designed buildings that flanked it, three on each side. Every March as the weather warmed up, students flocked to the grassy lawn between the buildings. The boys would take off their shirts and toss a football or play catch, and the girls would lie out and work on their tans in preparation for spring break on South Padre Island. Life was uncomplicated, even though Trent didn't feel particularly nostalgic about it. He realized now he was only half a person then, secretive and guarded, never fully himself with anyone.

He walked to the end of the mall and sat next to the Littlefield fountain. He looked up at the goddess Columbia and read the inscription etched into the stone:

*Short life hath been given by Nature unto man; but the remembrance of a life laid down in a good cause endureth forever.*

"You are absolutely no help whatsoever," he said to the goddess. He glanced at the tower and saw it was almost four o'clock. He made it back to Inner Sanctum Records just as Brendan was walking out the door.

"You ready?"

"As I'll ever be," Brendan said.

Trent tossed him the keys to his truck. "You want to drive?"

THEY RETURNED to the garage apartment and sat down on the sofa. Trent turned to Brendan and said, "I don't know what to do."

"That's what's going to make this so difficult."

"What are you talking about?"

"Before I say anything, you've got to know how I feel, right? I don't need to spell it out in so many words? Tell me you know without a shred of doubt."

Trent had a bad feeling all of a sudden, but he nodded and said, "I know."

"Okay," Brendan continued. "All afternoon I've been trying to decide what I want. And what's best for me. No matter how I frame it or slice it or dress it up, I always come back to the same place."

"What place is that?"

"I don't know what you've decided, but...." Brendan took a long pause. "Trent, I won't be seeing you again after today."

"I don't understand."

"I'm ready to come out. I'm going home to Houston next weekend to tell my parents. Then after that, it's time to take some action. There's a gay and lesbian happy hour in the Union on Friday afternoons, and a gay bar on Twenty-Ninth Street called Sally's. They have a beer bust every Sunday. I want to meet people and make some gay friends. I want to go on a date and hold hands in public. Stanton invited me to visit them in New York, and in two years I'm moving there. And someday, I'm going to meet a guy and fall in love. Maybe he won't be you, but we'll have a good life together."

"And what about me?"

"You'll become the greatest baseball player that ever lived. You'll be immortal. But there won't be any place in your life for me. Find a way to be happy, Trent. There's someone out there who can love you under those circumstances."

"But that someone's not you?"

"No. You have to play baseball. You just have to. But I can't live that way, not with all the secrets and lies. And we both know you'd never survive being the gay Jackie Robinson. So let's walk away now. A clean break. I promise I will never, ever forget you."

Trent stood up and looked out the window. A squirrel scurried along one of the tree branches with a nut in his mouth. Trent's chest ached, like it did the day his dad called to tell him Koda Patkotak had died—only this was a hundred times worse. He felt lost and didn't know what to do, but he had no intention of falling apart in front of Brendan. That much he knew for sure.

"I think it's best if I go home."

Brendan nodded. He got off the sofa and reached out.

"Don't," Trent said as he pushed Brendan's hand away. "I want to, but I just can't. I know it's selfish. I wish I could say I only want you to be happy, but if we're going to be completely honest with each other, I want you to be happy with me. I'm sorry I'm not the man you need right now."

"Please don't say that."

Trent felt his eyes tear up, and he turned his back on Brendan. The next thing he knew, he was walking toward the door and fleeing the garage apartment. He ran down the steps to the street and jumped into his truck. As soon as he had driven a safe distance from the Walsh house, he let go. His tears blinded him to the point that he had to pull over. He rested his forehead against the steering wheel and sobbed.

Eventually he pulled himself together long enough to drive home. He went into his bedroom and closed the door. He turned on the air-conditioning and cranked the knob to the coldest setting. He wanted the room to feel as much like home as possible. He crawled into bed with his clothes on, covered his head with a pillow, and fell asleep.

WHEN HE woke up, Trent was shivering and his head hurt. The room was pitch black. He rubbed his eyes and checked the alarm clock:

3:14.

It was the middle of the night. Trent got out of bed and turned off the air-conditioning. He went into the bathroom, took a piss, and for a moment forgot that he would never see Brendan Baxter again. But then he remembered everything and flushed the toilet. He went into the kitchen and opened the fridge. Not even some orange juice to drink. He closed the door and stood against the counter. Then he heard music coming from the living room. Elvis Presley was singing "What Now, What Next, Where To."

He crept across the kitchen floor and peered around the corner. A young man with long black hair was sitting on his sofa, looking at an album sleeve. Trent picked up a baseball bat from the corner and raised it above his head. He walked into the living room and said, "The front door's unlocked, so I suggest you get the hell out of here before I bash your head in."

The young man laughed. "Put the bat down, Nuka. Has it been so long that you don't even recognize your old friend?"

Trent couldn't believe his ears, but he lowered the bat and said, "Koda?"

"Why don't you have a seat?"

"Where did you come from?"

"Sit, and I promise to answer all your questions."

Trent looked around the room. He walked to the rocking chair and sat down. Koda looked at him and smiled.

"You're still eighteen," Trent said.

"One of the perks of dying young. Do you remember when we used to listen to Elvis Presley records in your room? Late at night, during the summer? Your little brother slept right through it. We both loved this song. 'What Now, What Next, Where To.' Pretty much sums it up, doesn't it?"

"Is this a dream?"

"Not really. You're half Eskimo. Don't you believe in the spirit world anymore?"

"So you're a ghost?"

"That's such a white man's term. Eskimos have been communicating with the spirit world for thousands of years. Turns out, it's not all for the tourists. It's in your blood, Nuka."

"Then why are you here? Why now?"

Koda laughed. "What? Things are going so great you couldn't use some help?"

Trent laid the bat on the floor and relaxed into the chair. "Okay, I see your point. It's good to see you, Suuna. I've missed you."

"I missed you too."

"I really screwed things up."

"Yep. I know."

"Tell me what to do."

"I think you already know what to do. Have you forgotten how we were raised? What's the most important thing to an Eskimo?"

"Family."

"And who is your family?"

"Those who watch over and protect me."

"What is baseball?"

"I don't understand."

"*What is baseball?*" Koda repeated.

Trent shrugged his shoulders. "It's a game, I guess."

"What's the most important thing to an Eskimo?"

"Family."

"And what is baseball?"

"A game."

The song came to an end, and the needle reset itself. Koda laid the record sleeve on the table in front of him. "Do I need to keep going?"

"No," Trent said. "I get it."

"Can you really lie to everyone about who you are? Your parents? Your brothers? Your teammates? The world? Can't you see how that will destroy you?"

Trent raised his voice in anger and said, "I don't know what else to do!"

"Calm down. I'm your friend, remember?"

"Everyone thinks I'm a coward because I won't come out and play baseball."

"I never said that."

"But you're thinking it."

"*No, I'm not.* I don't care about baseball, and there was a time when you didn't care about it either. You practically never even heard of it before you left the Slope. I care about you, Nuka. I care about what will happen if you live your life without a shred of honor, and that has nothing to do with playing baseball. The first test here isn't whether or not you can hit a ball or change the world."

"Then what is it?"

"It's whether or not you can love."

Trent felt like he was going to start crying. "I can."

"Then show me. And if you can't do it and still play baseball, then stop. None of us will think you're a bad person for quitting baseball, but we'll all think it if you lie about who you are for the rest of your life."

"Brendan won't let me quit."

"Whose life is it, anyway? Why does he get to decide these things? The last time I checked, you were in charge of your choices."

For the first time, Trent allowed himself to consider every possibility. He could tell his family the truth. He could ask Brendan out on a date and not care who saw them holding hands. He could sleep at night knowing that he wasn't a party to his own spectacular deception. And then he remembered something Quincy had said, just before Tony interrupted them: *That's because you imagine going through it alone.*

Trent stood up. "I know what I have to do."

"Wait. There's one more thing."

"What?"

"Something's coming. A big change."

"What kind of change?"

"I can't get into the details. I just want you to know that when it comes, don't be afraid. This is only the beginning, no matter what. Do you understand me?"

"I think so. Quincy said the same thing."

"Then listen to both of us. Say it for me."

"This is only the beginning."

"Good. Now get into your truck and go see Brendan."

Trent grabbed his keys off the side table. "Thank you. For everything."

"You're welcome. Oh, and by the way, I would have liked it, you know?"

"What?"

"If you had kissed me. I would have liked it."

Trent smiled. "Me too. Good-bye, Suuna. I'll never forget you." He ran out through the kitchen and jumped into his truck. The traffic lights going north were on the overnight schedule and blinking yellow, so he was able to race through the city on his way to the Walsh house. He couldn't believe what he was about to do.

When Trent arrived, he didn't bother parking in the street, but pulled directly into the driveway behind Bill's car. He immediately noticed that the lights were on in Brendan's living room, so he leaped out of his truck and raced up the steps. He knocked on the door and waited, bouncing on his toes, and when Brendan finally answered, Trent caught his breath and said, "Can I come in?"

"Of course, but...."

Brendan stepped aside, and Trent hurried into the living room. He turned to Brendan. "Would you sit down, please?"

Brendan took a seat on the sofa, and Trent remained standing.

"On the drive over here, I was trying to figure out when I first knew. Maybe it was when I walked into the record store and saw your smile, or maybe it was when we were sitting next to each other at Les Amis. I don't think it was either one of those times, though. I think it was when our knees bumped under the table. That's when I knew for sure."

"Knew what?"

"Quincy said life is a seesaw between distillation and dilution. I don't know how to distill it any more than this—I love you, Brendan. Those are my four words. I've been wanting to say it ever since we knocked knees under the table, but I was scared. Scared it was too soon. Scared you didn't feel the same way. Scared I wouldn't be able to live without you." Trent sat down and took Brendan's hand. "I'm done being scared. When I close my eyes and think about the future, I see you. If I play baseball, you're there. If I don't play baseball, you're still there. I can't imagine my life without you in it. The scenario you came up with, where we never see each other again, and you fall in love with somebody else? That's bullshit and we both know it."

Brendan stared down at Trent's hand and squeezed. "So what are you suggesting?"

"I'm yours, period."

"But what about baseball?"

"I'll quit if I have to."

"That's not going to happen."

"Then I'll play and come out."

Brendan looked up in shock. "Are you serious?"

"There is only one thing up for debate here, and that's whether or not I play baseball. You and me—we're not up for debate. We're a certainty. If you want a boyfriend who will hold your hand in public, I'm that man. If you want someone to move to New York with you, I'll move to New York. I will make any sacrifice you ask of me, and that includes quitting baseball."

"I just said, I won't let you do that."

"Then tell me not to. If you're willing to make all the sacrifices, just say the word now and I'll keep playing. But that means we go public. No lies, no secrets. Wherever I'm playing, wherever I get traded, I want you there."

"What about the fallout? If we go public, you're going to get booed and called names. People will send you death threats."

"I can handle it if you're with me."

"What if they run you out of baseball?"

"Then they run me out of baseball. I can handle it if you're with me."

"How can you be so sure?"

"Because when I made this choice—when I decided what's important—I didn't feel like shit anymore. Everything finally made sense. I'm not asking you to do this, Brendan. I'm offering to give up everything to be with you. But if you want me to keep playing baseball, if you'll be there to support me, then I'll sit down with the front office and tell them I'm gay. I'll tell them I have someone in my life, and that you'll be coming to the ballpark to see me play. We'll go on the *Today Show* and talk to Bryant Gumbel. Maybe Hutch is right. Maybe winning will trump everything else. Maybe it's time. Just tell me what you want me to do."

Brendan didn't hesitate. "Play baseball. I can be a lawyer anywhere."

"Is being with me enough?"

"Yes. A hundred times, yes. You're going to be bigger than DiMaggio. People will write books and make movies about you, and I'll be a part of that story. I don't care if the fans hate me or throw rotten tomatoes. I never wanted to be your Wallis Simpson, but I will happily be your Rachel Robinson."

"You have a thicker skin than I do."

"It's thick enough for both of us."

"I know I shouldn't ask this. I know I should wait until you say it on your own, but I can't. I need to know. Does this mean—"

"Yes, of course. I love you. Before the knees under the table. Before you walked into Inner Sanctum. Trent, I loved you before I met you. I've been sitting here for hours wondering how I could have been stupid enough to send you away, but for some reason I wasn't sad."

"That's because you knew I'd come back. I will always come back."

"But if you think being the Eskimo Slugger has been hard, wait until you're the Gay Eskimo Slugger."

"I'm not blind to what's ahead. If I couldn't handle the idea before, it's because I always imagined going through it alone. Is that the case?"

"No."

"Will you stand beside me?"

"Yes."

"When things get difficult, will you kiss me and rub my feet and tell me everything's going to be okay?"

"Yes."

"And when it's all over—when I put down my bat and walk off the field for the last time—will you grow old with me?"

Brendan smiled, and his eyes welled up. "Yes."

"Then it's settled. I'll have to postpone going back to Houston for a few days."

"Why?"

"Because I need to fly to Alaska and tell my family what's going on. They have to know everything before I go public. Then your parents will be next."

"Whoa. It's all moving so fast. They don't even know I'm gay yet."

"You're the one who wanted an adventure. Well, here it is. Once I tell the world I'm gay and that I'm in love with a man named Brendan Baxter, there's no turning back. You need to decide now. Are you in or are you out? But keep in mind, I'm not asking about you and me. I'm asking about whether or not I play baseball."

"I understand. We're not up for debate." Brendan leaned over and kissed him. "I'm in."

"Okay, then," Trent said. "Let's go home."

# Seventeen

BRENDAN SCOOTED to the end of the sofa. "Put your feet up." Trent toed his shoes off and lay down. Brendan began to massage his feet and asked, "So we're going to Alaska? Are you sure I should come along?"

"Yes."

"But what if they blame me, like Kieran did?"

"My family's not like Kieran," Trent said. "I told you, my dad is going to be okay with it. And so is my mom. But if I go home alone and tell her I'm gay, she won't understand. When she meets you and sees what I'm like around you, then she'll understand."

"Will you come home with me when I tell my parents?"

"Yes. We can go through this next part together too—and every part after that."

"What are you going to tell the front office?"

"That I have a family emergency and need to fly home, which is 100 percent true. When we get back, I'll drive to Houston and give it to them straight."

"So to speak."

Trent laughed. "You've gotten good with the foot rubs."

"I pop a boner every time we do this."

"Seriously?"

Brendan rubbed Trent's foot against his crotch as evidence. "What can I say? I associate your feet with sex now."

"It was really hot when you sucked on my toes while you were fucking me."

"I know. I guess that makes me a kinky perv."

"You want to hear what Hutch said? 'A guy wants a gentleman in the streets, and a pig in the sheets.'"

"I bet he's nasty in bed."

"He only likes to get fucked."

"He told you that?"

"Yeah. Seemed real proud of it too. Can't say I don't empathize, but make no mistake—I will pop your ass cherry someday. No question about it."

"You crazy Eskimo." Brendan dug his thumb into the sole of Trent's right foot. "I'm going to need a little more time to get used to the idea of getting fucked, okay?"

"No rush. We've got the rest of our lives."

"When are we going to Alaska?"

"Well, it's Tuesday morning already. I'll book us on the first flight out tomorrow. Can you take off work for a few days?"

"For this? Yes, I can take off. Fiona's mom is out of the hospital, and she owes me."

"Have you ever been that far north before?"

"Nope. I'm an Alaska virgin."

"Good. I'm glad your first time will be with me."

"I really want to take you into the bedroom and fuck you."

"What's wrong with right here? Bend me over the sofa and show me who the real slugger is."

They paused for a moment and then jumped up. Brendan undid Trent's shorts and let them drop to the floor. Trent peeled off his shirt, turned around, and bent over. He heard the clank of a belt buckle and the slide of a zipper, then felt Brendan coating his ass with spit. In a singular motion, Brendan slid his cock into Trent's hole. He grabbed Trent by the shoulders to deepen his position, and Trent lifted his foot onto the sofa to better the angle.

"Say it," Brendan whispered.

"I love you."

"No, the other thing."

"My ass is yours."

"That's it. Never forget it."

"My ass is yours."

And then Brendan fucked him from behind.


TRENT DROPPED him at the record store just before ten. He went home and booked them on a flight to Anchorage the next day. From Anchorage Trent would hire a plane to Barrow. He called the front office, and Sandra didn't press him about the delay. She must have heard something in his voice. There was only one other person he needed to talk to. He dialed the number.

Marcia picked up.

"It's me. Is Kieran there?"

"Yes. He was expecting you to call last night, so he's a little—"

"Can you just put him on, please?"

Trent heard Marcia cover the mouthpiece, then another line picked up, and the first line disconnected. After a long pause, Kieran said, "Hello."

"Hey. I know we said some things last week that are going to be hard to walk back, but I wanted you to hear this from me."

"Hear what?"

"I'm flying to Alaska tomorrow to tell my parents and my brothers that I'm gay. And then I'm going to come out. Publicly."

"So you're leaving baseball?"

Trent swallowed. "No. I'm going to keep playing."

"The club will never accept it."

"That's what they said about Jackie Robinson."

"Who are you kidding, Trent? You're no fucking Jackie Robinson. You don't have the stomach for it."

"Not alone, I don't."

"You're risking everything for a guy you met last week?"

"Yes. And don't try to make me doubt myself, because it won't work. I know exactly what I'm doing. This is who I am, Kieran. I'm a baseball player who's in love with another man. Those two facts are never going to change. And it just so happens that I agree with you about this club. The Houston Astros have no interest in being the home of the first gay player. You think I don't know that? But there are other owners and other managers and other players, open-minded guys who just want to win, and even some who don't give a shit about who I sleep with. I fully expect to be traded and I'm betting there's another team out there that wants me."

"That's a bet you're going to lose."

"Maybe. Failure is the one constant in baseball, so I wouldn't be surprised. But there are twenty-six teams in the major leagues. You can be right about twenty-five of them—I only need to be right about one. And even if I'm wrong, I can accept a future without baseball—it's never been a part of me the way it's a part of you. What I can't accept is a future without Brendan. I realize no one else sees him the way I do. I get that my certainty makes me look naïve or even a little crazy. But in time, the rest of the world will catch up."

"I'm sorry, Trent. I can't support you, at least not in the press."

"Well, actually, you could. You're just choosing not to."

"Do you have any idea what's coming down the pike?"

"Of course I do. We've been in the same locker rooms. We've heard the same fag jokes and the name calling. So what? There will be good stuff too. Maybe a few of the players will stand up for me. Maybe I'll change some minds. Or maybe I'll just win and shut everybody up."

"This isn't my battle, Trent. You're on your own."

"That's where you're wrong."

"I think we've said enough. You know how I feel about this. Good luck with your parents and… the rest of it."

"Good-bye, Kieran. I don't know how much longer we'll be playing together. I'll miss that part, at least."

"Me too. Good-bye, Trent. I'm sorry it ended this way."

IN THE afternoon, Trent packed his suitcase and picked Brendan up at Inner Sanctum just after four. They returned to the Walsh house, smoked a joint with Bill in the backyard, and told him everything. They flew to Anchorage the next morning, but when they arrived, all the flights to Barrow had been grounded due to weather. They were forced to wait throughout the night and into Thursday morning. After twenty-four hours in an airport, Brendan grew restless and kept moving around and sitting in different places. At one point they found seats across from an old Eskimo woman and what looked like her teenage granddaughter.

"What's today?" Brendan asked Trent.

"You mean the date?"

"Yeah."

The old Eskimo woman stared at them. Trent looked at his watch and said, "July 21."

Brendan groaned. "I hate this part of summer, when we've already blown past the halfway mark. Do you have any quarters?"

"No, but I have some dollar bills. We can get quarters out of the vending machine by putting in dollars and pushing the coin return button."

"Clearly you've done this before," Brendan said.

"All the time as a kid. There used to be an arcade in this airport. We always needed quarters. Why?"

"I'm bored and want to call someone."

"Who?" Trent asked.

"I don't know. Stanton, maybe. Or Bill. Or Quincy."

"Let's go get you some quarters, then."

They loaded up on eight dollars' worth and then found a pay phone. Brendan dialed Stanton's number, but the machine picked up. Bill couldn't talk because Grace's water had just broken, and they were heading to the hospital. Brendan dialed one more number and deposited a long string of quarters.

"Hi Quincy, it's Brendan. ... In Alaska. We're trapped in the Anchorage airport, waiting for the weather to clear up. ... We're going to see Trent's family. He has some news for them." Brendan listened to Quincy say one more thing and then handed the phone to Trent. "He wants to talk to you."

Trent put the phone to his ear. "Hi, Quincy."

"You're going to come out and play, aren't you?"

"That's the plan. I don't know who will want me after I make the announcement, but at least I'll be able to look at myself in the mirror."

"I'll want you," Brendan mumbled next to him.

"You're embracing visibility," Quincy said. "I couldn't be more proud of you." Trent heard a commotion in the background. "Oh my God, you won't believe what just happened. Tony ran out of here screaming that Suzie's gone into labor."

"Really? That's so weird. Brendan was just talking to Bill Walsh, his landlord, and Bill's wife just went into labor too."

"Everything's aligning, Trent. Can you feel it?"

"Yeah. It's a good day to be alive. By the way, I had a visit from the spirit world Tuesday morning. I'll tell you all about it when we get back."

"I look forward to hearing the story. Now travel safe and let me talk to Brendan again."

Trent handed the phone back.

"Hey. ... No, I won't. I promise— ... Okay, good-bye, Q."

Brendan hung up the phone and smiled.

"What did he say?" Trent asked.

"He made me promise not to make this all about me."

Trent laughed. "He knows you pretty well."

"Yeah. I feel better now. Let's get something to eat. Are you.... Never mind. You're always hungry."

They grabbed some hamburgers from one of the airport vendors and sat down in the food court.

"It's not too late to change your mind," Brendan said.

"I know, but that's not going to happen. Once I decided what's important, everything fell into place."

"Just like Bill said it would."

Trent nodded. "Clear waters."


AFTER THEIR meal, they returned to their seats across from the old Eskimo woman and her supposed-teenage granddaughter.

The girl smiled at Trent. "You're the Eskimo Slugger, aren't you?"

"Yeah. I'm Trent Days."

"I'm Vicki. And this is my grandmother, Ahnah."

"It's nice to meet you both," Trent said.

"Aren't you half Inupiat?"

"On my mom's side."

Vicki waved her bangle-covered arm. "I thought I read something. Are you waiting for a plane to Barrow?"

"Yeah. We've been here since yesterday. Is that where you're headed?"

"Yep. We were in Kansas City for the Native Languages Summit. We're storytellers."

"What kind of storytellers?" Brendan asked.

"Eskimo myths and legends, mostly. We don't have a written history, so everything gets passed down through an oral tradition. Ahnah speaks in the original Inupiat, and I translate the stories into English. Your dad's Carson Days, right? The English teacher?"

"Right. Did you have him in school?"

"Yes. He's the one who encouraged us to go to this conference."

Trent smiled with pride. "That sounds like my dad. I haven't lived there for ten years, so I'm a little out of the loop."

"Tell us one," Brendan said.

The old woman perked up. Vicki laughed and said, "Here? In the middle of the airport?"

"Why not? We're sitting around with nothing to do. I'm about to visit the North Slope for the first time. Tell me an Eskimo story."

Vicki leaned over and whispered into her grandmother's ear. The old woman nodded and sat forward. She looked straight at Brendan and said, "Tavrauvvaa atiba taimaffa, agga uumaruq sugruk aqaluktuq...."

"Once upon a time," Vicki said, "there was a great fisherman. He caught enough fish to feed his entire village. Everyone treated him with awe and respect, because his skills far exceeded those of normal men. The people he fed built him a grand igloo and offered him the most beautiful of their daughters, but the man would have none of it. The fisherman, you see, had a friend who was crippled. 'I cannot marry any of your daughters,' he said to the people, 'because I must take care of my friend, who cannot walk. I have known him since I was a young boy. He has no one else in the world and depends on me. He will always come first. I cannot abandon him.'

"Some were offended, but others called the fisherman noble and loyal. Then one day, the fisherman's friend got sick, and the people panicked. The fisherman would not leave his friend and catch fish for the villagers. After a few days, they went to see the fisherman. They called out, 'We are hungry and need your help.' But the fisherman refused to leave his friend and said, 'Catch your own fish. My place is here. I cannot abandon my friend.'

"The people went back to their igloos, and a few more days passed. The hunger in their bellies grew, and they returned to the fisherman and said, 'You must either feed us, or leave the village forever.' The fisherman was struck dumb. He could not believe the cruel nature of the people. 'Where shall we go?' he asked, but they were unrelenting. 'You are no longer welcome here. Take your friend, who is more important to you than all of us, and leave.'

"And so the fisherman wrapped some food in an animal skin and bundled up his friend as best he could. He picked him up and carried him out of the village. He walked for days and days, through endless snow and wind, as his friend got heavier and heavier. Finally, they reached the edge of the world. 'I have failed you,' the fisherman said to his friend. 'I could not keep you safe and warm, and now we are here at the edge of the world. I do not know what to do. We cannot go back. We cannot go forward. We are trapped.' His friend squeezed him tight and said, 'You have not failed. Step off, and let's meet our destiny.' The fisherman did not understand. 'But if I step off, we shall surely die.' The friend shook his head and said, 'Trust me. Step off.'

"The fisherman moved his right foot to the edge and stopped, but then stepped with his left foot and tumbled forward. The light of a thousand comets filled him up and burst through his pores. They rose together into the heavens, and the friend called, 'Look at us now! We shall outshine all the other stars in the northern sky!' Their human form peeled away, and they took their place in the firmament, where they became the guardians of Eskimo children everywhere."

"Wish upon the Two Friends," Trent said, "and all your dreams will come true."

"You know that story?" Brendan asked him.

"Of course. Every Eskimo knows that story."

The old woman sat back in her chair and mumbled something to her granddaughter.

"What is it?" Brendan asked.

"Nothing. She just likes your red hair."

A FEW hours later, the weather bureau lifted the travel ban to the North Slope, and Trent booked them on a small eight-seater to Barrow. He thought the pilot looked too young to have much experience, but at that point Trent would have paid for seats on a hot-air balloon.

The ban may have been lifted, but the winds were still strong, and the flight started out rocky. There were four rows, with one seat on each side of the plane. Trent and Brendan sat in the last row. Brendan was clearly freaked out by the whole experience, so Trent took his hand from across the aisle and said, "It's going to be okay."

"I hope so."

The pilot had left the door to the cockpit open, and Trent could tell something was wrong. Several large red lights were flashing on the plane's dashboard, and the pilot looked frantic and uncertain. Then they heard his voice on the PA system:

"I'm sorry, folks, but we have a fuel problem. In all the rush to get out of Anchorage, I forgot to check the reserve tank before we left, and... well, it's empty. I was hoping to find some flat terrain to set us down, but it doesn't look good."

Trent heard Ahnah yell from the front in Inupiat, and then Vicki translated, "How much time do we have?"

After a pause, the pilot said, "Five minutes. If I can't land it by then, we're going down. I'm sorry."

Brendan turned his head toward Trent. "We're going to die?"

"There's still a chance he'll find a place."

"But if he can't, we're going to die, right? Don't bullshit me now."

Trent nodded. "If he can't find a flat place to land the plane, we won't survive the fall, let alone the crash."

"Why aren't you freaking out?"

"I don't know. I'm sorry. I should never have brought you with me."

"Don't say that. I'm not sorry at all. If I could plan the last ten days of my life, they would look exactly like these last ten with you."

"This is what Koda meant by a big change." The plane started to rattle, and Trent yelled above the din, "Don't be afraid. This is only the beginning."

"What?"

"This is only the beginning!" he yelled louder. "Both Quincy and Koda told me that."

"Koda? The same Koda who died in the ice-fishing accident?"

"Yes."

"But you were going to come out and play baseball. You were going to change the world."

"That's someone else's job now. Don't you see? This was never about baseball. This was about us, Brendan. Finding each other. Starting something. Deciding what's important."

"So why is it ending?"

"Maybe it's not. Maybe Quincy was right."

Brendan laughed. "That would teach me a lesson, wouldn't it?" The plane shook from side to side. "He's not going to find a place to land, is he?"

Trent shook his head.

"How will I recognize you?" Brendan asked.

"What do you mean?"

"How will I recognize you in our next life?"

Trent smiled. "Don't worry about that. I'll recognize you. But remember, no matter what happens—no matter how lost we get—I will always come back to you. Do you hear me?"

"I hear you. We'll outshine all the other stars in the northern sky."

The plane sustained a steep drop in altitude and lurched to the left. Trent reached out and kissed Brendan for the last time. They looked at each other and said good-bye. Then the plane fell into a nosedive, something hit Trent on the head, and his story with Brendan came to an end.

# EIGHTEEN

*27 Years Later*

TRAVIS ATWOOD opened his eyes and bolted upright in bed. Of the many days he had dreaded in his life, this one topped them all. He took a quick shower and got dressed, then walked out to the front porch to get the Saturday newspaper. He looked across the street at the Walsh house and the several unknown cars parked in the driveway. He wondered how the boys were doing. Travis had moved onto the block six months earlier, when he got his job at a nearby auto shop and found a great deal renting a room from one of the neighborhood widows. Edith Wright had lost her husband Jon to cancer, and since they never had children, she rented her spare bedroom for $200 a month because she didn't like being alone in the house. Travis met Bill Walsh shortly after he moved in, and somehow over the months, Bill, his wife Grace, and their three sons had become Travis's new family. Then on Thursday night, seven days before Christmas, Travis came home from work and found Mrs. Wright crying. She told him Bill and Grace Walsh had been killed in a car accident. He had rushed across the street to be with the boys, but then their aunt and uncles showed up the next morning and told him to leave. Travis hadn't talked to them since.

He bent over and picked up the paper, then went back inside. Mrs. Wright was putting on her coat and getting ready to go out.

"I'm off to breakfast with my book club. Are you going to the funeral?"

"Yeah," Travis said. "I gotta head into work for a couple hours first, though."

"I'll see you there, then. Such a sad day. I remember when they first moved in across the street. Lord, I can't believe it was almost thirty years ago. Back when Jon was alive, they would invite us to supper parties. I was always the dumbest person in the room, but my goodness, I met some interesting people. Writers and professors and artists. Even a baseball player once. Of course, I never did understand half of what Bill was talking about, but he was such a kind man. And Grace—always the fiery beauty. I can't imagine what this will do to those poor boys."

"It's a sad day, that's for sure."

Mrs. Wright left the house. Travis sat down and turned the television to ESPN. The morning edition of *SportsCenter* had just begun. As they were about to cut to a commercial break, Kevin Negandhi said to Hannah Storm:

*—Here's a piece of baseball trivia for you, Hannah. I was reading the obituaries this morning, and guess who died?*

*—Who?*

*—Kieran Harrison.*

*—Is that the trivia part?*

*—Yes. Do you know who Kieran Harrison was, Hannah?*

Travis propped his feet on the coffee table and said, "He was a pitcher for the Houston Astros in 1983."

*—I have no idea, Kevin.*

*—He was a pitcher for the Houston Astros in 1983.*

"I just said that, idiot."

*—Why should I know who he is?*

*—Do you remember Trent Days?*

"He was the Eskimo Slugger. I still have the apron he signed for my dad."

*—You mean the Eskimo Slugger? The one who died in the plane crash?*

—*That's the one. He went to high school with Kieran Harrison. They played at the University of Texas and then were drafted together by the Astros. When Trent died, Kieran went into a tailspin. He started drinking. His wife left him. The Astros let him go. He even spent a few years in jail for a Ponzi scheme. Once in the rotation with Nolan Ryan, and today, dead at fifty-one from a failed liver. Baseball is a fickle mistress, Hannah.*

—*She is indeed, Kevin. Morbid story, but we'll be right back after a word from our sponsors.*

Travis turned off the television and then swiped a yogurt from the fridge on his way out the back door. He jumped into his truck, started the engine, and checked the rearview mirror.

Quentin Walsh was standing in the driveway.

Travis got out and walked toward the street. "How are y'all holding up?"

"I'm okay, but Jason has gone all Silent Bob on me, and Cade is walking around like someone tased him. Where have you been?"

"Keeping my distance, Q. Your Aunt Julie doesn't know me from Adam. I'm not family, and as much as I want to be there for you three right now, it's not my place. I have to respect that."

"Jesus, don't you get it? You're more like family to us than Aunt Julie will ever be."

"Your brother's home now. He'll take care of things."

"Oh, right. Only you would say that, Travis, because you're the only one who hasn't met him yet."

"Stop that, you hear me? Cut him some slack. He can't be half as bad as you make him out to be."

"You have no idea what a self-centered moron he is."

"It's not possible that your mother and father raised a monster."

Travis heard the muffled sound of a text message. Quentin reached into his pocket and pulled out his phone. "I gotta go. You'll be at the funeral and the cemetery, right?"

"Yeah," Travis said. "I'll be there."

Quentin put his phone back. "And afterward, everyone's coming over to the house. Please be there for Cade. And to run interference for Jason."

"I'll be there too. Hopefully, I'll get the chance to meet your brother."

Quentin sneered and said, "My sympathies."

He walked across the street, and Travis continued on his way to Groovy Automotive. When he pulled into the shop parking lot, he grabbed the carton of yogurt off the passenger seat and walked into his bay. He kept a couple of clean spoons in his toolbox, so he fished one out and peeled the top off the yogurt. He ate a spoonful and looked around. Topher Manning, the mechanic who worked in the bay next to his, was missing. He looked a little further, and sure enough, Topher was sitting in Ed's bay, listening to the radio. Travis walked over and joined them.

"What're you listening to?"

"Shhh," Topher said. "It's almost over."

—*After spending a week with Brandon Flowers and the Killers, I'm in awe, and not just of their talent, but of what they've done with it. For me, there are really two kinds of music. There's the stuff you listen to while you're folding laundry, and then there's the other stuff, the music that demands your full attention. The Killers are, and always have been, in that second category. This is Stanton Porter, reporting on location for NPR Music.*

Travis spooned some more yogurt into his mouth. "What's the big deal?"

Topher turned to him. "The Killers, Travis. Only the greatest rock and roll band of our generation."

"I thought Linkin Park was the greatest rock and roll band of our generation."

"It depends on who you ask, I suppose. I thought you had a funeral to go to."

"I do. In a couple of hours."

They walked out of Ed's bay and back into the space between their own.

"She asked about you," Topher said. "Trisha, I mean."

"I'll text her."

"You'd better. She's my sister, so don't be a douchebag."

"I'll probably see her tomorrow, anyway. We have a standing date on Sundays."

"I don't want to hear about it."

"What are your plans for Christmas?" Travis asked.

"I'm driving to Dime Box and spending it with my mom."

"Is Trisha going with you?"

"Probably. My roommates Robin and Maurice too. They've spent every Christmas with us since their parents disappeared ten years ago. Why? What are you doing?"

Travis shrugged. "I don't know. I was supposed to spend it with…. Never mind."

"Why don't you come with us? My mom puts together a pretty good spread, and then we usually head over to Peter's house in the evening. Trust me, the Moses family knows how to do Christmas."

"I don't think I'm up for it this year. I'll probably just stick around the house, in case the boys need something."

"You're not their brother, Travis."

"I know that. But Quentin caught me on the way over here and said Cade isn't doing so hot."

"He's the youngest one?"

"Yeah."

Topher picked up a wrench and started to work on a Ford Mustang. "Well, it's your choice. Stay here and mope if you want. Did you meet him yet? The older brother, I mean."

"No. I reckon sometime today."

Travis worked through two oil changes and a multipoint inspection. Then he returned home and got dressed for the funeral. He didn't have the proper clothes, but he made do with a pair of black pants and a white short-sleeved shirt. He didn't even own a tie.

By the time he arrived at the church, it was pretty much full. Travis took a seat in the last row. He thought maybe he'd get a glimpse of him, but all the students blocked his view. As he sat listening to the preacher, he thought about his own parents, who were also dead. Travis didn't kid himself; he still carried a lot of anger toward his mom and dad. He couldn't say that he liked either one of them, but he never denied that he loved them. Tony Atwood was a pathetic excuse for a father, but he also made a mean chicken-fried steak. And since Travis thought his red hair helped him stand out in a crowd—well, he had his mother to thank for that.

When Travis arrived at the cemetery, about a hundred people were already huddled around the dual graves. He walked the perimeter until he caught a glimpse of Jason and then Quentin, who was holding Cade's hand.

And there he stood, right beside them. Tall, with black hair like his father, and a tiny cleft in his chin. The older brother leaned over and said something to Quentin. Travis couldn't explain what was going through his head, and he almost started to cry. He'd done plenty of that in the past two days, but these wouldn't be tears of loss or mourning. Instead, in the midst of all the sadness, looking at this man he'd never met before, Travis felt giddy. He'd known a few moments of happiness in his life, but this was a different thing entirely. This was a kind of joy Travis had never experienced before. Cade saw him and tried to pull his hand away from Quentin, who managed to hold on for a few seconds. Then Jason saw him too, and Quentin let go. Cade walked around the crowd and up to Travis. He held out his hand and said, "Please."

Travis took it and allowed the boy to lead him back to the family. He made eye contact with the older brother, who smiled at him. Travis almost started laughing, because he reckoned the guy could get anyone to do just about anything with a smile like that. The five of them stood together for the rest of the sermon, which involved more prayers and more incense. Then, after the preacher finished up and everyone chimed in with their last amens, the older brother reached over to Travis, offered his hand, and said, "I'm Ben Walsh."

BRAD BONEY lives in Austin, Texas, the seventh gayest city in America. He grew up in the Midwest and went to school at NYU. He lived in Washington DC and Houston before settling in Austin. He blames his background in the theater for his writing style, which he calls "dialogue and stage directions." His first book was named a Lambda Literary Award finalist. He believes the greatest romantic comedy of all time is 50 First Dates. His favorite gay film of the last ten years is Strapped. And he has never met a boy band he didn't like.

Please visit Brad on the web at http://www.bradboney.com or follow him on Twitter at http://www.twitter.com/BradBoney

# THE
# NOTHINGNESS
## OF BEN

## BRAD
## BONEY

# THE RETURN

## BRAD BONEY

CPSIA information can be obtained
at www.ICGtesting.com
Printed in the USA
BVHW061933180319
542985BV00024B/557/P